SKIN

Also by Catherine Bush

Blaze Island

Accusation

Claire's Head

The Rules of Engagement

Minus Time

for Terri –

CATHERINE BUSH

stories

best wishes,
Cat V Bush
April 24 - 2025

GOOSE LANE EDITIONS

Copyright © 2025 by Catherine Bush.

All rights reserved. No part of this work may be reproduced or used in any form or by any means, electronic or mechanical, including photocopying, recording, or any retrieval system, without the prior written permission of the publisher or a licence from the Canadian Copyright Licensing Agency (Access Copyright). To contact Access Copyright, visit accesscopyright.ca or call 1-800-893-5777.

Edited by André Alexis and Bethany Gibson.
Copy edited by Paula Sarson.
Cover and page design by Julie Scriver.
Cover images: (background) Hannah MacLean, unsplash.com; (details, left to right) istock.com; Kyaw Tun, unsplash.com; Francesco Ungaro, Pexels.com; and Anne Lambeck, unsplash.com.
Excerpt from *A Lover's Discourse* by Roland Barthes. (Roland Barthes, *Fragments d'un discours amoureux* © Éditions du Seuil, 1977). English Translation Copyright © 1978 by Farrar, Straus & Giroux, Inc. Reprinted by permission of Hill and Wang, a division of Farrar, Straus and Giroux. All rights reserved.
Printed in Canada by Marquis.
10 9 8 7 6 5 4 3 2 1

Library and Archives Canada Cataloguing in Publication

Title: Skin : stories / Catherine Bush.
Names: Bush, Catherine, 1961- author
Identifiers: Canadiana (print) 20240434080 | Canadiana (ebook) 20240434110 | ISBN 9781773104317 (softcover) | ISBN 9781773104324 (EPUB)
Subjects: LCGFT: Short stories.
Classification: LCC PS8553.U6963 S55 2025 | DDC C813/.54—dc23

Goose Lane Editions acknowledges the generous support of the Government of Canada, the Canada Council for the Arts, and the Government of New Brunswick.

Goose Lane Editions is located on the unceded territory of the Wəlastəkwiyik whose ancestors along with the Mi'kmaq and Peskotomuhkati Nations signed Peace and Friendship Treaties with the British Crown in the 1700s.

Goose Lane Editions
500 Beaverbrook Court, Suite 330
Fredericton, New Brunswick
CANADA E3B 5X4
gooselane.com

For all who listen

Contents

- **9**   Benevolence: An East Village Story
- **81**   Skin
- **85**   Animals
- **89**   Voices Over Water
- **97**   The International Headache Conference
- **105**   Touch
- **107**   Breath
- **119**   Camouflage
- **137**   Roxanne (after Edmond Rostand)
- **167**   Mortals
- **169**   Derecho
- **209**   Glacial
- **221**   In the Park, the Great Horned Owl Summons His Mate

Benevolence:
An East Village Story

Last night, in the small house by the shore of Lake Ontario where I live now, I was sorting through books, pulling ones I intended to discard from the shelf, when my hands found themselves in front of *A Lover's Discourse* by Roland Barthes. The 1980s, those were my days of reading Barthes. As my fingers reached out, then riffled through the long-unopened pages, something fell to the floor. A small piece of paper, one ragged edge, as if ripped from a notebook. I picked it up. These were the words handwritten on it, in a dark, looped script: *The subject experiences a sentiment of violent compassion with regard to the loved object each time he sees, feels, or knows the loved object is unhappy or in danger.* On the reverse I found this: *So let us become a little detached, let us undertake the apprenticeship of a certain distance. Let the repressed word appear which rises to the lips of every subject, once he survives another death: Let us live!*

The words were Barthes, I was sure of it, just as I was equally convinced that the writing, not mine, belonged to Chris. Chris. I dropped the paper. Even now, after all this time, I recognized his hand.

Why now? Why this?

If the book had been at my bedside when he vanished from the Ludlow Street apartment in New York City all those years ago, I would have shaken out its pages, hands all over it as if it were a body. If it had been in the stack piled on my desk, I would have done the same. I had shaken so many books as I picked them up, my fingers ransacking them as I zigzagged from room to room in those jagged days after his departure. If he had returned this one to the shelf, I might not have searched it. Surely I would have examined this one, yet the small rectangle of paper, wedged deep inside, tucked up against the spine, had remained hidden. There was no sign of it above the binding when you pulled the book from the shelf. A note he'd placed there on purpose for me to find, because he assumed I would look as frantically as I did, or a forgotten scrap, words written to and for himself? Which made it, nevertheless, a message.

September 1987, my first day at the Beverley School, Carroll Gardens, Brooklyn. At the far end of a hallway, I caught sight of a slim boy in an overcoat that belled around him, making him, from a distance, look like a cross between a youthful professor and a spy. The girl at his side, taller than he was, dark kinks of hair cascading over her back, bumped against him, the two of them colliding into each other with the absorbed, dreamy, demonstrative theatricality of certain teenaged couples.

When I entered the staff room, that first morning of my life as a substitute English teacher, anxious and wanting to self-medicate with another cup of coffee, I walked in on talk of how Chris Sienowicz, who had spent the previous year living with his grandparents in New Jersey, was now shacked up with his girlfriend Jazmin Molnar and her mother in their Fort Greene apartment. The boy in the overcoat. Had I seen him? Maybe the math teacher, with his skinny tie and rutted forehead, asked that.

"Yes," I said, because, funnily enough, I just had. What I didn't say was, You mean the beautiful boy.

"First the foster family didn't work out, then the grandparents, we'll see how long this lasts," muttered the Latin teacher, waist cinched with a wide belt, snapping across the floor in her high-heeled boots.

"You've met the mother. Give him a chance." Let's say this was the biology teacher, hunched over her coffee mug, sheets of paper spread across her knees.

I barely knew these people. We'd met for introductions. It was a small school. Private. Everyone on staff knew who Chris was.

The school had lost its English teacher at the last minute due to pregnancy complications. The art teacher, Celia Hahn, knew my husband and, perhaps because he'd occasionally taught college art history, had reached out to him. From the south of France, where he had moved two years before, he'd called to tell me about the job. In those days, I was barely making ends meet by temping: legal proofreader, receptionist. As far away as he was, my husband had perhaps intuited my fragile financial state. When he wanted, he had keen powers of perception, empathy, even generosity. And, since I lived in what was still essentially his apartment, subletting it, he had a vested interest in seeing me employed, his on-paper wife, the Canadian with the Ivy League degree, in New York on a green card that I owed to him.

Twelfth-grade English was to be my last class of the day. Fifteen minutes before it was due to begin, I entered the staff bathroom and, in my lace-up boots and vintage dress, splashed water over my face, trying to still my twenty-nine-year-old, manically beating heart. I was an actor performing the part of a teacher. I'd made it thus far, corralled the sea of hormones of the twelve-year-olds, spoken of passion to the fifteen-year-olds. No one had yelled at me. In another part of my life, I told solo stories on stage: about a woman who knits gargantuan sweaters for possible lovers, a woman who calls the numbers on lost pet posters, another about an artist who takes part in a tuna-fish tasting session in midtown for money, a thing I had actually done while looking for love among the tasters.

SKIN

Five years before, I'd been the star of a downtown movie, an underground hit. At eighteen, I'd crossed an international border and arrived at Yale, knowing no one, imitating the dress codes of others, changing outfits by the day, slipping between them because I had no idea who I was. All I'd known upon arrival in New Haven was that I wanted to put a country between myself and the particular family dysfunction that seemed the cause of my unhappiness—and remove myself from a romantic relationship I didn't know how to leave. You're lucky, I told myself then, as I had when the film made such a splash. And I repeated the words to myself in the staff bathroom of the Beverley School. That I had been hired at all seemed a fluke: I had only taught theatre in summer camps. Yes, I had the English degree from Yale. In college I'd played Nina in *The Seagull*, the ingenue it goes without saying, to a ripple of success. I told the principal I had always wanted to teach. They were desperate. I was broke and available. And Celia Hahn vouched for me. Luck, I told myself, took many forms. In the staff bathroom, I patted my face dry, adjusted my make-up, set off down the hall.

When I entered the classroom, quiet resounded, because no one was there. I waited, checked my schedule, frightened that word had got out about my newness, my substitute-ness. After ten minutes, I headed to the office, ready to admit defeat, only to discover the scheduling glitch, so that when I entered the actual classroom, late, the air was raucous and a few had already left. I felt them pheromonally, their judgment, their raging insecurity meeting mine. All I had to do, I told myself, was hold their attention, in other words, perform for my life.

At the back of the class, beside the tall windows, Chris Sienowicz and Jazmin Molnar leaned their heads together. Jazmin picked up a pen. Chris mimicked the gesture. With limpid curiosity, his gaze met mine. I apologized for my lateness. I wrote my name on the blackboard.

"Hello," I said. "I'm Ms. Larsen."

He showed up at my office door one afternoon in late September, saying he needed my advice. It was a tiny office, little more than a closet, filled with books, old assignments, file boxes, a room that should have housed two teachers. The second desk was so buried in stuff that a teacher might have been entombed there; you'd never have known. A warm day. Minutes before, I'd been up on a chair, propping the window open with a ruler, reaching through the bars. Horns barked from down the street. Overcoat billowing around him, Chris took the empty chair beside the filing cabinet, set a cup of takeout coffee on the desk, and announced that he needed to read more poetry.

What kind of poetry? The shelves around us overflowed with the belongings of the woman I had replaced, anthologies, nineteenth-century Americana, my knapsack and coffee mug the thinnest graft over her possessions. Chris's small hands reached for his takeout cup. He took a sip. He had a noticeable, prolonged way of meeting your gaze and holding it. Was it tactical, I wondered, or unconscious. In class, he spoke up, unlike Jazmin who never put up her hand, but he didn't hog the conversation. I would have said he had an ability to read and respond to the psychological temperature of a room.

He pulled a small, soft-sided notebook from his overcoat pocket. Contemporary poetry, he said.

Adrienne Rich? Audre Lorde? Louise Glück? Did he write poetry? A little, he said, scribbling down these names. I'd bring in books for him if he wanted, I said, if they weren't in the school library. I plucked a volume of twentieth-century American poetry from a shelf. Generosity rose in me to meet the teacherly authority that I struggled to inhabit.

"Jazmin is training to be an opera singer," Chris said as he took the volume from my hands. "I bet you didn't know that, and because she's so quiet in class, you don't expect it either, but she has this incredible contralto voice. She goes into Manhattan for voice lessons twice a week. She practises in the living room while Vikta, that's her mother, and I cook dinner. Verdi, Purcell. Mozart. Vikta's teaching me how to cook. She's Hungarian, so things like stuffed cabbage and goulash. She says I'm getting good."

Pride entered his voice. I wondered why he wanted to assert these things to me so strenuously. Perhaps he knew or sensed the way his current living situation was being discussed, or might be discussed, and wanted to counter it.

He told me that he and Jazmin had been together since shortly after he'd left home, in the tenth grade — grade ten, I would have said in the country where I'd grown up. They'd known each other since middle school. They were good together. His face flushed as he spoke. He'd been living with a foster family in Park Slope, he said, but they hadn't wanted him sleeping with Jazmin, not even at her place, and that wasn't going to wash, so he left and moved to his grandparents' place in New Jersey, which was okay, but the commute across the river was awful, and he hadn't wanted to transfer schools, because of Jazmin. So then Vikta told him he could move in. He was staying over a lot anyway. It was good for him to be around Jazmin, she was so clear about what she wanted to do with her life. They were good at supporting each other.

"Vikta's very old-world European," Chris said. "Do you know what I mean by that? Warm and blunt, and practical. She saw how it would be better for both of us, for me and Jazmin. Less disruptive."

"Better for you to move in?"

"Yes." He grinned.

There was a performative quality to this act of self-narration, his voice ranging from light-hearted to sober, which made me wonder to whom else he'd offered himself like this. The story of him and Jazmin. In any case, I felt flattered by his trust. I asked if Jazmin's father was in the picture and Chris said, no, he was a jazz musician, and a junkie, and Jazmin's mother had cut him out entirely not long after Jazmin was born. As I listened to Chris, I tried to decide if he and Jazmin were scholarship students. I guessed, from his version of her story, that Jazmin might be. As for Chris, I couldn't tell.

He canted forward, hands in the pockets of his coat, pulling the sides close to his body, eyes still on me. "Aren't you going to ask me why I left home?"

I said, growing aware of my hands, my feet, that it was up to him to decide what he wanted to tell me.

"My mother's a painter, quite a good painter, actually, she's had a few solo shows. She's also an alcoholic, high functioning but blackouts, et cetera. We don't get on, we maximally don't. And she's a real estate agent, that's how she supports her art, she loves old houses and she loves to sell things —she's very good at it. Watch out, when you meet her, she'll probably try to sell you a brownstone. My dad's not really around, he kind of checked out of the domestic sphere, but they're not divorced, not even separated. He comes home for brief visits then goes back to LA. My mother calls him even to his face The Invisible Man—then she takes his money. He spends most of his time out there, making industrials."

I said I didn't know what that was.

"Films for corporations about new products. Cars, computers, pharmaceuticals."

He told me how, from the time he was eight, his mother, Patricia, would send him out after school to buy supplies like milk and toilet paper. He'd leave his younger sisters, Renata and Charlotte, playing together under the dining-room table and set off by himself down the block with the money his mother had given him. The first time, before ushering him out of the house, she'd warned him to watch out for pederasts, explaining to him precisely what that meant. Again, his wide-eyed gaze met mine.

"Did anything ever happen to you?" I asked as I rose to my feet.

"You mean did anyone ever attack me in the street? Or lure me into their car? No, they didn't."

He began to drop by at the end of the day, never more than once a week. On his first return, he hiked the empty chair closer to my desk before folding himself into it. Hands clasped, overcoat flowing around him, he launched into Elizabeth Bishop's "One Art," reciting from memory the poet's litany of loss, telling me when done that the poem had moved him to tears. Pulling myself together, I said the poem had a habit of doing that to people. It had made Jazmin cry as well, Chris said. I handed him Rich's *Dream of a Common Language*, which I'd brought from home at the beginning of the week—which wasn't anything like Bishop, I said, but something else, and, thanking me, Chris slipped the book into his coat pocket, as if we'd entered into a kind of private exchange, poetry for poetry. Could I recite something for him? he asked. After a flustered instant, I offered him Larkin, not the one about parents fucking up their kids, but "The Trees," all the way to its final line: *begin afresh, afresh, afresh.*

"Nice," Chris said, on his feet. Swaying back and forth, he told me how, when he was six, he'd taught himself never to fall asleep on his back because corpses lay on their backs and if he fell asleep on his back he might die in his sleep. The only way he'd been able to sleep was by listening to voices on an all-news radio station. Even if a newscaster was talking about murders or missing children, the voice had soothed him into drowsiness.

"It's better for me not to sleep alone," he added.

Why tell me that?

Part of my mind floated off. I was still learning to pace myself, through all the class prep, the consuming energy of the classroom, which both fascinated and exhausted me. I wanted there to be a remainder, some part of myself left to devote to my old life, which I wasn't ready to give up entirely.

Vikta was smaller than I expected, her accent more pronounced, when, the evening of the first set of parent-teacher meetings, she seated herself across from me in the classroom. Her checked jacket and slim skirt set could either be called classic or old-fashioned; a thick veil of musky perfume hovered about her. Dark eyeliner. I tried to imagine her in a jazz club. She did not mention Chris. Jazmin's work was exemplary and thoughtful, her handwriting impeccably neat, I said; this part, speaking about Jazmin, was easy. Vikta announced that Jazmin would be applying to music schools: Juilliard, Berklee. I listened for and found her practicality, steely and indomitable. I wondered if I should bring up Chris, but when Vikta didn't, I didn't.

I was packing up my bag at the end of the evening when someone burst through the door. There'd been only one no-show. "I was held up with a client." A surprisingly deep voice. The woman shook out coppery, streaked hair that fell to her shoulders. She came within inches of my face to introduce herself. Chris's mother. Patricia. The long hair gave her a girlish cast. The large, masculine forehead did not, yet her belief in her own powers of seduction made her seductive. She was nothing like my mother. She did not sit but loomed over me, tall in her heeled boots. I told her Chris was brilliant, and she nodded, as if his brilliance were self-evident and certainly no credit to me. She shrugged off talk of college and the requisite tests before admission, saying she'd figure it out.

"Was she drunk?" Chris asked the next day, back in my office, seeming to shrink into his chair when speaking of her. I said I didn't think so. "We still talk," he said. He squirmed inside his overcoat, an item of clothing I'd never seen him without. Part of me wanted to tell him that he was free to take it off if he wanted. I was sure, if he'd wanted, he would have done so. Apparently, the math teacher had once tried to make him remove the coat in class and Chris had refused. According to the Latin teacher, he'd worn the coat the entire previous year as well. Security blanket, armour, second skin, it wasn't any business of mine why he wore the coat so obsessively. Did he wash it? It didn't smell. Inevitably there were jokes in the staff room: Did he take off the rest of his clothes and leave on the overcoat when in bed with Jazmin? I never saw another student tease him about it.

Something caught Chris's eye. Upon arrival that morning, I'd dropped the book I'd been reading on the subway onto the desk: a slim, hand-stitched volume by the artist who'd been a child hustler and would become an activist before his death. Image of a prone body on the cover, William Burroughs quote on the reverse. In fact, I shouldn't have removed the chapbook from the apartment at all, because it was a rare edition that belonged to my husband, and he'd asked me to treat such items in his collection as the precious objects they were. I'd taken it because I harboured a small, ongoing, reactive desire, in relation to my husband, to do as I pleased, and Tyler, my art critic friend, had mentioned the book to me a week or so before, which had aroused my curiosity and made me pull it from the shelf. Chris picked up the chapbook, opened it.

"Is this yours?" Eyes wide, he began to read.

"My husband's."

"Oh." At this, Chris looked up. "I didn't know you had a husband." Then he returned to the book, flipping through its pages, the precise nature of his avidity being difficult to gauge.

That steady gaze again. "Ms. Larsen, if I'm careful, can I borrow this for the weekend?"

Caught out, I could have said, I'm sorry, Chris, it's not mine to lend.

It struck me that perhaps I ought to hesitate before offering a high-school student a book of monologues about gay sex and cruising and life on the streets. Yet the book wasn't an instruction manual, it was fiction. What kind of person hoards art? And what would it mean to say no, to dismiss his interest? Rebuff him?

What if he damaged the book or failed to return it? If so, I could attempt, hard as it might be, to find another copy. Once more I longed to be generous. To make, when all else failed—when it felt, as it sometimes did, as if other forms of affection had withdrawn from me—kindness my lodestar. If I was going to err, the voice in my head said, better to err on the side of kindness.

"Can't you tell your husband you forgot it here for the weekend?" Chris said.

"If I lend it to you," I said, "you have to promise to have it back to me by Monday. No bent pages, no coffee stains. It has to be intact. All right?"

"I understand," Chris said. "Absolutely."

He held out his hand. Startled, I shook it.

As he slipped the book into his satchel, I was pulled back into a memory of being sixteen, standing in the shower, wanting to open my arm with the knife in my hand because the boy I was seeing, in his insecurities and jealousies, had accused me of infidelities with people I barely knew—older boys, athletes, a friend's brother who lived out of town. The week before, my boyfriend had passed me his diaries to read; in them, he threatened to find the shotgun his father had hidden and kill himself. I had no idea, as I stood in the shower, if any of what he had written was true, if there was a shotgun, or if, in his own despair, he was messing with me. At sixteen, having no prior experience of anything like this, I had no idea what to believe or what to do, other than that I had the knife. I could not have gone to my father, the distant economist, for advice. I feared him enough to make it impossible. Nor could I have confided in my mother, who had once told me that my entire adolescent life was incomprehensible to her. I could not bear to speak to my friends, because the accusations, untrue as they were, haunted me so much I didn't want to repeat them to anyone. In the shower, I drew the knife along my arm until a red line bubbled, wondering what I'd do if my boyfriend really blew his brains out.

I had no intention of telling Chris about this episode, about the boy who'd threatened to kill himself but didn't. I said nothing yet was pulled back into the heat of a promise I'd made to myself as the blistering shower water sluiced over me and I'd dropped to my knees,

SKIN

blood running down my arm: I would never forget the intensity of those feelings, the longing, the panic, the shame, I would always take their depths seriously, in myself and others, never diminish or disparage them.

I opened my office door, ushered Chris out, wished him a good night.

The following Monday, he returned the borrowed book, unblemished, by slipping it under my office door. No word, no note accompanied it. As Thanksgiving approached, and the year wound down, he began to skip classes. Not just mine. His failure to stop by my office hurt the most, although I couldn't speak of it, as if I'd failed some special assignment at being interesting.

In class, Jazmin sat beside his empty seat, taking her assiduous notes. I called on her sometimes, simply to hear the sound of her voice. When Chris was there, he seemed to have done the readings or else, when he spoke, covered for himself effortlessly, and though I debated asking him to meet me after class, I could not, as I watched the two of them vanish out the door, bring myself to do so.

In the new year, after a few good weeks, his absences began again. When I asked about him in the staff room, others shrugged. Because this had happened before. Apparently he was spending a lot of time in the library. One day I walked past, and there he was, headphones pressed to his ears, dark head lowered, a notebook in front of him, small hands tapping, not writing, not drawing. I thought about entering the library but did not. At least he wasn't out in some alley getting high. The Latin teacher, she of the cinched waist, said, He always sounds convincing when he says he'll pull it together and you want to believe him but, after all this time, what's the point?

At last, unable to help myself, I asked Jazmin to stay behind one afternoon. She kept her gaze down, bristling when I asked if she knew what was up with Chris. He's fine, she said in her soft, resistant voice.

At the end of January, I turned at a knock on my office door to find Chris waving a small sheaf of stapled pages in his gloved hands. "I'm sorry, Ms. L, I couldn't write about *Romeo and Juliet*. Have you read Hyde's *The Gift*, about how we give value beyond capitalism to art, about gift economies and economies of reciprocal relation, I happened to be reading *Bartleby* at the same time, and it's all in there, too, only in the form of failures of reciprocity, and Hyde doesn't talk about *Bartleby*, so I really wanted to connect them for you."

It was as if the weeks of his absence were shoved into an envelope, sealed, posted, and we were picking up where we'd left off. I was swamped with relief. Swamped with something.

"Couldn't you somehow work *Romeo and Juliet* into an essay on failures of reciprocity?" I asked. "Seems like there'd be a fit."

"Read what I've written first, okay? Then if I have to redo it, I will. I have read *Romeo and Juliet*. Quiz me. I'll memorize a scene if you want that. Do you know there are school boards that have banned *Romeo and Juliet* for promoting teen drug use—not teen suicide pacts?"

He bristled with a manic energy that didn't, to my mind, seem drug-induced but spurred by some internal anxiety.

"Is everything okay?" I asked.

Chris held out one gloved hand. "Look what Vikta gave me for my birthday. Deerskin. They're soft as butter. Try them on. You have to feel them for yourself."

"Chris, I don't need to —" but he was already pulling the gloves from his hands, passing them over, and it seemed ridiculous to refuse: They were a pair of gloves, just a pair of gloves, his gloves, soft, warm from the heat of his hands. I wanted no one to see me trying on Chris's gloves. I tugged them off and handed them back as swiftly as I could.

"They're beautiful," I said.

"And this sweater, it's cashmere, she gave it to me for Christmas."

When he flung open the wings of his overcoat, I almost leaped back, convinced he was going to ask me to touch the sweater as well.

There was something he needed me to affirm about Vikta, who was not, after all, his mother but whom perhaps he had fixed on as a kind of mother.

"When was your birthday, Chris?"

"Last Friday."

He had, I realized, likely turned eighteen. An adult. Yes, he said, when I asked. Had he had a good birthday? Yes, he said. He and Jazmin had gone to see *Sans Soleil*. Which I hadn't seen, I said. But I must have seen some of Chris Marker's films, Chris pressed, and I said yes, of course, again with the sense that he sought some approbation from me.

I retreated to my desk and laid his paper atop all the other papers written as I'd instructed, on *Romeo and Juliet*, not Lewis Hyde and Melville's *Bartleby the Scrivener*.

"Can I expect you back in class sometime?" I asked.

"You know, you mustn't take it personally when I cut class. It doesn't have anything to do with you." It was like being pinned, as if he could see right into the place where I did take his absence personally.

"But I can expect you back?"

"I hope so," he said. "How's it been going for you so far this year?"

Disconcerted, I told him everything was going fine.

"Can I ask you something else, Ms. Larsen?" He stood in the doorway, small body leaning against the frame, one gloved hand holding onto it. "Maybe this is an inappropriate question, and if it is, you'll tell me, but I'm curious, where do you live?"

I felt his question enter my body. I did not know if it was the kind of question a student should ask a teacher, or if a teacher should offer a reply. I lacked a certain kind of experience. I tried to calculate in terms of harm: Did the greater harm lie in answering or refusing to answer? I said, "The Lower East Side."

"I see you walking to the F train sometimes," Chris said.

Saw me from where? Did this mean he watched out for me?

"I feel kind of stuck in an art rut," Chris said. "It's what I know. Art, art history. There's poetry, which interests me, but I'm thinking I should broaden my areas of study, especially if I want to write essays, like eclectic, philosophical essays, like the one I wrote for you. I'm taking Latin, in part because I want to learn about medieval mysticism, but I'm wondering if I should have taken physics or biology, because neurology is also of interest. Then there's landscape gardening, especially the design elements. You don't happen to know any landscape gardeners, do you?"

"Not offhand," I said, taken aback by this barrage. "I could ask around, but you can always look in the phonebook."

"I'll see you later," Chris said, with a little wave, closing the door behind him. He was not really shutting me in, I could have flung the door open as soon as I heard him retreat down the hall. But I didn't. I collapsed in my chair. I picked up his paper and thrust it in among all the other papers, where it dazzled like a coin half-buried in the thick of a pudding. I pulled it out, read the first sentence, instantly wanted to read more. I stuffed it back in the pile. Was I a real teacher or someone pretending to be a teacher? I placed my hand atop the whole stack, as if I could flatten them all. It was almost five, dark hastening outside.

I pulled on my coat. But I didn't leave. I pulled cookies from a box I kept there and stuffed my mouth with them. I switched on the hot pot to boil some water and make myself a cup of instant coffee, and when I took a sip, scalded my tongue. I switched on the desk lamp. I pressed my hands deep into the pockets of my coat. I paced. I was supposed to care. It was my job to care, and to be careful.

I often felt uncharismatic in those days. Love, the kind of love I longed for, seemed to have failed me, along with the professional success I'd aimed for in coming to New York, eager, right out of college, to throw myself into whatever processes of transformation had already begun. With the film, I'd had success, a heady one, and had assumed there would be more, that I had initiated a process, and would keep floating upwards, only it hadn't happened like that.

There must first be some further transformation I needed to achieve: I was searching for this transformation. This was what I told myself. I didn't know where or how I was going to find it, but the desire to do so pressed like a blade against my chest.

I packed up my bag. On the other side of the door, a janitor, singing softly in Spanish, rolled a metal bucket along the hall. Once more I told myself: I'd made it through six months and not been driven by my students from the classroom. I'd bought myself a year's worth of financial security.

When at last I stepped into the hall, stomach growling with hunger, I spotted a lone figure sitting on a bench, farther along the hallway, coat buttoned to his chin. The doors were locked. Or should have been. The janitor ought to have asked him to leave hours ago.

"What are you doing here?" I asked when I reached Chris's side.

"Waiting for Jazmin."

"Is she here?"

"At her voice lesson."

He'd told me her lessons were in Manhattan. "Why can't you wait for her at home?" As soon as I said the word *home*, I regretted it, because the word made him flinch.

"Chris, it's almost seven. Have you had dinner? Listen, I have a car." My friend Jack had loaned me his for two weeks while he was in London. "Why don't you come home with me and I'll make you dinner, then I'll drive you back to Jazmin's." As soon as the words were out, I was desperate to withdraw them. What had I been thinking? I hadn't been thinking. He looked so forlorn. Hence my compassion. Something must be up with Vikta: This was what I surmised.

Chris stared at the wall. "I didn't think you had a car."

"A friend of mine is out of town and needed someone to keep an eye on his. On second thought, let's try a restaurant. Somewhere near here. Tell me where. Then I'll drive you to Jazmin's." I was trying to hide how flustered I felt.

Chris stood up slowly. "I'd prefer to go to your place."

He told me, as I threaded Jack's car towards the Williamsburg Bridge, hands tight on the wheel, that as soon as they were through school, he and Jazmin were moving to Paris. "Jazmin wants to study voice with someone there. Or Montréal if we can't afford anything in Paris. We went to Montréal as a family when I was a kid. It's very European. French. Cosmopolitan."

He was speaking to me as though I knew nothing about Montréal, which made me laugh, because by then I'd told him I'd grown up in Toronto. Meanwhile I was scrambling to overcome my phobia of driving off the edge of this bridge like any bridge and plunging into the water below. A voice in my head shouted at me that I should stop, wherever, heedless of traffic, tell Chris to get out. *Get out!* Another voice said, Stop projecting. Stop catastrophizing. All I was doing was spending an hour or two with him, distracting him. I was taking him into Manhattan where he needed to meet up with Jazmin.

"We can't afford anywhere here. Anyway, Vikta thinks it's a bad idea, our moving in together. Even if I found somewhere, Vikta told me she wouldn't let Jazmin move out. Vikta says it's the wrong thing for Jazmin to do and she'd stop supporting her. I asked Jazmin to marry me. It's not like we just met —"

I wanted to yell at him, too, but kept my eyes on the road. "Does Jazmin want to move in with you? Does she want to get married?"

"Yes," Chris said. His voice made me turn.

Perhaps in the beginning Vikta had been charmed by him, taken in by his plight, but now saw him as an impediment, even antagonist. His unruly romanticism felt dangerous to her. Even I, his confidante, turned cynical in the face of it. Maybe Vikta was trying to placate him with gifts before making a move. I wondered what Jazmin wanted. If she even knew what she wanted, tugged between her boyfriend and mother.

"I don't think Vikta wants me there anymore," Chris said. "Like I'm sucking Jazmin's energy or distracting her. Vikta's very practical, I told you. She thinks I'm not practical. Maybe I'll go to a hostel.

Patricia will laugh at me when she finds out. She'll drive in every nail that she can, then say, You still have a room here in case you've forgotten. She was fine in the beginning. She was glad I wasn't living at home."

"Chris, you're not going to end up in a hostel."

He said nothing.

"Will you tell me why don't you want to live at home?"

"Patricia and I, we get into terrible fights. It got physical. It's a lot better if I'm not there."

"Physical how?" But, staring out the window, braced against the passenger seat, he didn't say anything more, and I decided this was not the moment to press.

When we came off the bridge onto Delancey, I sped through a red light, which, given the flick of his eyes, Chris noticed but didn't mention. I drove past shuttered storefronts as I circled one block, then another, searching for a parking space. I could give up and drive him directly back to Fort Greene. I wanted badly to do this. I explained to Chris that my husband lived in the south of France. We were married but lived separate lives. His attention focused at that. A man pulled a grill over a bakery window, like the cascade of a metal waterfall. We could go to a restaurant, one in my neighbourhood, the Mexican one. A quick meal. Then, either he would head off to meet Jazmin or I would drive him back, back to a place where he felt he wasn't wanted. Though it was winter, children played mysterious games in the pools of orange light beyond their stoops. I saw Chris in them.

He seemed reluctant to go directly to the restaurant. "Don't you want to drop off your bag?"

We were on my street. We exchanged barely a word as he followed me up the four inside flights. He watched as I jimmied the key into the lock, pulling the whole door towards me until the key caught at its precise angle and turned.

Benevolence: An East Village Story

❖

The apartment, the two conjoined railway apartments with separate entrances, was at the rear of a building on Ludlow Street. My husband had rented them both, back when it was obscenely cheap to do so, knocked a hole in the wall between them, linking rooms where the windows opened in daylight over a parking lot and, across the street, a schoolyard, a miracle of Manhattan sky.

Through the door on the left, you entered the main bedroom. The door to the right led into the kitchen.

On entering through the right-hand door, Chris might have thought the small spare room, beyond the kitchen, was my bedroom, the room that had become mine when my husband, though he was not yet my husband, and I stopped sleeping together, where, face stuffed to a pillow, I sobbed myself to sleep at night and, during the years of my marriage, listened to my husband fuck others in what had been our shared bed. We had come to an arrangement, an arrangement, I'd told myself as I lay on the spare-room futon, touching the wedding ring on my finger, that had benefits for me. I could live like this. I had lived like that.

On my own in the apartment, I kept the futon in the spare room rolled out on its frame, pillows piled upon it. Occasionally out-of-town friends stayed over. Sometimes, I slept there for a change, as if a different bed might change me. Beyond that room was a small bathroom: toilet, rickety shower stall replacing the bathtub.

I looped my bag over one of the hooks by the door. Across the kitchen, a series of black-and-white photos hung on the wall above the table, a few photos that my husband had taken along with stills from some of the independent films I'd acted in. Chris walked towards them. In the largest one, I'm in a black leather jacket, torn fishnets, wearing a very short blond wig. This was the film that won all the awards, the one that had a commercial run in North America and Europe, *Invitation*, in which I played Angie, crack addict, former flower-shop owner, who sets off in search of her brother in the wake of her father's death. Briefly, four years before, when I was twenty-five, there'd been posters with my face on them plastered all over the streets below Fourteenth Street. Sometimes people, recognizing me, had stopped me on the sidewalk.

Those were the months when I had felt the thrill of minor fame, the shock of convincing my director, so many people, even my husband, that I could become someone so unlike who I was. Somehow I had done that, or we had, the group of us coming together on the streets of New York and Hoboken, under the hot lights in rooms with men behind cameras, repeating the lines, finding the trick of communal neurochemistry and projection that had allowed me as I knew myself to vanish into someone else. Angie, haunted and craving, pounding flower stems with a hammer, my throat raw from smoking so many cigarettes on set. I'd done that. We had. Every decision I had made to reach that point in my life felt justified. I'd lived those months in the thrum of an alchemy that fuelled my body from the moment I woke up until I collapsed at night. I lived in awe. And I'd believed, I'd wanted to believe, that something like it would happen again. There had been other roles, some minor, some satisfying. But none with the immanence of that one.

Chris stepped towards the image of my cocked blond head, cigarette teetering between my fingers.

"That's you." His incredulity. Sometimes it takes people a while to recognize me. "I didn't know you acted."

I nodded. "Now you do."

"Do you still act?"

"Not so much."

"I saw that film. I had no idea that was you." He was taking me in, with wonder, so that, standing there in my kitchen, in my work clothes, I felt re-encountered, as if I'd inadvertently stripped. I was almost thirty, embarrassingly alive to his admiration. And confirmation: I had, indeed, done that. "Will you be in something else soon?"

"Senior English class."

I moved away from the door and explained about the double apartment. Cockroaches rustled into their cracks. A faint smell of gas from the stove filled the air. I took Chris as far as the living room on the near side, which contained a desk and the flowered sofa that my husband and I had dragged up from the street in the earliest days of the AIDS crisis, when people still joked, only they weren't joking, that even a sofa might give you AIDS. Hauling its weight up each flight of stairs, how we had scoffed at them. I did not lead Chris through the open doorway into the study that held my work desk and a wall full of bookshelves, where I'd stuffed the Wojnarowicz chapbook back on the shelf. There was no door between this room and my bedroom, the double bed on its box spring, the red velvet curtains closing off the hand-built closet, where my clothes and underclothes lay strewn across a chair.

What had I been thinking in bringing Chris to the apartment? By indicating where my actual bedroom was, I was, however, gesturing to something else. I didn't know why it had taken me so long to recognize it. The spare room swelled. I was certain that Chris, in whatever new light he saw me, was aware of it. My husband had never said, Don't get a roommate, though I'd always thought he'd prefer I didn't. And I'd never wanted one, despite my financial need. But here was a different need, not mine. It was possible, I knew, to live quite separate lives in the apartment because I'd done so. I could do this again. We could do this.

Chris stood still, as if any shift or expansion of his own desire would throw what he wanted out of reach.

*

Seated in the same office chair as for my job interview six months before, I told the principal that we both knew the circumstances were unusual. I had worn a vintage suit and sensible pumps to this meeting. That morning I'd taken my Chinese grocery store wedding ring out of the bathroom medicine cabinet and, as I sat there, worked it around my finger. I explained that I had reason for concern about

SKIN

Chris's current living situation based on things he'd said and the fact that he was only irregularly coming to class. I was prepared to offer the spare room to him in order to help him finish the school year and graduate high school. I realized that there was much of his history I didn't know, nevertheless, given that once again he seemed to be teetering, I had what looked like a possible solution. I listened to the timbre of my voice. Conviction. Actor. I wasn't attempting to go behind the principal's or anyone's back, I said. I'd told Chris to speak to his parents.

It might have been useful to have been able to produce an actual husband or partner, someone to sit in the chair beside me in my woollen suit, to make the situation look more conventionally familial, but I did not have that. I told the principal truthfully that my husband was living in the south of France.

A man in his forties whom I presumed to be gay, he had an ability to project neither instant judgment nor overcompensatory friendliness when dealing with the school's students. I'd witnessed him in action. He picked up a tennis-ball-sized rubber brain from his desk and squeezed.

I said I wished there were a word for the kind of solicitude I felt. If *aunt* had been a verb, I would have used it.

We both knew, even if we didn't say it, that Chris was no longer a minor. He was free to make his own decision about where he lived. I was only temporarily affiliated with the school. If I'd had any chance of being hired on permanently, perhaps I lost it at that moment, although I didn't yet know if this was something I wanted, if what I was doing could be construed as self-sabotage.

"You've talked to him," said the principal.

"Yes," I said. "He seems to think the move will allow him to focus on school. Surely that's a good thing."

Benevolence: An East Village Story

❖

I had met the man who would become my husband on a bus coming into the city from Newark airport. I was, in those first months post-college, living in an Upper West Side flat with college friends, auditioning, reading scripts for a midtown non-profit theatre; one of us was trying to form a theatre company. Six years older, part-time academic, photographer, art critic, Michael, seated next to me on the bus, begged for my number. An appealing extrovert, he tugged me downtown to see art, film, dance, theatre. Bands and performances in East Village clubs. Opening up a world to me, he introduced me to people he thought I should know, film directors, performance artists. We went dancing until all hours at Danceteria. Three months later he asked me to move in with him.

Five months after that, he told me the relationship wasn't working. I sat at the kitchen table. Michael's lips moved but I could no longer hear him. I was twenty-three. I told him, It's like you're breaking me up with my life.

Melodramatic, yes, but that's what it felt like. The next day he told me he'd changed his mind.

I had already begun to sense the ways in which he liked to be kept off-kilter, while I wanted the opposite. For a while I was able to mimic this quality of his but I couldn't sustain it. At first I told myself that the electricity racing up my back when he spoke to some other man or woman was simply my insecurity talking, like the night in the basement cavern of 8BC when I caught him chatting up the blond ceramic artist in a leather halter top. Then I accosted him.

Six months after the first breakup he told me that although he liked me well enough, he didn't think we were suited to being together as a couple. I had just been cast in a film that a friend of his was directing so I was free to move into the spare room on the other side of the apartment, he said—only I needed to understand that he was going to be sleeping with other people. That was the way it was, at least for now, how he felt compelled to conduct his life. He moistened his lips with his tongue as he spoke. There was a strong seam of self-interest in him, I'd always known it. Behind their little glasses, his eyes glittered.

I flew back to Toronto, though I'd never found great comfort in the company of my parents or the house where I'd grown up. In those days the cheapest way to fly between Toronto and New York was to take a flight from Newark to Buffalo then travel the rest of the way by bus. It was on the way back that I got stopped. The border grillings were always worse when travelling by bus than air. From the depths of my wallet, the customs agent extracted a folded pink deposit slip from a New York City bank made out in my name. He couldn't accuse me of working illegally, he had no proof of that, but he could accuse me of lying, of not being the temporary visitor I said I was.

Bag over my shoulder, I had to walk back across the border bridge to the Canadian side and beg the driver of a bus heading to Toronto to let me board. Near tears, I told him I had to get home. From the Toronto bus terminal, I called my mother, distraught because everything I had thought to be my life lay out of reach.

In New York, unless I spoke about it, no one guessed that I was not American. I had learned to shift my vowels, the very cadences of my voice. At the Bay Street bus terminal in Toronto, I ripped all the used pages out of my datebook. I took the subway north and prevailed upon my mother, when she met me by car, to lend me the money to book a direct flight back to New York. At the house, acquiescing to my mother's suggestion, I signed up over the phone for a course in social work at a local college and was given a registration number that anyone could check for its veracity until I cancelled it. We drove to a consignment store where I replaced my vintage dress and lace-up boots with polyester office wear, every gesture rippling with anxiety. At the airport drop-off my mother kissed me on the cheek, patted my shoulder, wished me luck.

That night, after stripping off my consignment clothes in my small room and wrapping myself in my silk dressing gown, I told Michael what had happened. I still had a strong urge to confide in him. If I closed my eyes, I remained convinced that the apartment around me might go up in flames, as I'd feared that afternoon when climbing the stairs out of the Second Avenue subway station. I dreamed often of fire burning the apartment to the ground and leaving me homeless.

Why did I want to return to this life, to a man who did not want to be with me, whose infidelities had broken our relationship? Because it was my life and I wanted to be whoever I was becoming in it, which was the closest thing to feeling at home that I could imagine. Michael poured me a glass of Bordeaux from the open bottle on the table and kissed me. Then he offered to marry me. On edge and still aflame, I thought I must have misheard him. He said, We can discuss it in the morning.

The thing was, despite our differences, we lived well together. Even if we did not like to do the same things in bed. I was smart and knew little about art, thus, he said, I was his ideal reader and he had come to depend on me to edit his articles. I loved the way the apartment's rooms opened one upon another, light-filled, and experienced my life in them as a form of luck. Michael seemed genuinely gratified that the introductions he'd made for me were paying off.

Was it masochism to accept such an arrangement? The next night, as I lay on the spare room futon, restlessly turning, I decided I would accept his gift in the form that it took. In the spare room, in the kitchen where I often found Michael's coffee grounds dumped in the sink, out on Houston Street, in my blond wig in front of the camera, I called upon the raw edges of my unsettledness, found the necessary urgencies, searched for the romance in beneficence until I found it. I made something of what I had. In the bathroom that was my husband's, mine after he left for France, hung a print taken on our wedding day by a photographer friend of his: On the steps of city hall, Michael smiles beatifically in his dark suit, as, head tucked to his shoulder, clutching a bouquet of daisies, I lean against him, skinny and hopped up on gratitude in a white velvet wedding dress.

SKIN

❖

I told my friend Magda, the video artist, the two of us shouting at each other, scrunched in our black leather jackets in a bar on Avenue A, that because I'd been the beneficiary of someone else's altruism, I felt compelled to pass it on. Chris was a senior, smart, a bit troubled, bad home life. He had a steady girlfriend whose mother didn't want him living with the two of them. I had the unusual luxury of an extra room. He would only be there for a few months. I was going to make sure he made it through the school year.

"What kind of person would I be if I didn't make the offer when I knew I could?" I answered for myself, I would be a bad person. If, at that moment, other things were missing from my life, namely a partner, a true husband, here was a chance at something else. I chose benevolence. I wouldn't have listened to any opposition even if she'd offered it.

I buzzed Chris in one Saturday afternoon and listened to his footsteps climb the stairs. Before that his father had called from LA, not so much to vet me as to work out financials. He wanted it to be clear that his son wasn't indigent. Nor was I expected to cook and clean for him. He would have an allowance, pay rent. His father didn't thank me for taking him in or ask me questions about myself. The conversation was brief. Remarkably, Chris's mother didn't get in touch at all.

He arrived with a single knapsack over his shoulders. Leaving him to settle himself in the spare room, I put together some pasta and salad for supper. At the end of the meal, Chris thanked me politely.

"You okay?" He fixed me in his gaze. As if he were the parent and I the teenager.

I said yes. "You?" I asked.

He told me he'd wash the dishes. That night, as I undressed in the bathroom on my side of the apartment, hook in its eye to lock the door, clothes slung over the edge of the tub, I violently chastised myself. What had I done? The next afternoon Chris showed up with a fortress-sized block of toilet paper rolls, holding the package out as a gift.

I offered him the desk in the living room next to the kitchen, my desk being the one on the other side of the wall, in the room with the built-in bookshelves that rose to the ceiling, my husband's Persian carpet softening the floor, the room next to my bedroom. I rigged up a curtain to hide my bed, another curtain between the front rooms, but told Chris he had free rein of all the books. I jimmied a curtain in front of the spare-room doorway so that he, too, had privacy. I found myself listening to him. For him. Whenever the bolt of the door leading into the kitchen opened to his key in the lock, the sound resonated as if inside my head. He was quieter in the apartment than I expected. When I told him to try me if he needed any help with his homework, he gave me an amused smile. He asked if I had a typewriter he might borrow.

First thing in the morning I struggled into some sort of clothing before pushing the curtains aside and making my way around to the kitchen where I would often find Chris already up, dressed, in his overcoat, sleeves pushed to his elbows, lighting the burner under a stovetop espresso maker as cockroaches scurried back into the walls. The top rattled. Steam rose. He adjusted the gas flame. I mumbled good morning, having already brushed my teeth and peed, wondering if he had heard me pee. I wondered again if he wore the overcoat to sleep in. Even first thing in the morning his skin was smooth, as if he needed to shave only every couple of days. I couldn't help noticing. I asked him how he was doing. Fine, he said. The coffee was strong. He told me his mother had taught him to make coffee. I wasn't his mother. Under the coat, he wore the cashmere sweater that Vikta had given him. I wasn't Vikta either. One morning, as I poured coffee into a thermos, I asked if I'd heard a transistor radio in the night. Chris nodded, and I remembered him telling me in the fall how he needed a talking voice to fall asleep, how he didn't like to sleep alone. The next day he appeared with a Walkman.

After breakfast, we set off, our voices echoing down the stairwell. My neighbours would have registered his presence, including my friend Jack who lived two floors below. I dropped a note of explanation under Jack's door. On the street, men had already gathered outside the small warehouse beside my building, chatting and calling from a cluster of upturned milk cartons. Salsa music blared. People lined up farther down the block to buy crack. Past the bodega, the deli, the homeless woman who'd once hit me over the head with her umbrella, up to Houston, down the steps to the F train. As Chris's overcoat lifted in the acrid sirocco rising from underground, I inhaled the scent of his deodorant.

Once we arrived in Brooklyn, Chris hung back on the platform, hands in his coat pockets, and let me go ahead, as if this were something we'd agreed upon, and I went, without looking back, through the turnstiles, up the stairs. When I next saw him, he would be in class with Jazmin, small body, dark head drawn close to hers.

I kept an eye on Jazmin, who maintained her silent intensity but avoided looking at me. I wondered if she resented me, if other students knew of the change in Chris's living arrangements or if Chris and Jazmin kept this to themselves. I did not hide what I was doing from the rest of the staff. I left a note about Chris's move into my apartment in their mail boxes. I mentioned the extra room. I wrote that my husband—note, the husband—had agreed to the arrangement. Most people said nothing. I kept wearing my Chinese grocery store wedding ring. To the wasp-waisted Latin teacher, I said that the situation with Jazmin and her mother seemed to have unravelled, making it difficult for Chris to concentrate on school work, and that as soon as they graduated, Chris and Jazmin planned to move in together. I said that I wanted to do what I could to help him make it through high school. I added that his father paid me rent. And the thing was, he did seem to have settled. He was back in class—not just mine but theirs.

Benevolence: An East Village Story

❖

Beside me on the vinyl sofa, the two of us alone in the staff room, Celia Hahn, long, sand-coloured hair raked on top of her head, crease between her eyebrows, picked at the cushion seam between us with her paint-spattered fingers.

"How's it going with Chris?" Pluck went her fingers.

"We meet in the kitchen. It's virtually two separate apartments. He lives an independent life." I had a hunch that Celia, who showed at a gallery on Eleventh Street and who knew that my husband didn't live with me, had been to the apartment, for parties, back in the days when Michael lived there.

"Do you cook meals together?"

"Sometimes I make enough for both of us." In truth, I wasn't much of a cook.

One afternoon, the first week after Chris moved in, I'd run into Celia on the F train platform, both of us on our way back into the city, and she'd asked me where Chris was. I told her I had no idea. Probably somewhere with Jazmin. In the staff room, as on the platform and the train crossing the bridge into Manhattan, I felt the probe of her curiosity. I had the wild thought that she was spying on me, intent on reporting back to Michael.

"Jazmin's mother is probably thanking me for taking him off her hands," I said. "And it may be that Jazmin is happier for the space as well."

"Do you ever hang out with him?" Celia's fingers, granted their own life, went on plucking at the seams of the sofa. Pluck, pluck.

I stood, shoving my hands into my pockets. "You mean do we go out and do things together? We do not."

When Jazmin stayed over, on weekends, sometimes after a voice class, they kept to themselves. Sometimes I met and chatted with them in the kitchen. They washed their own dishes, mine, too, on occasion. I told them to be careful coming back after dark. Even on weekends, they rose early and had often left the apartment by the time I got up.

At night I wore ear plugs. I tried to hold onto to my feelings of benevolence the way one might hold onto a lover. To swallow altruism like a drug.

One evening I came home late from school to the darkened, empty apartment, switched on the light in my bedroom and knew instantly they'd been in my bed. Everything had been left neat but the comforter was folded under the pillows and a hand towel lay crumpled at the foot.

I smelled sex. I imagined their naked teenaged bodies stumbling heedlessly from room to room, from futon to sofa to bed. Their fucking. I dropped my bag. I didn't undress. My own orgasm was quick and fierce. Afterwards, clambering to my feet, I bolted into the bathroom. Sometimes, standing in front of that classroom of eighteen-year-olds, I'd think the one thing, perhaps the most essential thing they did not know about me was how time passed through me. It still stunned me, at nearly thirty, this new, inescapable velocity. Nothing was inconsequential because everything becomes unrecoverable.

There had been other men since my husband. In the years when we lived together, for all that I dated, I found it hard to bring anyone home, even though my husband kept telling me that, to him, it didn't matter. For some months a willowy printmaker named Anna kept him company on his side of the apartment, then a scrawny young sous-chef named Teddy, who worked in a Sixth Street Italian restaurant. On my side, I kept a box of condoms stuffed at the back of a bedroom shelf. Meanwhile we documented our marriage assiduously in photo albums, ticket stubs, receipts. We wore the cheap rings we'd bought at the Chinese grocery store. I stayed up late editing Michael's articles, padding about the apartment in my silk dressing gown, drinking the wine he bought, reading the books he suggested I read, growing ever more familiar with the smells of his body, when he liked to shit, the timbre of his voice when he grew livid with frustration. He told me stories about running unchecked as a boy around building sites in suburban Ohio while I told him of tobogganing sorties, hurtling down hills in Toronto ravines, leaping off once before the toboggan smashed into a tree. He made me chicken soup and tended to me when I took to my bed with a fever. Sometimes we kissed. Yes, we kissed. Sometimes we jerked each other off. In our immigration interview, we spoke of our shared life, each other's likes and dislikes, each other's parents, how happy we were to have met each other, affirmed each other's eye colour. Blue, that part was easy. And, yes, I paid him rent.

A few months after I received my green card and my husband set out for France, I met the phenomenologist in a restaurant on St. Mark's Place. At the Café Mogador the tables were packed so close together our elbows bumped. It was a relief to spend time with someone who did not see me through the lens of the famous film, who knew me as the creator of solo pieces that I had begun to perform in small places like Darinka or Dixon Place, along with the text and dance collaboration I was working on with my choreographer friend Vivienne. If I was surprised that someone so naturally reserved was studying the cultural meaning of adulthood, which seemed such a chaotic phenomenon, I welcomed people's contradictions, along with the steady pulse of his attention, so unlike the wild ride of my love life with my husband. This steadiness sustained me, sustained us for months, more months, long enough that I began to imagine life going on like this. I allowed myself to relax into happiness. I loved the beautiful expressiveness of the phenomenologist's hands. Then something crept into his voice when he spoke about my friends. One night, he told me that he was distrustful of the performative. He stopped coming to see any of my shows. From my bed, in the apartment where he liked to spend time since it was far larger than his, he lobbed the words, *my friends*, at me as if they were a weapon, then as if my particular friends were anathema to the kind of adulthood he wanted, which required our privacy, our mutual solidarity, at last as if my having friends at all were a betrayal.

Some weeks after I told the phenomenologist that I could not go on like this, I invited home a man who came up to me, full of praise and energy, as soon as I stepped off the tiny stage at Darinka after performing the lost-pets-posters monologue. Once inside my apartment, he pushed me onto the bed, pinning my arms. When I protested, he slapped me, hard enough to shock, told me he'd seen how I was on stage and in that film, understood my inherent submissiveness, knew I wanted this. Gripping my arms, he turned me onto my back. I screamed and somehow, I don't know how, Jack, who lives two floors below, heard me.

I sat shivering in Jack's kitchen, the room strident with clarity, drinking shot after shot of whiskey in my hastily pulled-on clothes, as Jack's dog licked my calves—Jack, with his Irish lilt and fringe of black hair, who might have had an affair with my husband, who liked lovers who spoke little English and lived in far-off places like Istanbul and Buenos Aires, who kept a small votive area in a corner of his living room hung with portraits of those who'd died. Pablo, whom I'd known. Miguel. Daniel. I wanted to call Vivienne, howl and bury myself against her shoulder, but she was on tour, dancing with her boyfriend, also a choreographer, with a bigger reputation and a company of his own. I paced and cried out to Jack: Is this how things are going to be from now on?

Arriving home, I let myself into my side of the apartment, hung up my coat, climbed out of my work clothes, tugged a slippery dress over my leggings. After nudging my lips with a darker lipstick, I came around to the kitchen to discover Chris at the table, where he often liked to work, overcoat pulled tight around him, pale neck bent. I'd known he was there from the buzz of his Walkman. He waved as I entered. I leaned over his shoulder. Latin verbs, about which I knew next to nothing. The sight of him pleased me. Somehow I'd managed to create this pool of calm. He didn't go out much, other than with Jazmin and very occasionally a childhood friend named Ben from Park Slope. He'd gone home once for dinner at his mother's insistence and spent the next day in bed. In the apartment, he behaved like someone who had learned never to call too much attention to himself while doing his best to please. Sometimes I'd catch him scribbling or sketching in his little notebook. Some nights he cooked for me, with fetching pride, the dishes that Vikta had taught him: noodles, chicken paprikash. It struck me that he was used to living among women. Glad of the company, I brought home unusual cheeses for us to try: ammoniac-scented French rounds, ash-laced Humboldt Fog. I let him play his mix tapes, then shared mine, exposing him to local bands he hadn't heard of.

As I stood chugging water at the sink, Chris pulled aside one of his earphones and asked if I was heading out. Yes, I said, I was off to an art opening with friends, up on Tenth Street, including Jack, who had popped his head into the stairwell that morning and so I'd introduced the two of them. Impulsively I asked, "Do you want to come with me?"

Earphones around his neck, Chris leaped to his feet.

Had his mother ever brought him to art openings, I asked at once, panicking. Yes, sometimes, Chris said, closing his workbook, stuffing his notebook into his coat pocket. Was his mother likely to show up at an opening in the East Village? Chris shook his head. Having conjured the invitation, I didn't see how I could retract it, unless I fell down in a faint. One saving grace: Celia had told me she wouldn't be there.

It was a Thursday night, which meant Jazmin would be at her voice class. Before long, Chris would head off to meet her. As we made our way in a stiff wind, north up First Avenue, all I wanted was for the schoolboy flapping at my side to vanish. No, I wanted gratitude to flood him, for him to look back on this moment from some point in the future and be moved to his marrow by all I was doing for him. I cast another glance at him: his full lips, his slightness, the dark spray of his hair.

From the entrance of the storefront gallery, I spotted Jack midway down the room, clustered with leather-jacketed Rodney, who'd directed most of the films I'd been in, including the famous one, and Tyler, the art critic, with his soft cheeks and blond locks. When I approached, Chris at my side, their scrutiny of him felt feral. I'd already mentioned Chris to Tyler. He and Jack would be saying something to Rodney. I kissed Tyler and Rodney, introduced Chris as a student who was boarding with me until the end of the school year, mentioned that he was interested in art. "An international student?" Rodney asked. "Are you at NYU?"

"High school," Chris said. "The Beverley School where she teaches." He held out his hand, charmingly. "Ms. Larsen's my benefactor."

"You're teaching now?" Rodney asked as Chris set off for the folding table that served as a bar to fetch us drinks. "Ms. Larsen?"

"Stop it," I said.

"Nice one," Rodney said, nodding in Chris's direction.

They were not in a bathhouse, watching him materialize through a haze of steam, though they might as well have been. "Rodney, quit it. He's renting the spare room in the apartment. He's got a shitty home life."

"And, darling, you brought him to an art opening," said Rodney. "How culturally magnanimous of you."

I punched him in the arm.

With his head on Rodney's shoulder, Tyler spoke wistfully, staring after Chris: "That's exactly what I wish I'd been like at his age."

Steering Chris away from the alarming clump of them towards the paintings, I caught sight of a man about my age—our gazes snared. Even as Chris and I stared at the canvases, their broad brushstrokes and almost cartoon-like figures, my body awoke to the man's glance. What is it? Chris asked. Nothing, I said, even as I wanted to turn away from him and amplify this feeling. The man's gaze passed over the two of us. I stepped away from Chris.

"It's okay," Chris said. "Don't worry, I'll be off." As if aware of the man, or my discomfort, Chris turned with a wave.

Coming together, the man and I launched into a conversation about the paintings, the texture of their darkness, their brushstrokes, both of us noticing, at the same moment, a mysterious daub of turquoise on the canvas in front of us. I did not know how to introduce myself. Performance artist. Teacher. I did not know how to channel what I was feeling, lust and its stir. When the man, a sculptor who made his living in a metal-work shop, asked if I wanted to join him for a drink, I said I had to prep to teach the next day. He told me he lived with his ex and couldn't invite me home with him. Nor could I invite him back to my apartment.

I walked home alone in a bitter wind.

Yet I had done this to myself.

When I unlocked the door and entered on my side, yellow shone through the open curtains and the broken-open wall that led to the other half of the apartment. I recognized the glow as that of the lamp on the kitchen table, which I didn't remember leaving on.

In that glow Chris stepped into sight.

He wasn't wearing his overcoat. That was the first shock. Never before had I seen him without the coat, even in the apartment. He was clad only in T-shirt and jeans. He must have been cold, for, in winter, the apartment was never truly warm. The shape of his body was newly visible. He said hello as I hung up my jacket.

I thought, If I say anything about the coat, he'll bolt. I didn't ask why he was alone or where Jazmin was. He asked how the rest of the opening had been. Fine, I said.

"You didn't go out with anyone afterwards?"

"Seems not," I said.

I made my way to the kitchen, where a bottle of beer stood on the table beside the book Chris seemed to be reading, one of mine,

Speed and Politics by Paul Virilio. He must have taken Barthes's *A Lover's Discourse* from the shelf because it, too, lay on the table, cover up, spine cracked open. I touched the cover but didn't move the book.

"You're reading Barthes," I said.

"Is that okay? Is that one yours?"

"Of course it's okay," I said.

In the nearly two months since Chris had moved in I'd never before seen him drink anything alcoholic. Had he purchased the beer on his way home, at the bodega across the street? Two more empties stood in the sink. Hooked over the back of the kitchen chair where he'd been sitting was my old leather jacket, the one I'd grown tired of and left on a peg by the door. I'd told Chris that it was his if he wanted it. I hadn't exactly been trying to nudge him out of the overcoat though, yes, to offer another option. He'd never before shown any interest in the jacket. Now the overcoat hung on a peg.

Chris took a swig from his beer, as if this, too, were an ordinary thing for him to be doing on a Thursday evening. "I'm finding the Virilio very seductive, his notions about speed defining civilization — on a personal level, he's making me think about movement and trajectory and circulation."

I wanted to say to him, You're eighteen. What do you know about velocity? Or trajectory? "That's great."

"I'm sincerely grateful for everything you're doing for me," Chris said. "Everything you're introducing me to." At this I blushed, because wasn't this exactly what I'd wanted him to say?

"I'm trying to be kind —" These ridiculous words burst from me.

"Oh, you're kind," Chris said, and I wondered if he was mocking me.

At the fridge, I cracked open one of my own bottles of beer and took it with me into the living room. I pulled my wedding album from a shelf. Back in the kitchen, I laid the album on the table and peeled apart its laminated pages.

It had taken me years to see how I look younger in these photos, to see not just a different version of my adult self but how time passing alters how we perceive time. There Michael and I are, in our wedding clothes, toasting each other in this very room, seven years in the past. I had already explained to Chris something of the nature of my marriage but I wanted him to confront these parts of my life, the palimpsest of complicated layers I'd already lived in this place.

Chris peered at the photo, then pinned me with a look. "I'd do something like that for someone," he said.

"With luck you won't have to," I said.

He asked if there were photos of me wearing my cast-off leather jacket, which he'd slung over the chair. I turned pages until I found one, taken outside the Limbo Lounge, the already vanished bar we'd all loved on Tenth Street near Avenue B. Beside me, Vivienne throws an arm over my shoulder. I'm gesturing, hand in the air. We are being performatively demonstrative. Michael smiles through his little round glasses, hands in the pockets of his bomber jacket. You can't see the flame of his attractiveness in it or feel his need for the affirmation of his attractiveness. He's about to turn thirty-two, two years older than I was as I stared at his photo with Chris. Behind us, there's a blur of someone else, not yet a ghost, a glimpse of Pablo, who had been Michael's friend as well as Jack's lover before he died. I did not tell Chris that Pablo had died.

Taking in these images with Chris became a reminder, not that I ever forgot, that for all my husband had done for me, there was one thing he had not done. Every so often the absence nagged, but, because of what he had done, I had never felt entitled to insist on the claim. He'd never put my name on the apartment lease. As the months and then years passed and my husband did not talk of returning, I reassured myself by thinking that, in those days of so much death and dying in New York, it was reasonable to assume that he might wish to stay away.

Slipping his bare arms into the sleeves of the leather jacket, Chris backed away from me, across the kitchen. "Ellen, how do I look?" Ellen. He had never before called me by my first name.

From my perch by the sink, aware of my bones tight inside my skin, I said he looked great. I did not say, Don't call me Ellen.

"Have I ever told you about the time a friend of my mother's tried to seduce me, when I was thirteen?"

"No," I said.

"It was at one of my mother's parties, where things can get kind of wild, especially if my dad isn't around. She likes to bring together this mix of real estate people and artists. It turns her on. Usually I'd hang out for a while, then go to bed. This time, I was already in my room, door closed, lights out, when I heard someone coming up the stairs, I guessed they were looking for the bathroom, but my door opens and someone walks in and climbs into bed with me. It was Mira, this friend of my mother's, she's a photographer, her hands smelled like fixative, she was really trashed. She starts kissing me, tongue and all, running her hands all over me. It was kind of hilarious, I don't think she had any idea who I was." He'd taken a seat again at the table, shrugged off the jacket, T-shirt pulling loose around the waistband of his jeans, eyes on me.

"What did you do?" I asked. While my mind went: Hilarious?

"My mother's pretty self-consumed but maybe she sensed something, because all of a sudden, she barges into the room. The light goes on and she starts laughing. Mira rolls over, and she starts laughing, too, then she passes out, right beside me on the pillow. I left, went to my mother's room, shut the door, turned on the radio. I assume my mother spent the night in my bed with Mira. She never came to her room. I don't know what Mira remembers, though sometimes when I knew she was in the house, I put a chair against my door before I went to bed."

"What did your mother do?" Had he been wearing anything in bed that night, I wondered, when the photographer was fondling him?

"She made kind of a joke about it the next day."

"That's it, a joke?"

"She was really drunk, Ellen. It is kind of funny, come on."

I said, "If I say it's funny will you also admit it's kind of not funny?" At thirteen, making out with my first boyfriend in the ravine behind his house, on leaf mould, twigs, broken branches, what had unnerved me was being half-stripped, in broad daylight, close enough to the path that anyone passing by could have caught sight of us.

Chris rose to his feet and stood there, swaying like a reed. "Do you want me to?"

"It's not about what I want, Chris."

Something poured from him, a sudden, liquid submissiveness I'd never felt from him before, as if he were offering himself to me entirely, his body saying: Do with me whatever you want.

Had he been like that, the night with the photographer?

"Good night, Chris," I managed to croak. "I'm going to bed."

I'd asked him before, but I tried again the next evening. After dinner. About college. I tried not to belabour the point but I needed to make it. Why not apply to college? At least apply, what's the harm in it? There are late admissions. I would make a list of places. All over the country. It doesn't mean you have to go, but this way you'll have options. What bad thing is going to happen because you decide to apply?

He didn't need to apply to college, Chris insisted, because he was going to Paris with Jazmin.

One night, it was mid-March by then, I heard him arguing on the phone. I was in bed on my side of the apartment, Chris on the other side, in the living room beyond the curtain, but because there was no door it was impossible not to hear him; there were two phones, one on my side, one on his, but only one line. Come on, he said, with a note of irritation that surprised me. How cutting his voice became, belligerent, even domineering. We can go anywhere—a tonal shift, this spoken in supplication, with an agonizing wistfulness. I stuffed in my earplugs and rolled towards the wall. At breakfast the next morning he seemed subdued, but in class, he and Jazmin were seated side by side at the back of the room, as usual, chatting amicably, or so it appeared. The next evening, Thursday, Chris came home late by himself. When I encountered him, in his overcoat, in the kitchen, he looked pale and seemed to be making an effort to speak, a false cordiality; he didn't want to be drawn out. The next day, Friday, for the first time since the beginning of the year, he and Jazmin were not sitting together.

I had no chance to talk to him until that evening. He was in the apartment when I got home, at the kitchen table. I asked if something had happened with Jazmin—an argument?

"We broke up," Chris said.

In addition to his obvious distress, I had to fight my own shock. "Isn't there a way to work it through? You've been together for so long and have all these plans."

"No, it's over," Chris said.

"Was it your decision or Jazmin's?" I took a seat beside him. "It seems so sudden. Are you sure it's irreparable?" He hadn't come to me for advice, and he wasn't doing so now. I didn't know how much to ask, bewildered because I, too, had counted on the endurance of their relationship, on the strength of Chris's romanticism, however youthful, so that it felt as if an edifice in my own life were falling apart.

"She doesn't want to go to Paris."

"You don't have to go to Paris. Couldn't you stay here if that's what she wants?"

"It doesn't matter, it's over."

He spent the rest of the evening in bed, curtain drawn. The next morning, with no sound from him other than the buzz of his Walkman, I stood outside the curtain and asked if he wanted anything. Still in the throes of my own bewilderment, I made him a mug of coffee and set out a plate of eggs and toast on the kitchen table, called to him, heard him get up as soon as I left the room.

Was it that Jazmin had decided to listen to her mother, whatever her mother wanted her to do after high school, I asked him later, over bowls of ramen noodles, broth laden with chicken and mushrooms and bok choy.

"I guess, in part," he said. Then, more sharply, "That's not all of it—"

His sharpness made me retreat in my attempts to draw him out.

The next day, Sunday, I asked if there was anyone else he could talk to—what about Ben, his Brooklyn friend?

Haggard over a mug of coffee, Chris shrugged.

But on Monday morning he was up without my needing to rouse him, dressed, in my old leather jacket, waiting for me to make him coffee and offer him food. I'd expected more withdrawal, that I'd have to cajole him out the door, or leave him to himself, but, clutching a thermos, he stayed close at my side as we left the apartment. I chalked this up to the fact that, however much pain and turmoil he was in, however fragile he felt, he held onto enough sense of a home that he felt able to venture out into the world. And, despite everything, the fact that he was still coming to school made me glad.

I had to stand at the front of the classroom, knowing what I knew, Chris distracted and mute by the window, Jazmin, puffy-eyed, refusing to look at me, occupying a seat in the front row, having displaced a girl named Briony. Did Briony know what had happened? Surely everyone in that classroom guessed or knew, given their choreography.

On a Saturday, maybe a week later, I let myself into the apartment on the kitchen side, hands full of shopping bags, to find Chris staggering from counter to table, empty bottles everywhere. He turned, an up-ended bottle of beer pressed to his lips. He must have consumed to the dregs every unopened bottle along with every half-open bottle of alcohol I'd left in cupboard or fridge. I pulled off my coat. Without saying anything other than a curt hello, I dropped the groceries and, grabbing a paper bag from under the sink, began to gather up the empties, bottles crashing against each other. Two days before, a fug of pungent smoke had met me in the hallway when I returned; as I'd entered through the door on my side, a drone of words and wild bursts of laughter wafted towards me, the smell even thicker inside the apartment, drenching everything. That time, when I entered the kitchen, Chris, red-eyed, had leaped to his feet as his friend Ben bolted out the door. I flung open the windows, Chris flopping at my heels like a puppy, so close I almost fell into him. Sorry, so sorry, he kept repeating, giggling as pigeons scattered into the air.

This time, things felt different. He dropped the beer bottle and picked up a wine bottle, straining for dregs.

"Isn't that enough," I said, thinking of his alcoholic mother. I set the bag of empties by the door. "Want to talk?"

He shook his head. "Not really."

"Then maybe you should put yourself to bed."

He grabbed a plate from the dish rack and threw it at the wall, missing the photographs. "Don't feel responsible for me." His knees buckled as he collapsed, beseeching me in a series of high-pitched bursts to forgive him, clutching my legs so hard I was frightened I'd fall over. "I'm sorry, I'm sorry."

I pulled myself out of his grip. He seemed to be scrambling for the dustpan. I helped him to his feet, as best I could, which meant touching him once again, and manoeuvred him into the spare room, which was scattered with his belongings, underwear, sweater, books, cassette tapes. When I tipped him into bed, he curled on his side, like a child, clutching his Walkman. "I don't know what to do," he said.

I pulled the covers over his shoulders, all the way up to his neck, before retreating, unable to perform the gesture that hovered in the air, the maternal gesture of laying a hand on him, rubbing his back.

I didn't want to say stupidly mollifying things, like, You'll be okay. I did not want to belittle whatever he was feeling. Maybe he was terrified that I would throw him out. "Chris, I'm the one who's sorry," I said.

When he turned, his words incinerated me. "Don't be kind."

Across the apartment, in my bed, in the dark, I tossed from side to side. The wail of a siren passed along Essex Street. Chris must in his own way have been thinking about time. The end of the school year. What, given the combustion of his relationship, was he going to do now? Where would he go?

Perhaps he pictured me handing him his packed knapsack the morning after school ended and showing him the door. Shouldn't he want to leave? I asked myself, pulling the comforter over my body. Find another place to live. With roommates his own age. Do the things that people his age did. Get a job if he needed one: waiter, dishwasher, busboy. A breeze blew over me. I had signed no contract with his father because I'd wanted the flexibility to ask Chris to leave when or if things became unmanageable. Were they unmanageable? He'd told me how beautiful he found the apartment, the light in it, his face brightening as he spoke. Of course he liked living here, given the freedom he had to come and go, and the space, even the privacy to go through whatever he was suffering. In the dark, I wondered if I should tell him that, if he wanted or needed to, he could stay a little longer, through the summer, until the end of August, if that would offer him a necessary respite, when everything else in his life was so at sea. Wouldn't that be what a good person would do? I asked myself. A kind person?

When I told Chris he could stay on for the summer, his face broke open. He asked me if I was sure and when I said yes, a new wave of relief and pleasure crested over him. He dropped the book he was reading and stumbled to his feet.

"And it's fine with your husband?"

"Yes," I said, although I hadn't consulted with Michael, nor had I yet written to tell him I'd invited Chris to remain for a few more months.

"I'll cook you dinner. I'll cook for you every night until you tell me to stop."

"We can go out to The Hat for a meal," I said. "Or get takeout quesadillas and bring them back here."

"Let me cook for you. I'll make you whatever you want." Standing, we were nearly the same height, eye to eye, so close, his slim face overflowing with emotion.

"What if I want takeout quesadillas from The Hat?"

"Then I'll run down the street and get them for you," Chris said. "Do you? I'll go right now." He made a lunge for the door.

He was the one who brought up the subject of college, a few weeks later, mid-April by then. We were in the kitchen, Chris making supper, some kind of dish with soba noodles from a recipe in one of my cookbooks that he'd pulled from a shelf. "I'm thinking about applying to City College."

From my seat at the kitchen table, I seized on his words and said that I was pretty sure there were places that went on accepting late admissions until they'd filled every spot. I didn't know for sure about City College but I'd check. The principal and guidance counsellor would help. His grades should be okay. And where they weren't, he could explain. Or the principal could. In the fall he'd aced the SATs, taking them only because Jazmin had, yet useful now. I'd help him with his admission essays, I said, although he probably didn't need my assistance.

"What if I don't have enough money to pay for college?"

"There's financial aid. Scholarships. Surely your parents will help. And, if you need to, you can work part-time. Didn't I just get you a job?"

I had got him a job. The day after I'd told Chris he could stay through the summer, Tyler had called, wailing about the loss of his long-time assistant, who'd quit in the middle of transcribing a series of artist interviews for a book that Tyler was writing on the already vanishing East Village art scene. Did I know anyone who could take over? I thought immediately of Chris, who possessed an astonishing ability to touch type accurately and at phenomenal speed, fingers whipping over the typewriter keys as he sat at the little desk in the living room, a feat he'd learned at secretarial school one summer, he said. His mother had made him take the course.

Despite some hesitation, I gave Chris's name to Tyler, telling Tyler he'd be great, as long as the job didn't take too much time away from his school work, which had to come first. I explained about the breakup, Chris's vulnerability, how the work might provide a useful focus away from school.

"Got it," Tyler said. "I'll give him a try."

"But, Tyler, don't you dare, ever, think about touching him. Nothing. No flirting even. He's a high-school student. My student. I'm entrusting you with him."

"Oh my God, Ellen," Tyler said. "I'm in love. Matthew, you've met him, the gallerist, we got together, and it's so good, I am in an absolutely absorbed and joyful state here and will not be making eyes at your little high-school student, however delectable he is. I am very careful these days and will not endanger him."

"Tyler!"

"Relax, Ellen."

I told Chris that the work ought to be interesting, and Tyler was definitely interesting; I also said that he was a terrible flirt and promiscuous, and so Chris needed to be extremely careful around him. Hot-cheeked, I felt as if I were his mother, explaining to him about pederasts. "And if you have sex with anyone, anyone at all, please, please use a condom."

"Ellen!"

On Tuesdays, Chris arrived home around suppertime from Tyler's place on Sixth Street. While it seemed to me that he could easily have done the transcriptions from the apartment, using my tape recorder and headphones, Chris said, after their initial meet-up, that Tyler refused to let either tapes or transcriptions leave his premises so the work had to be done there.

When, after a couple of weeks, I checked in to see how things were going, Chris said Tyler watched over him like a hawk but mostly left him to himself.

Over the phone, Tyler said, "Oh my God, Ellen, your lodger can type like an angel *and* he knows about art."

"Like I said." And so I allowed myself, despite misgivings, to feel reassured. The thing was, the money—and Tyler was paying Chris the wage he would have paid any assistant—did seem helpful. It gave Chris an autonomy and self-sufficiency beyond my power to give.

In the kitchen, tossing soba noodles into a pot of boiling water, Chris said, "The problem with college is that it saddles you with an albatross of debt." Before I could protest, he added, "Tyler says the world would be a better place if there were more autodidacts in it."

"You're already an autodidact. Autodidacts can go to college. You'll meet people. Have you been talking to Tyler about all this?" I pictured Chris at Tyler's newly purchased computer and Tyler standing at the edge of the desk, magisterially lighting a cigarette. "Tyler went to college."

Chris stirred the noodles. "He's impressed by how much I've read. His position is if I keep reading and have someone like you around, I'll be fine. I'm learning lots. Maybe I don't need to go to college. But, you know, Ellen, that's Tyler's shtick. The real question is, do you think I should go?"

I was distracted. *Someone like me around.* I pushed away the bouquet of tulips I'd set in the middle of the table. "What does Tyler mean by 'someone like me around'?"

"Oh, you know, Ellen. Mentor. Intellectual guide. You give me things to read. You bring me to plays." Chris poured soy sauce and peanut butter into a bowl.

"One play."

"Maybe you'll bring me to another play."

"You don't need me to go see plays. You can go on your own. When you're at college. And after. With your friends."

"So, okay, like I said, I think I'll apply to City College. Aren't you pleased? I thought you'd be pleased."

"Yes, yes, very pleased. But why not think beyond here." I gestured, arms out, towards the window. "Consider other places. Broaden your horizons. We can make a list together."

"I think I'll start by applying to City College," Chris said.

I had taken him to a play by a friend of mine, over at The Kitchen, now in the far reaches of Chelsea. I'd been offered two free tickets and told myself it would be educational, a play about Black cowboys. Bill Pickett. Nat Love. Two men drawn to each other in an all-Black trail company. Meanwhile, I was working on a new piece of my own. After one of my Sunday night performances, the director of the performance space up on Ninth Street had come up to me and offered me a spot, which meant the chance to create something new and get out of the small clubs where I usually performed.

And so, on Tuesdays, when Chris was at Tyler's, I abandoned my school work and, eager but anxious, wrote at my desk, before standing to declaim to the empty room. At night I wrote in bed, curtains drawn, speaking the words aloud to myself in an undertone. The idea had come to me swiftly. In this new monologue a woman turns into a fox and roams the transformed streets of the East Village, unable to return to her former life. She is both a fox and not a fox. She can recall all that she has lost yet not reclaim it. Fox-like, she lives wild in the alleys, following friends who no longer recognize her. She tries to determine whether she has a soul and what the idea of a soul means to her. What love means. The voice of the piece felt different than my previous monologues, the writing more rhythmic; I felt as if I were listening to something and responding. Was I speaking to Chris? Not exactly, although I was aware of his presence as I wrote, of wanting to hold his particular quick and restless attention, while drawing on it, too. When I began to rehearse, I locked myself in the bathroom and turned on the cold tap so that I could run lines without being heard, but of course Chris noticed and confronted me one night in the kitchen.

"Ellen, what are you doing?"
"I'm working on something."
"What kind of something?"
"A piece I'm performing."
"You're performing? When?"

The first night of the three-night run, we walked together up First Avenue to Ninth Street, Chris practically leaping at my side. On the bill with me was a queer artist named Ian, whom I knew a little, presenting a solo show about his relationship with a series of squirrels in Tompkins Square Park. For so long I had tried to keep Chris out of this part of my life; I had wanted the privacy to slip out late and unencumbered to see a show up on Avenue A or be among the women at the WOW Café, where I'd also performed. I had not wanted him to see me trying out new material, like the monologue about the winged woman, trying and sometimes failing, exposed at a mike on a tiny stage with flimsy curtains and jerry-rigged lights, in front of an audience packed onto sofas or crammed on chairs and sometimes not very many people at all. I hoped he never spotted my name in small letters on posters wheat-pasted to telephone poles. Yet once Chris found out that I still performed, he peppered me with questions. Given the impossibility of shutting him out entirely and his dismay that I had tried to do so, I decided to use him as my audience when I rehearsed. Let him be my dramaturg. I told him to sit on the sofa, night after night, which he did compliantly, dark hair longer now, my leather jacket loose around him, listening, it seemed, with his whole body. We did our school prep afterwards.

I like that part a lot, Chris would say with fervour, ticking the air with his index finger. Then he'd notice some out-of-sorts detail, blossoms on the trees when there shouldn't be blossoms. He'd say, That part feels loose. Or he asked questions revealing knowledge that shouldn't have surprised me coming from him but did: Ellen, do you know that a group of foxes is called a skulk? And you've heard of the Japanese myth about the fox wife?

"Yes," I said, "and, of course, yes." It was hard to know who I was, standing in front of him like that, in my own living room, or what I was becoming, because, whatever else I felt, I was swept with admiration, even as an impression of Chris in the classroom never left me.

On stage, in that small ground-floor black box, despite the lights that made it impossible to see anyone, the beam of his attention met me and I spoke — not to him alone but him among others, the friends, the strangers, unnerved by the intensity of his attention and somehow calmed by it. I tried not to think too much about that calm. In those days I did not use props; I stood at the mike in my favourite pair of boots, black, knee-high lace-ups, and told my story, tugging on it, seeking its tautness, its moments of swerve, feeling how it registered in other bodies.

Afterwards, when people came up and formed a circle around me, I knew their enthusiasm was real, that something had happened in the room, the truthful thing I sought to make happen, just as in Ian's piece, hilarious on the limitations of human relationships, there had been a final, gutting tip into heartbreak. Magda swung me into her arms, Vivienne kissed me, Rodney patted me between the shoulder blades then gave me a hug, all of us surging together in our black leather jackets. After the circle broke up, Chris stepped forward, colour in his cheeks, in my cast-off leather jacket, to touch my leathered sleeve before backing away as if I'd given him an electric shock.

"You were so good. I loved it. There's one tiny thing I'd change — a point where I feel you could be funnier, it would add something tonally, when she first sees that friend and sniffs the air."

There was a roar in my ears. Through the roar I heard Chris reciting one of my lines, which he'd memorized in its entirety. He'd helped me shape the piece. He had. "Thanks, Chris."

Something must have registered on my face.

"Ellen, you're not angry with me, are you?"

"No, I'm not angry with you. You've been extremely helpful."

"Please don't be angry."

Magda whirled back into sight, shouting as she often did. "You coming, foxy lady?" She named the bar where some of them were going for drinks, before exclaiming, "You must be Chris." She enveloped him in an outsized hug that made him, in turn, switch on his repertoire of charm and good cheer.

I told her it was a Thursday night, I had to teach the next day, I hadn't done a whit of preparation. I had to perform again the next night. And the next. "One drink?" As Magda spoke I grew aware of the reed-like sway of Chris's longing.

"Saturday night, at the end of the run, we'll go out then, promise me that," I said.

"Are you ashamed to be seen with me around your friends?" Chris asked as we made our way back down the avenue, my limbs adrenalized, mind still processing the evening. I wanted to shout: *All I want to do is to go out with my friends and drink and feel loved!*

"No," I said.

Chris went quiet. I reminded myself about his breakup; perhaps I wasn't being sympathetic enough. "Look," he called as we approached Houston, pointing across the street to a boxy television that someone had set out at the curb, near the corner of First Street. Not far off were the basement steps that once led down to the now-closed Darinka. Chris dashed across traffic. Caught off-guard, I dashed after him. "It works." There was a sign taped to it to that effect. "You don't have a TV. We can take it home and watch Letterman. And if you don't want it in the living room, I'll keep it in my room."

Home, he'd said. *My room.* While I still thought of him as sleeping in the spare room. For a few more months.

I had chosen not to have a television; I was a snobby downtown girl and Chris seemed to be craving some suburban idyll.

I said, "You're not even asking me if I want a TV in my apartment." With the television cradled in his arms, he looked eager, young, the cord snaking around his knees so that I had to stuff the snake against his elbow to stop him tripping on it.

Back at the apartment, I tried to block out the sounds of Chris on the other side of the open wall, moving things about, the coffee table, a lamp, piles of magazines. I was trying to decide why I'd chosen to give the twelfth-grade students a Shirley Jackson story in which a man goes about New York City performing good deeds for seemingly altruistic reasons only to have his motives upturned at the end. I wanted to know what they'd make of it. What Chris would make of it, if he bothered to read it. A burst of static travelled through the doorway, clarifying into the rising roar of a laugh track, then another sound, a scatter of kernels in a saucepan, popcorn. I hadn't even known there was popcorn in the apartment, but Chris seemed to be making some. I wanted to shout at him. The smell of oil and butter and bursting kernels wrapped themselves around me.

"Come on over," Chris called. He was sitting on the sofa, where he'd sat obediently to watch me rehearse, now with his hand in the bowl of popcorn at his side.

"Is this your idea of domestic bliss?"

"Not precisely," he said. "But it's good, isn't it? Isn't it at least a little bit celebratory?"

I sat and took the popcorn bowl when he passed it to me. There was nothing to drink in the apartment. Neither of us had replaced any of the alcohol that Chris had consumed in his drunken binge.

And so this was my life, my altered life, and out of it had come the fox woman monologue. Greedy, I wanted more of that, more like that.

On his feet, Chris switched off the overhead light, leaving only the standing lamp beside the sofa to shed its soft yellow rays.

"Can I ask you something?" Seating himself once more, he picked up the popcorn bowl from the space between us. "You can say no if you're not comfortable and it doesn't have to be tonight, but there's something I've been thinking about ever since the breakup. Wanting. Something that would be extremely helpful and relaxing. Would it be okay if I had a bath?"

The only bathtub in the apartment was in my bathroom, surrounded by all my unguents, the privacies of my bodily life. Chris went on stuffing his mouth with popcorn, the flutes of his fingers wandering through the bowl. I had no idea what show we were supposedly watching. A kind person would have no trouble saying to an eighteen-year-old distressed by a breakup, Yes, you can have a bath. A bath. It was just a bath.

"Sure," I said. I got up to clear away my toiletries.

"It doesn't have to be right now," Chris called at my back.

I set out a clean, folded towel from the pile on the shelf above the toilet. I tugged on my leather jacket.

"What are you doing?" Chris asked, on his feet, stopped at the border of my bedroom, which he'd have to traverse to reach my bathroom. "Where are you going?"

"You're welcome to have a bath," I said, "but that doesn't mean I need to be in the apartment while you have one."

Benevolence: An East Village Story

❖

I nearly tripped while running across Houston. This time, I cut west along Fourth Street, to Second Avenue, where, on the corner, I bumped into the painter Irene Antonio, whom I knew vaguely through my husband. In her pink mohair coat she drew close and mentioned that she was on her way from drinks with Javier Toller, the filmmaker. I knew Javier, didn't I? A week ago, in Toulouse, Javier had met Michael, my husband, and his new French girlfriend for dinner. Apparently, the girlfriend, a dancer, had just moved in with Michael. I wasn't sure why Irene felt compelled to tell me this. Because she thought I'd want to know, because she assumed I didn't know?

I hadn't known about the girlfriend. There was no reason to think that my husband wouldn't share the news when he was ready. Still it was a shock to find out this way, as Irene must have seen. I tried to solicit details but Irene knew nothing. She waved, and, like the awful little emissary she was, departed, trotting along Fourth Street. The poster of a pink triangle shone from a street lamp. And all the while I couldn't stop imagining Chris in my bathtub. I wondered if Michael had asked the dancer to move in with him as quickly, as persuasively, as he'd once asked me. She was likely young, and no doubt beautiful. Of course, the news ripped a new seam in the evening. It made me lonely, magnified my uncertainty. I tried to take comfort by telling myself that if they'd moved in together, in some quaint French village, it was even less likely that Michael was planning an upcoming return to New York.

Back at the apartment, having walked as far north as Twenty-Third Street, I stepped into a humid darkness. I assumed that Chris, after turning off all the lights, had gone to bed. That's when I noticed, through the open curtain, beyond my bedroom, the limbs splayed on the floor of my study, wan in the streetlight between my desk and the bookshelves. Chris turned his head.

"Have I ever told you how when I was fifteen I wanted to live in a lighthouse?"

SKIN

"Chris." Perhaps I shouted then, dropping my jacket onto the bed. "What are you doing?"

"Sorry, Ellen," he said. "The bath was lovely. Thank you. Then I saw the light, the way it fell across the wall, and I had the impulse to lie here, because it reminded me of something." He was naked from the waist up, in jeans, wet hair tumbling over my husband's Persian rug. I pushed past the bunched-up curtain, wanted to yell at him to get up, get up right away, stop being so ridiculous, so flagrant. Had he been planning to lie there all night, until whatever hour I arrived home and found him?

"When I was fifteen I painted my bedroom walls ultramarine, the walls and the ceiling. It was extremely beautiful. I'd lie there and imagine myself surrounded by the sea at night, I was in my lighthouse, the waves down below. I was a lighthouse keeper, living all alone on my island, my light blinking. I wanted to be a lighthouse keeper, tending a garden, saving people from wrecks. That was my dream. Then do you know what happened?"

"I have no idea."

"My mother decided the walls would look amazing with putti painted all over them. You know, like cherubs in eighteenth-century paintings."

"I know what putti are."

"One day I arrived home from school and she'd painted these fleshy babies with no drapery and anatomically correct little penises all over my walls. She's a good painter, so it was like being surrounded by really good fake Fragonard. She told me my girlfriends would love them."

Girlfriends. I noted the plural. Three years ago, when Chris was fifteen, I'd been sleeping on my own in the room where Chris slept, listening to the click of the door when my husband came back very late. I'd told Chris a little about this.

"Were there girlfriends when you were fifteen?"

"One girlfriend. Mostly. Anyway, my mother was ecstatic, she kept repeating that she'd created this work of art just for me. I ought to feel honoured. But, to be honest, I felt violated. It's hard to feel like you're in a lighthouse when you're surrounded by a bunch of naked putti painted by your mother. I tried to tell her this, but she told me to stop being so selfish. She was my mother and an artist. One day when I knew she was out, I stayed home and painted over all the putti and made everything a sea of dark blue again."

"What happened then?" I crouched near him in the dark.

"She yelled at me and called me a philistine. She got really angry. Enraged, actually. She grabbed me and tried to throw me down the stairs. In the end she threw me out. I mean, she grabbed my coat and literally tossed me out the front door of our brownstone. I fell down the steps. We were both so angry. I don't know if she thought I would stay away, but I did."

"She physically assaulted you."

"Can you help me, Ellen? I need you to help me stay in my body. I've been having trouble with that lately. Can you touch my wrist, right here, where my pulse is."

"Chris, I can't do that," I said.

"Yes, you can," Chris said. "Please."

"No, I can't, Chris."

When I was twenty-three, the first time that Michael broke up with me, I'd rented a room in a nuns' hostel in Chelsea with a glow-in-the-dark crucifix hanging on the wall. Penniless, I rented it so that no one in the world knew where I was and I lay for a day and a night in the dark, as if paralyzed, staring down at myself, imagining other lives, who I might have been if I'd never left Toronto, until a kind of animal terror filled me, a sense of my whole body vanishing.

"Where did you go the night your mother threw you out?" I asked Chris as he lay on the floor in front of me. I'd told him how I'd spent a night in a room with a glow-in-the-dark crucifix; I'd made the obvious joke about not being able to stop seeing the light.

"Green-Wood Cemetery."

"Why didn't you go to a neighbour's? Or your girlfriend's?"

"I couldn't. The cemetery seemed safer than the park. I had to climb over a fence to get in. The gates were locked."

"Weren't you frightened?"

"I climbed into a tree, I imagined I was back in my room, in my lighthouse."

"But then you ended up in foster care."

"Because of the neighbours. They're okay people. They filed some kind of report. They heard the fighting. They saw or heard her throw me out. Social workers got involved."

"Only you, not your sisters."

"It's always been worse between the two of us. I can't love her the way she wants to be loved, something like that."

"You can't love her?"

"She loves me, but not in the way I need to be loved."

"Are the walls of your bedroom still dark blue?"

"She left them like that and never tried to paint them again."

On the floor, eyes closed, he lay for a long time without moving. The skin at the base of his wrist was very soft. Through my own skin, I felt the quiet beat of his pulse. At last, lifting my fingers, I clambered to my feet. "Get up now, Chris. It's time for you to go to bed."

On First Avenue, in early June, we ran into the choreographer Agnes Rivard, whom I hadn't seen in almost a year. From a sling, strapped to her front, peered a small, dove-coloured head. I hadn't even known she was pregnant. A week later, Chris and I stepped through the front door of our building, laden with grocery bags, to find Persephone, the toddler who lived in one of the ground-floor apartments, running pell-mell towards us and the open door. Chris was the one who dropped his bags and scooped her into his arms, chuckling at her in such a way as to distract her from the shock of being intercepted mid-flight, singing out her preposterous name.

When he settled her onto his hip, then swung her back to her mother with ease, as perhaps he'd once lifted and held his own little sisters, something unexpected flew into me. I had never felt the longing for a child until I did, the swoop happening, right then, in Chris's presence.

The desire to love like that. I began to dream about babies. In the dreams I was holding them. Nursing them. They pressed against my breastbone. I tried to fight the longing, and still it came back. Nor had I understood before how this particular longing could magnify my sense of time passing, how my awareness of my body would transform—every swing of hormones heightened, the viscousness, the blood—and Chris in front of me, there in the morning when, wrapped in my silk dressing gown, I padded into the kitchen, handing me a cup of coffee. The pull all through my body.

I dreamed about him.

Even when he went out by himself in the evening, as he sometimes did, telling me he was off to meet his old friend Ben, he was usually up before me, always dressed, in jeans and T-shirt, if no longer wearing his overcoat, often washing my dirty dishes left in the sink the night before. If by chance I was up before him, I'd hear him rustling behind the spare room curtain. I wondered what he wore to sleep, underwear, or nothing at all, if he was standing there, naked, at that moment. Because we each did our own laundry, never together, Chris hauling his out in a black plastic garbage bag while I took mine down the street in an old leather duffel that had once belonged to my father, what I knew of Chris's clothing was what I saw on him.

Taking the mug of coffee he held out, I tried not to stare at the dip of his larynx above the collar of his T-shirt, the bob of his Adam's apple as he swallowed from his own mug, the furrow of his eyebrows as he passed me the carton of milk, the neat slope of his fingernails.

At school, I assigned Zora Neale Hurston and Harper Lee. I would miss so many of them—the younger ones as well as those in the twelfth grade. Nico, half in love with her Brazilian father who made art out of garbage; Rachel, who offered surprisingly philosophical commentary from beneath thick, dark bangs; the druggy yet earnest boys. At the end of June, I would be done. In September, the woman I had replaced would return. I was working on a new monologue about a woman who travels to the moon, using objects that would become props or costume: a globe, a bowl of water, an animal pelt, a pair of silver shoes. Soon I would turn thirty and go back to temping.

But before that Chris and I would celebrate: celebrate his getting into City College, his making it through the school year. He told me, joyously, about the essays he was going to write, how he'd be my dramaturg for the new piece, or my director, that he wanted to go to the beach, to Coney Island or out to Rockaway, we would go to the beach and celebrate together. Yes, I said.

Two more weeks to get through. We were so close.

One afternoon, dropping by my office at the end of the day, something he almost never did anymore, Chris pulled the door closed, and when he did, I scrambled to my feet, told him to open it, both of us taken aback by my sharpness. Perhaps my abrupt response could be attributed to the fact that I had been circling apartment ads in *The Village Voice* when Chris appeared.

It was his mother's birthday on Saturday, Chris said as I stuffed *The Voice* into a drawer. He wanted my help buying her a present, while I calculated something I'd guessed but not known for certain, that the age separating me from Patricia, who was turning forty-two, was the same as that between Chris and me.

"I want to buy her an antique Japanese kimono. There'll be some in the vintage shops in the East Village, won't there? Can you help me choose one?"

It seemed a request he could easily have made back at the apartment but I didn't say that. Somehow mentioning our life in the apartment while at school felt too intimate.

"Happy to help," I said. And yet I was puzzled. Some complicated desire seemed to be at work. "Isn't an antique Japanese kimono rather an expensive gift?" For a woman who, by his own account, had treated him so badly.

"It's what she wants."

If I was taken aback by his desire to buy such a gift for his mother, with whom, as far as I knew, he'd had minimal contact in the months that he'd been living with me, if his acquiescence to the extravagance of her desire surprised me (where did she think he'd get the money—unless she knew about his job working for Tyler and felt she deserved the proceeds from it), I nevertheless felt I lacked the right to intervene or discourage him.

"She's planning a birthday party," Chris said. "She's calling it a party even though I'm pretty sure it's only going to be the five of us." His mother, his father, Chris, his two younger sisters. "It's a lure to get me to go back."

The gift could be celebrating the distance he'd travelled from her. Was travelling. With it, he might be making a kind of psychic offering for the pool of happiness that, it seemed to me, we had both somehow stumbled upon in those late spring and early summer days.

"I'll see you later," I said as Chris let himself out the door.

At the back of a boutique on Seventh Street, he held up a kimono, stroking the cloth: dark blue, woven in a pattern of waves, the silk, when I touched it, soft as skin. Three hundred and fifty dollars when I glanced at the tag. Beautiful, yes. For a price. I fingered through the small collection and pulled out another, red, the pattern more garish, the silk harsher, half the cost, but Chris shook his head. "Not that one, Ellen."

"Isn't the first one kind of pricey?"

"Yes. Well."

Annoyance, then jealousy surged through me, childish and unrestrainable: Despite all I'd done for him over these last months, he'd never attempted to buy such a gift for me. Nothing but a block of toilet paper. Could you call a discarded television set grabbed from a street corner, a television that he watched, a gift? But I was not his mother. I was his teacher. Of use to him. Of service. Where did beauty come into it? I was being unfair, I knew. Even if he'd offered me such a gift, I would never have accepted it.

I left Chris absorbed in the kimonos and propelled myself towards a rack of dresses, pulling out one whose silver sheen caught my eye. Short, sleeveless, it answered to my immediate desire: I ducked into a dressing room, wriggling, behind the flimsy curtain, out of my cotton dress and leggings and lifting the glittery fabric over my head. If the dress fit, I would wear it that night to the party that Celia Hahn and her girlfriend were throwing; the dress would carry me into whatever future awaited me at Celia's party, the future I needed to be waiting for me.

Chris's voice called from outside the curtain. "Ellen, hey, I want to show you something."

I zipped up the silver dress. I stared at myself in the mirror. I piled my hair on top of my head. That morning, I'd been the one up first. The curtain had not been pulled in front of the spare room. There was no sound from inside and so, passing in front of the doorway, I'd glanced in to find Chris staring at me, torso bare, entangled in the sheet, pillow clasped to his chest.

In the gap between mothball-smelling ranks of old clothes, he was modelling a jean jacket, the expensive kimono folded over another rack. He gestured to the patch inside the back collar. "It belonged to someone named Buzzy Reichgut. Isn't that the most incredible name? Ellen, listen, I want to be Buzzy Reichgut, live on Ludlow Street on the Lower East Side, and go to City College. He's a very mellow fellow, easy to get along with. You'll like Buzzy Reichgut. You'll see." He reached down and touched the hem of my dress, the two of us shining in the mirror, side by side. My body felt thrummy and vibrant. Sensations crawled across the top of my head. "That's a fantastic fabric, the way the leaf pattern woven into the silver shows up in some light not others. And, excuse me, but I have to say, you look really hot in it. Don't you think we look fabulous together?"

"Chris," I said. "Don't." There we were, as if in a photograph. But there are no photographs; I took no photographs at all during the months we lived together. "I'll buy you the jacket."

He turned radiant with pleasure, thanking me effusively. And I asked myself: Can't gratitude at someone else's pleasure be enough?

I didn't know what the sales clerk, tall and slim, with her out-of-time, carefully tended beehive hairdo, made of us. Perhaps she thought we both looked young. She might have assumed we were a couple, or on the verge of becoming one. I might have thought so, looking at us. She asked if everything should be rung up together. I said no, even as Chris, wearing the jean jacket, countered that he would pay for the kimono and, pulling a folded wad of cash from his pocket, counted out three hundred and fifty dollars in bills as I watched.

He asked the beehived shop clerk if she'd wrap the kimono and leaned in close as her slim fingers folded tissue paper around the cloth. His attention was such, and her awareness of his attention, that I might have said they were flirting with each other, despite the way our arms brushed.

Out on the street, Chris said, "I wish you could come with me to the birthday party, Ellen. I know it's impossible, Patricia wouldn't like it, but I feel so much calmer with you around. You know that, don't you?"

A breeze blew a newspaper into my feet. "Yes," I said. "And you know it makes me glad." The days marked themselves on me like handprints. Six more days until the end of the month. Four more days of school.

"Maybe we could meet up afterwards for a drink? I know you're going to a party, but after. It would give me an out. If things get weird, when they get weird, I can say I have plans and go."

"It's not going to make your mother happier if you tell her you're going out for a drink with me."

"I'll say I'm meeting a friend. Who needs to talk something over. The whole time I'm there it will make me feel better."

I'd half-wondered if he might spend the night in Brooklyn, while recognizing that this was no doubt wishful thinking.

"Come on, Ellen, I want to be Buzzy Reichgut and meet you at a bar for a drink. One drink."

"No bars," I said, before relenting, allowing myself to be charmed, naming the little French diner on Essex Street around the corner from the apartment, even as the traffic lights blinked and I thought: You cannot, cannot be the father of my child.

I broke away from a cluster of people and made my way across the rooftop of Celia Hahn's building in my silver dress and boots, empty martini glass trailing in my hand, alcohol sluicing through my bloodstream. Fireworks broke through the night sky. There would be ten more of these exploding nights, until the Fourth of July. No one could wait. And I thought: I can't do it, I can't. I can't wait. What, under the circumstances, is the greatest kindness? The necessary kindness?

I would ask him to leave by the end of July. No, by mid-July. Surely asking him to leave as soon as possible was the best thing. The kindest.

I stood near the edge of the rooftop, facing the sky. I'd say I had changed my mind. Yes, I had been opened in new ways, and, yes, I'd watched him settle, but I needed to pull back in whatever way I could—to protect him. Protect myself. I'd say I was going travelling, as soon as school was done, and he needed to be out of the apartment. To Mexico, no, to Italy. My husband wanted him gone. Or he could stay, but if so he absolutely had to be gone on my return. I'd help him find another place to live. Lights spangled from street corners to the south. Flashes of light broke over me. I would hurt him. At my back, people laughed and smoked whatever they were smoking. Danced. I would be as good as saying, You cannot hold onto a home. Once again you have failed. You are dispensable. Or I have failed. To be too kind or not kind enough? I sucked at the dregs of my martini, seeking conviction. He'd never leave unless I asked him to. I would not go to meet him for a drink. I'd stay late at the party, as late as it took even if that meant breaking my word.

 I toyed with asking Celia if Chris could stay with her for the summer, given how much time she spent at the home of Juanita, her girlfriend, the ex-cop turned philosophy PhD student, who, buzz-cut, was waving her long arms above her head in the dark. But if I said anything to Celia, I'd be admitting that things were not as calm as I'd insisted. Or not calm in the way I had insisted. And Celia, holding up a full martini shaker, metal sparkling, shaking her hips, every shake a slam into my body, would inevitably latch onto the illicit, because, whatever she thought about it, she desired the illicit, and searched for it every time she looked at me.

 Someone called my name. Stumbling towards me, Rodney threw himself into my arms. "Where's Chris," he slurred as if he'd expected Chris to be with me, but before I could say anything, he told me, fumes of alcohol pouring from him, that John had died that afternoon, John O., who'd played my brother in the famous film. Two days before, Rodney and I had talked about visiting John in hospital. We'd gone once, brought white peonies, which I'd chosen, and found John lying in bed with his eyes closed, skin peeling from his hands, Malcolm, his lover, in the chair at his side. On screen, John had an intermittent incandescence; when it wasn't there, he seemed only tall and awkward; when it was, you couldn't look away. In the film that had made both our names, directed by Rodney, we'd found a version of this gift together. Body pressed to mine, Rodney broke into sobs. Head on his chest, arms around his girth, I rocked him back and forth, his leather jacket creaking with grief. Through my tears, a small note of wonder rose in me about where Tyler was: He ought to have been at the party, he was a good friend of Celia's,

SKIN

he knew Rodney far better than I did, knew John, might have slept with both John and Rodney, but I hadn't seen him all evening. All around us the sea of the night exploded.

A young man in a jean jacket threaded his way through the empty restaurant. I knew him. I had no idea who he was. I'd arrived late, Chris even later. In the kitchen, through a swinging metal door, the chef shouted at someone in French.

"So sorry, Ellen, I got delayed." He pulled out the chair across from me. "Tell me you haven't been here long." There was an effervescence in his manner that I didn't recognize. The one other diner in the restaurant turned. Was it Chris's agile movements, his vivid beauty on display? He had that effect. You would notice him in the street. People did. I'd seen them do it. "Nice dress." He smiled as he sat down. He was drunk. I smelled the alcohol on him.

I had a glass of seltzer water in front of me by then, an attempt to cool my nerves. But when the chef, a beanpole of a Frenchman, appeared at our table and Chris ordered a beer, I asked for a shot of whiskey, and a plate of frites, at which the chef shook his head; the kitchen was closed. I tried again, this time in French, telling the beanpole that I wanted something to soak up the alcohol, a basket of stale baguette slices, anything. After giving me a once over—hair pinned to the top of my head, strands tumbling, cheeks pink—he offered a curt nod.

"There was dancing," Chris said. "She really wanted a dance party even though it was only the five of us. That made it hard to get away." I tried to fix my attention. His mother had hung a disco ball in the living room, he said, climbing onto a chair that his sister Renata braced for balance, while Charlotte, at fourteen, the youngest, practised solo dance moves on the other side of the room. Meanwhile his father, in a corner, made balloon animals, for which he had a surprising knack, twisting long balloons and round ones into giraffes or sausage dogs or animal heads, at Patricia's request.

She'd made a cake, Chris continued, which she set out on the dining-room table after dinner, a big, fat slab covered in white icing. She'd directed Chris to put Stravinsky's *Rite of Spring* on the stereo, and when the first chords began, she took a huge carving knife and sliced into the cake, which oozed gobs of red jam.

"How is that celebratory?" I asked, tossing back my whiskey.

"She was having fun, Ellen," Chris said. "She has a flair for the dramatic, as we know. Think of it as some kind of performance art — and she loved the kimono, like really loved it. She put it on right away. After the cake. She wanted to dance in it. I didn't tell her you helped me choose it, but I'm glad you did."

"I didn't," I said. It seemed clear to me suddenly: Patricia had wanted to dance with Chris, not anyone else. This was at the heart of, the point of her whole performance.

"Yes, you did," Chris said. "I couldn't have done it without you. And you bought me this jacket and told me I could be Buzzy Reichgut and come out for a drink with you."

All the while I was struggling to figure out how to say what I needed to say. Because Chris wasn't Buzzy.

"She's going to help me go to college," Chris said. It took me a moment to realize he was still speaking about his mother. "She promised to pay for everything. She knows people, she knows people on the art faculty at Bennington, she has a friend in the art history department, she's already spoken to him about late admission."

"Wait a sec, Chris," I said, like a ship at sea, a crosswind swerving my path. "You've never said anything about wanting to go to Bennington. Or studying art history. In the country. Up in Vermont."

"We've been talking about it, Patricia and I, the last few weeks. She came up with the idea. I think it could be a good thing, don't you?"

Something lanced me. Through the lancing the sea rushed in. When had he been talking to her? Had he met her, had they spoken on the phone when I wasn't around? And I saw how, from Patricia's perspective, it was a brilliant strategy for re-staking a claim on Chris, drawing him back into her orbit, leaving him indebted to her, while pulling him far from whoever or whatever she thought I was. Despite my shock, a sober part of me felt relief: If Chris went to Bennington, wouldn't that be a good thing for me as well?

"You don't need your mother's help to go to college," I said. "Nothing you've ever told me about her makes her seem dependable. Why do you think that will change? What about your plan to go to City College?"

"Even if I do go to Bennington, it doesn't mean I can't come back. For visits. It doesn't have to have any effect on what happens with us."

"Chris," I said, my mouth full of fur.

He reached for my hand, twisting his fingers between mine, just as the frites arrived, stunning and greasy. "Ellen, you know what's happening. You know I love you. I've been in love with you for months. I told Jazmin I couldn't stop thinking about you."

Heart in my groin, groin in my heart, I said, "You really shouldn't have done that."

If something in him stumbled, he pressed on. "Come on, Ellen. I see you. I feel you."

"One more week. We have to hold all this together until the end of school."

"And then what?"

"And then you graduate. Concentrate on that. Don't think about anything else."

What I longed for was to roll back time, two days, a week, back to those days and nights of unstable, fragile calm, except that whatever I wanted was already hurtling away.

"Tyler wants me to go with him to LA."

The air swept out of me. "What do you mean by that?" I asked.

"He's moving out there. He's opening a gallery. He told me he'll give me a job."

"Chris." My body shook. "Are you sleeping with Tyler?" Everything he'd said so far dissolved like a house of cards.

"No." He almost shouted this. "I'm not." But I didn't know whether to believe him.

"Because if you do sleep with Tyler you have to be extremely careful. Tyler's smart and funny but promiscuous, I told you. He likes to chase people and seduce them. And then he drops them. Cuts them right out. I've seen him do it over and over. You could end up dead."

A week ago on Sixth Street, Tyler, in his long leather coat, had stepped towards me open-armed and told me I looked ravishing while saying nothing, not a word, about moving to LA.

"He told me he'll buy me an airline ticket."

"So we at least know he wants to sleep with you."

Chris said nothing. My rib cage felt like a prison. His father had a place in LA. Why shouldn't Chris go out there? I didn't know if he was tossing the prospect of Tyler at me as a dare, if he was tossing all these things at me, simply to see how I'd respond.

"Don't do it, Chris," I said.

"Why not?"

"Because putting yourself in Tyler's orbit is dangerous."

"What do you want me to do?"

I closed my eyes. "I want us to get through next week. I want us to manage to do that without everything imploding. Please, Chris. I want it for your sake."

"And then what?"

"And then we can have a conversation. Right now I want us to stand up. Things will look very different in the morning."

"You want me to leave. You think it will be better if I'm not there."

"Chris, please, let's talk in the morning."

"Are you inviting me home, Ellen?"

"Let's walk back to the apartment."

I stood up, waving to catch the chef's attention, but Chris was on his feet as well, stumbling to the cash register at the end of the counter, pulling out a handful of bills from his pocket, always a fat packet of bills on him now. And I did have this thought: Was all the money from Tyler?

When he met me at the door, I had to look away as I thanked him. I longed, one way or another, to walk through time. Forward or backward. If a pack of wailing cop cars had come speeding past on Houston, I wouldn't have heard them. As we made our way up Essex Street, Chris leaned into me, as if there were still comfort to be found in the vicinity of my body. I let him lean, felt my body move into the slim, warm contours of his. I wished I were drunker than I was, my feet not my feet, my numb arms not my arms. I thought to say, but didn't, Perhaps he was in love with the apartment and not with me at all.

How many times had I walked down this block, my block, by day, at night, by myself, after a show, with Michael, with others, but never late at night with Chris. Someone slammed the door of a cab. The sound echoed. At the front door of the building, I pulled out my keys and let Chris step ahead of me into the small vestibule where the mailboxes were.

"Go upstairs," I said. "Go to bed, get some sleep. I'll see you in the morning."

His face crumpled into puzzlement.

"I'm not coming with you," I said. "Go upstairs. I'll be fine."

"But it's your apartment."

"Chris, go upstairs now. Please."

I stood in the doorway. I waited until he put his own key in the lock of the second door and, with a glance over his shoulder, stepped into the hallway, until that door clacked shut behind him. After a few more heartbeats, I heard his footsteps begin to climb the stairs. I had no idea what he would do next—trash the apartment in my absence, tear through my belongings in a manic search, pursue me as I set off at a run towards Houston.

I made it on foot back to Celia's, up on Tenth, laughter still volleying from the rooftop, audible above my ragged breath. In party time, it wasn't that late. Not surprisingly, no one answered the buzzer.

I tried shouting, despite the hour; earlier they'd been lowering keys from the rooftop in a wicker basket tied to a string. At last, another leather-jacketed resident returning home took pity on me when I told him I'd been at the rooftop party, gave him Celia's name, and Juanita's, and the number of the apartment up on the fifth floor, whose door, when at last I tried it, turned at my touch. A woman I didn't know stumbled out of the bathroom. A pair of red pumps lay abandoned in the middle of the kitchen floor. Everything around me looked glazed. In Celia's all-white bedroom, with paintings by her and others covering the walls, I sat on the edge of the bed, trying to re-root myself in an elemental kindness, only I didn't feel kindness at all. I rolled onto the bed, tugging the duvet over me, willing sleep to carry me out of this delirium, and the next thing I knew, someone was leaning over me, Celia, stoned and perplexed, her long hair in my face, perfumed with pot. I sat up wildly. It seemed crucial to make something clear to her. That I had been transformed? That Chris had been? No. "I'm not sleeping with him." I shouted the words. "I'm not sleeping with him."

In the morning, I roused myself from Celia's couch before either Celia or Juanita were stirring. Outside, sunlight plunged so brightly it scoured my party dress and fishnets, blistered the avenue as I wove past those already up and about their missions with dogs and muffins and takeout coffees. I stopped to buy Italian pastries, guzzled a bottle of water, still uncertain about what lay ahead. As soon as I entered the apartment, I sensed the silence. I stumbled from my side into the kitchen, the curtain to the spare room pushed open, every trace of him gone except for residues of trash in the bathroom and kitchen cans. I called his name. I searched the kitchen table, both desks, my bed, my books, for some kind of note. I went through the garbage with my bare hands. There was no phone number to try. At last, as evening came, I collapsed onto my bed, as if a current inside me had arced and shorted.

SKIN

❖

In the days to come, I would finish the school year. I didn't want to admit to the principal that Chris had left my apartment, that I did not know where he was. It had been Chris's decision to leave. I'd had nothing to do with it. I couldn't say that. He wasn't at school. He would still graduate, I assumed, he'd done enough work in all his courses, even if he failed to hand in his final assignments. In those last days, as I stumbled through my classes, trying to avoid my colleagues and the staff room, I kept hoping that Chris might show up at my office door, waving a sheaf of typewritten pages like a flag, even though I knew this to be a figment of wild hope. I was aware of Jazmin, in class, far off in the middle row, in line to hand in her final assignment, and I felt a terrible, contradictory sympathy for her as I stood in front of all of them, acting with a fierceness I barely knew I had.

When Patricia called the apartment, a week or so after Chris's disappearance, asking to speak to him, this was my way of discovering that he hadn't been in touch with her, that she, too, had no idea where he was. I should not have expected sympathy, and I didn't receive any, even as I tried to offer what I could, only to be met with her voice hurling the words at me down the line, "What did you do to my son?"

I tried to reach Tyler. The line went to voicemail. I tried again and again. I even took myself up to Sixth Street and banged on his buzzer. The next time I called, the line had been disconnected. I pleaded with Rodney, who in those days had thrown himself into ACT UP meetings and protests, to help me find a number for Tyler, if he had indeed moved to LA. Plucking up my courage, I told Celia what had happened, that Chris had left the apartment and vanished.

Her cheeks pinched when I told her I was frightened Chris had run off with Tyler.

"He's not here," Tyler said, when at last, weeks later, I did receive a voicemail and frantically returned the call. His voice sounded scratchy in an unfamiliar way, acidic, defensive, as if he wanted to hurl whatever accusations I might be harbouring back in my face.

"Was he there?" I demanded. "Are you opening a gallery? Did you offer him a job?"

"He's not here, Ellen," Tyler repeated in his newly scratchy voice, "and I have no idea where he is."

Celia was the one who told me, a few weeks after this, it was late July by then, that, out in LA, Tyler had been admitted to hospital.

I began to pack. The day after my birthday, when I had gone to the beach with friends and left them to walk by myself into the waves, I pulled a stack of books from a shelf and set them in a box. I threw out things I thought I would no longer need, culled my books from those that belonged to my husband, even though I didn't know yet where I was going or what I would do. When I walked the streets I knew so well, I felt as if my skin had changed. I felt unrecognizable to myself.

Don't go, Magda said to me. Vivienne said, Don't leave us, and, There's someone I want to introduce you to. But I told them I couldn't stay.

There is the time of minutes and years in which I went on looking for Chris, in phone books, then performing online searches as the years passed. I told myself: Even now there are those who, dead or alive, leave no internet trace. Twice I returned to the apartment to visit my husband and his new wife, and I've returned several times since they left the city, once with the man I lived with for many years, to stand across the street and stare at the towers that surround our building now, leaving no glimpse of open sky. I've walked the streets,

SKIN

searching, in a surge of bodies crossing at the lights on Houston, on the F train platform, in some trick of the light, among the places where the clubs I performed once were, as if, even now, Chris might appear. Then there are the moments in which, crossing First Street, I've slammed into the places in my body where gratitude and grief co-mingle with the violence of Chris's departure—his pain, his desire, whatever it was that impelled him into flight. I wouldn't, until now, have called this compassion. On these streets, I've looked for a way to forgive myself. For what? Let's say, for all my youthful myopias.

Skin

After her divorce my mother flew to Tanzania. The particular kind of evangelical Christianity that she embraced used foot washing as a form of baptism and she criss-crossed the country, washing the feet of men and women and children, many surprised but most eventually willing to be taken up by the ministrations of this tall, devoted woman.

Six months later she returned to Toronto and left the church that she'd so recently joined. Yet her impulse to wash others' feet didn't waver. She approached an organization that assisted newly arriving refugees and asked if she could offer her services to those who came through its doors. Of course not all those seeking the organization's help wanted to have their feet washed. Yet there were some who allowed themselves to be led to the plastic chair that my mother set up in the corner of an office. She spread a towel on the floor in front of Ibrahim from Idlib. Gently she peeled off his socks, which were as new as the winter boots sitting beside him, and invited him to lower his feet into a basin of steamy water. Lifting his right foot into her lap, she began to soap the cracked skin, working her fingers into the webbing between big toe and second toe, second toe and third, tugging on each toe as she went.

He faced her with a look of frozen uncertainty. Each day of the last week had been a besiegement of the unknown. The woman holding his foot took out a file and began to rub at the hard callouses of his heels. She pressed a finger to a place on the ball of his foot that sent a jet of feeling through him, so powerful it made him cry out. Then some part of him, braced for years through the bombings, shellings, since the first time he'd huddled as a child in terror under the kitchen table, experienced a small release. My mother massaged each of his feet in turn with almond oil until his skin was silky, drew his socks over them and sent him back to the world, wiping tears from his eyes, his gait at least briefly different.

When friends asked us how our mother was doing, we tended to be vague, embarrassed by her strange preoccupation. Yet my mother insisted that everyone who arrives in a new country deserves to be touched and where better than the feet, that vulnerable, overlooked, nerve-rich part of the body.

When we were children, she never kissed us as she put us to bed, she unkinked our toes. If something happened during the day to upset us, some unhappy schoolyard incident, she had the ability to find the place on the sole of the foot that called up the moment, a pain that with the pressure of her fingers seeped away. She deduced our moods from the pattern of our wet footprints across a tiled floor after a shower.

Later, when I was about to become a mother myself, she told me that her own feet were the most sensitive part of her body. With every step she took, a sensorium burst to life, shooting up through her soles. The grass that she crushed underfoot thrust itself against her. The experience was so overwhelming that she did everything she could to dull it: wore shoes with the thickest tread she could find; scrubbed the soles of her feet with sandpaper; never went barefoot. To my surprise she confided that her feet were the most eroticized part of her body; she couldn't come to orgasm without a gentle, continuous brushing of her left metatarsal arch. My father, it seemed, had grown tired of her peculiarities.

On his deathbed, my father called for my mother. Barely conscious, he kept repeating her name. When at last she appeared, she pulled a chair up to the end of his bed. She unfolded the sheet at the bottom of the mattress and laid a hand atop each of his ankles. He made small cries like a wounded creature as her wet sponge touched him and she pressed her fingers slowly and methodically to his wasted flesh.

Animals

Through the night heat, a heavy-set man approached me, a hitch in his stride. Uneasy, I debated veering off the sidewalk to avoid him, the empty street filled only with the sound of air-conditioners whirring in the darkness. I was clad in a thin dress, after the mind-frying fever of this day and the day before and the day before that. From side to side the man swayed. I did not want to assume menace on a quiet block so close to my home. And there was the dog, my companion, sniffing at the edge of a garden with a fervour I could only presume was fervour. As the man drew close, she tugged me towards him.

A sheen of sweat clung to his moon-white face. He had large, uneven teeth. His stomach pressed against the buttons of his short-sleeved shirt. Everything about him made my muscles clamp even as my dog nudged closer.

The man dropped to his knees in front of her. He was a baggage handler at the airport, he told me, fingers ruffling my dog's white hair. The day before, a flight had arrived from the Middle East. From Jordan. Did I know where that was?

Yes, I said, hand coiled tightly around my dog's leash.

He was unloading luggage on the blistering tarmac when he came upon a cage, he said. Inside a dog lay limp and unresponsive. For seventeen hours the dog had been in transit, seventeen hours in the belly of a plane through searing heat and freezing temperatures.

There was no water in the cage. How could anyone have been so careless?

The man held out his hand for my dog to sniff. I loosened my grip on her leash. Above us, leaves rustled in the dark.

He did not know what to do, the man said. He tried calling out. He spoke softly to the dog in her kennel. He tugged on the cage door but it was securely locked. A beautiful black dog with long legs, she was still in transit, according to her luggage tag. Someone had dropped her off in Jordan. She needed water. Trapped in her prison, she had not yet reached her destination. What good would it do to call the number on the front of the cage and tell whoever answered that their dog was dying?

And so she was his, for the moment. Her fate lay in his hands.

He called 911. He did not know what else to do, the baggage handler said. He told the woman who answered that he needed an ambulance. Someone was dying.

Moments later, through the undulations of heat, a man appeared on the tarmac with a pair of pliers and cut the wire of the cage door open. Joyful and relieved, the baggage handler returned with a bowl of water, knelt, and offered the water to the unresponsive dog. He crumpled a piece of paper towel and, parting the dog's lips, gently squeezed drop after drop onto her gums.

I imagined all this: the baggage handler, his moon-like face and large hands, squeezing drops of water from the paper towel patiently into the limp dog's mouth. He wanted to stay with her, to comfort her, he said, but he had to return to work.

Before leaving, he wrote a note that included his number and tucked it behind the luggage tag of the dog's cage. The next day he received a message from a woman in Winnipeg. She and her husband had been reunited with the dog at the airport. *Overjoyed...* she texted. *Without you...*

In the dark, as he knelt before me, the baggage handler began his story once more, this time with new urgency. How he had called an ambulance and told the woman who answered, Someone is dying.

What else should I have done? he asked me, his voice rising as he stumbled to his feet.

No, he asked *us*, my dog included in his gaze, as if he were demanding benediction or absolution or needed to be witnessed in his own moment of emergency.

He had come to Canada as a young man from Serbia, he told us. He had grown up on a farm. His father had owned the land, a small, poor holding. He had owned animals, too. Goats, pigs, chickens. The baggage handler and his family had left the country in 1995.

I thought about what I knew of that part of the world in those days, the war, the rapes, the massacres, and wondered what the baggage handler had known as a boy of all that was happening not far from his home. I wondered what reason his parents had given for leaving Serbia and what his father had said to him about the war when the boy brought him a flask of coffee in a far field, an old dog with a limp following him everywhere, past the rifle in the barn, through the stiff grass and around the bee-buzzed yard. What had he said to the old dog in those hours before his father sold off all the animals, including the dog, and they abandoned that life to make the move across the ocean?

The baggage handler cupped my dog's head in his hands. He brushed his lips to her ear. He kissed her forehead.

You must be good, he whispered. Be good.

Voices Over Water

A young man and a young woman are walking along the top of the Scarborough Bluffs. They stride quickly over the bright grass. A breeze buffets them. Beyond them, the land drops off, the lake wide as an ocean to the horizon. The young woman, my grandmother, wears a dove-grey skirt that she has made herself, cut fashionably high above the knee, like the skirts of smart young women she's seen dashing about London streets. In a couple of weeks, she will lower all her hems in mortification because no women in Toronto are wearing skirts as short as hers. Before they left England, with the last of his savings, my grandfather purchased a new black bowler hat. He pushes the hat down over his forehead so the breeze doesn't bear it away.

Below, the lake breaks against boulders, surges and retreats. In the distance the water shines crystalline blue, its surface fractured by tiny waves. They have no money but right now this doesn't matter because the clear air and unsalted water scintillate with possibility until the two of them become light-headed with excitement. My father, curled inside my grandmother, feeds on their excitement, growing slowly. My grandmother feels him shift. Rose, they will call the baby, or Thomas.

With his bowler hat perched on his head, my grandfather looks taller than ever, a firm, broad-shouldered, somewhat self-conscious man. There is no one else around. He turns to my grandmother, opens his arms, dances a little jig. "We're here," he shouts, "we're here!" Then, as if to welcome their new un-English life, he doffs his bowler hat and hurls it—like a cricket ball, a baseball?—over the edge of the cliff where it sails, before plummeting to the surface of the lake.

What if someone saw the hat, my grandfather worried as soon as he had thrown it, and thought there was a body beneath it, a suicide or death by drowning, and called the police? He imagined his hat drifting west, past the water filtration plant, the houses and the boardwalk along the Beach, out again around Ashbridges Bay, towards the islands that surround Toronto's harbour. Perhaps his hat would float across the lake as far as Rochester, or along the shore, westerly, past Hamilton, to Buffalo. Someone, picking it out of the water, sodden but still holding its bowler shape, might wonder who had lost the hat, and where. Could it have floated all the way from England, travelling the kind of distances that bottles sometimes did?

    I imagine it washing to shore on the stony beach not far from where my grandfather sent it spinning into the air. A young man who smells of bricks and sweat, who wears a paper-thin collarless shirt with the sleeves rolled up, squats and stretches one sunburned arm to pick the waterlogged hat out of the water. Curious, he sniffs it, pokes it, presses his ear to it, listening, as you might press your ear to a shell.

Voices called my grandparents back across the ocean to England, like Marconi's first radio signal from Cornwall to Newfoundland.

    During that first year in Canada, my grandfather designed radios, his designs nestling in rooms all across the expanse of the country: pride-of-the-parlour radios housed in oak cabinets with doors that opened; matter-of-fact kitchen radios with round speakers like mouths chattering from a sideboard or shelf; a novelty radio for a lady's boudoir that spilled jazz from a speaker shaped like a heart.

Without my grandfather, the radios would have had no voices. He was responsible for where the speakers went and for making sure all the parts that must go inside fit. It was fearless work and he was extremely good at it. The designs had to be flawless, because there were no maquettes, no trial runs. In the name of efficiency and the speed of new communication, each design went right into production.

Four years later, my grandparents left Toronto with their packed bags on a train bound for New York, because the ship they were to travel on sailed from there. In Niagara Falls, New York, they climbed off the train onto a windy platform where a customs inspector met them and took the steamer tickets out of my grandfather's hands. He looked at my grandfather, the tired hunch to his shoulders, his swollen fingers. Perhaps the customs inspector could smell the trace of gas that still seeped from my grandfather's skin, because he had begun working for the gas company, digging lines through soil that had once been sand at the bottom of the ancient, ice-age lake. Sand leaked from the splits in his boots. His designs hadn't faltered, it was just that the radio company had gone bankrupt. Men all around him were losing their jobs as well. Destitute, starving, they haunted the streets. Trying to keep the future in sight, my grandfather had turned down a three-month contract on another design job only to find out that the three months were probation and the job would have continued after that. He thought of himself now as an unlucky man.

Hair pins held my grandmother's dark hair in place. She stood there nervously, refusing to feel ashamed. A small, sturdy, dark-haired boy pressed himself against her legs.

"So you're taking him home to make a proper Englishman of him, are you?" the customs inspector asked.

"Yes," said my grandmother. This man had the power to refuse them, land them penniless in Toronto again.

SKIN

The man sized them up, as if to make sure they were not going to step off the train with their bags in Utica or Rome, or disappear into a New York warehouse, down the crowded streets under the elevated trains, in some desperate, last-ditch attempt to start another new life.

The boy stared back at the man, at the wisps of pale grey curling as if from out of the man's head, a cloud of vapour rising like a thin beard if beards grew upwards. His father had told him about the Falls. Now he had seen the Falls! In England, during the war and after, he would crouch in the tiny parlour or the backyard bomb shelter, ear pressed to one of the new radios that his father had designed, smaller, compact radios for the Marconi Company itself. Greedily my father listened for news of Canada, traces of its far-off voices. He told himself: I will go back.

The room is very still. Outside snow is falling. A streetcar rumbles past along College Street. The young man lies in bed, pressed against the warm body of his wife, utterly content. With his arms, like this, around her swollen waist and his hands on her abdomen, he can feel the child swimming inside her. In the closet, on the far side of the room, hangs her white nurse's uniform. Nursing is her passion, her calling. He is halfway through medical school. Hints of the England he has left behind still echo in his voice.

"We have to go somewhere," he says as she turns to face him. Her skin under his fingers is very warm. "We'll take a trip. Where shall we go?"

"Moose Jaw, my darling." She laughs softly. "Winnipeg. Vancouver. Or London. Take me to London."

"We'll fly," my father says. "We'll board a plane and be there in hours." He imagines her eyes, which he can barely see in the dark, their exuberance, the way they pull cheerfully tight at the corners when she laughs, which he loves. He loves the round, fierce lilt of her Canadian voice. When he touches the skin along her hairline, he feels beads of sweat. She struggles with the sheets as she sits up and asks him for a glass of water, although when he comes back into the room, with the water and a bottle of aspirin, she is lying down again.

"We'll go to the Rockies and climb a glacier together," she tells him, on her back, staring up at the ceiling. He knows she is the kind of woman who would do just that.

"We'll go to Corsica and lie on the beach and eat fresh sardines," he says. She shivers. Her hair is dark and glossy. Her skin, when he touches it, burns under his fingertips. A fever. A cold, not the flu. If they are lucky.

"I'm all right." She smiles. Her eyes glitter in the darkness. "I'll wait until the aspirin kicks in."

"Casablanca," he says as he pulls one of his own cardigans over her nightgown. "California." There is a world of places they can go, places that call to them. They will be explorers. He works her arms, which tremble in his grasp, into the woollen sleeves. In the bathroom, he moistens a washcloth, goes down the tiny hall to the kitchen where he fills a saucepan with water. On his return, he stops and takes the thermometer out of the medicine cabinet.

She is under the covers with her knees bent. She has stopped shivering. Her lips, when he slips the thermometer between them, are terribly dry. Sweat has soaked and flattened the hair around the edges of her face. The heat rising from her body feels perversely like some kind of radiance. "As long as I don't dehydrate," she says very clearly, in spite of the thermometer in her mouth. She pushes back the covers. He pulls the thermometer out and switches on the tiny bedside light.

None of his medical training or hers has prepared him for the fact that the temperature of a human being can rise so high so fast.

"I feel as if I'm floating in a lake." She laughs again.

They don't have a car. He helps her swallow some water and suggests that he should call an ambulance.

"You know that feeling when you're frightened fish are nibbling you. You think they're going to eat your arms and legs." Her whole body trembles.

SKIN

Ordinarily he'd think the best thing to do in the case of a fever would be to run a lukewarm bath, then he would sponge her down, but this has happened so fast, and she is pregnant. She tells him that her body feels like it is swelling. He wants to help but she is tossing back and forth in the bed. "I'm here," he tells her, "I'm here," pressing the cool washcloth to her forehead, although her eyes, travelling over him, don't seem to see him. He runs into the kitchen, through the air in the hall that still drifts with the smell of their pork chop dinner, calls for an ambulance. The ordinariness of their plates still piled in the sink, their hairbrushes on the bureau, no longer anchor them. None of his training or hers, he realizes in horror, is any promise of inviolability.

She is lying very still but her skin, when he touches it, is hotter than ever. There is no sound of traffic from the street. "Please take me out of the water," she whispers. Her body gives one short spasm.

The taste in his mouth is pure fear. If there were a lake, he would dive into it and pull her out, both of them gasping, he would drag their bodies and possible lives to shore. The sheets he holds in his hands as he crouches by the bed are soaking wet. Her skin is soaking wet. He feels as if he is standing at the top of a cliff, watching his wife and child drown.

He packed up everything he owned in Toronto and stored the boxes in the basement of a friend's house on Sullivan Street. In one box he stuffed the photographs and letters, all signs of his life with Nora, and sealed it tightly. He wrote to his parents explaining what had happened but could not bring himself to call them. He flew to Burma. In the Rangoon airport, a team of Burmese doctors met him, small, pleased, self-possessed men who shook his hand. They escorted him out into the torpid air and led him to a waiting Jeep. They drove north straight away, into the green hills.

He worked out of a white canvas tent, vaccinating people. Except for the children, the people who were afraid of the vaccinations hid their fear. Nevertheless, he felt it in their stiff arms. Once vaccinated, did they believe themselves safe? Outside the tent, strange birds sang in the trees. The thick air permeated his skin. He was relentlessly careful of his own health because he felt betrayed by all forms of luck; he had to look after himself because nothing else would. He did not eat local dairy products or vegetables that he could not peel, always dissolved chlorine tablets in his water or boiled it first. He did not walk without shoes or even wear sandals because of what might lie underfoot. He stayed away from radios, anything that brought news from other continents.

Sometimes he watched the monks in their bright orange robes, holding out their wooden bowls, only the shadow of their hair remaining on their shaved heads. He did not long to be one of them but he longed to walk through the world as they did, stripped clean, carrying a kind of silence around them. At least, in this country, he did not have to talk about what had happened to him. He could begin again.

In Maymyo, he worked his way through a crowd and watched men in bare feet run over a path of stones with fire laid underneath them, stones so hot they should have burned the men's feet but did not. The men walked in a trance: Was this what saved them, and if not, what did? In Pagan, he stood on the brink of a small hill in the dying light, watched the sun catch on the gold leaf of the spires, a field of old and empty temples that stretched out across the land as far as the eye could see. A bird that resembled a swallow flew out of one of them. My father stared at the temples but didn't see immortality—even if some ancient ruler had built them believing this grandiose gesture would reward him with endless life—just the tender beauty of slow decay.

The saturated air changed his skin, the very quality of his skin. He stopped lurching awake on his thin bed in the middle of the night, phantom water pouring over him, dreaming of a drowning body, a drifting bowler hat. Perhaps he would stay in Burma forever. There was nothing to stop him. He travelled down the Irrawaddy by boat. In Rangoon, he found a room to live in.

One day, in the Rangoon marketplace, he stopped at a stall full of lacquerware, picked up a small owl, the black lines of its face and wings etched through a patina of gold leaf, haggled seriously with the vendor, and bought it. The next day he went back and bought a matching one. The owls reminded him of Pagan: the temples, the birds flitting out of them. He bought a small lacquerware cup, a lacquerware bowl. Nothing he bought was very large, and the objects did not give him any sense of material accumulation. Instead, he collected them like talismans, because they held stories; he began to imagine himself telling these stories. He cupped the objects in his palm and felt them hum.

He kept his purchases in his suitcase under the bed. One day, he left the suitcase out, lid propped up, in a corner of the room. Crouched on the floor beside the suitcase, he wrapped the owls carefully in socks to protect them, nestled the bowls in an old, soft T-shirt or two.

In the late afternoon, when the sun turned deep yellow and the air had cooled, he walked the length of the market. At last, he came to the silk vendors' stalls where he marvelled at the glistening bolts of Burmese silk. He pointed to a cascade of blue-green silk, thick as a waterfall, stopped, asked the vendor to unwind instead a chute of white silk studded with red and sky-blue, silk that my sister would one day fashion into her wedding dress.

When he returned to his room, he realized in surprise that his suitcase was half full, packed with his clothes, his socks, the objects he had bought. He tucked the package of silk inside. From beneath his mattress, he retrieved a small transistor radio. He switched it on, swivelling through the crackle of static until a voice called out.

The International Headache Conference

They met at the International Headache Conference.

Constance was near the end of the migraine aisle, conference dossier clasped under one arm. At this end, far from the medications, were the heads: a head with a metal vise clamped over one side; a head with a nail drilled through one eye; a head with a knife protruding from the base of the neck. At a nearby podium, a woman whose pain had been compared to that suffered in the last moments of a fatal heart attack, as a ventricle of the heart collapsed, intoned into a microphone: "You cannot see it, but the pain is real."

The heads were fake but more comforting than anything else Constance had seen. She wanted to caress them, cradle them in her hands, run her fingers over the metal vise, the rammed-in nail, the blade of the knife, because at least these things made the pain visible.

There were days when she would stare at her face in the bathroom mirror, seeking evidence of the pain, days when friends came up to her on the street and said, You look great. At home, confronting her eyes, her skin, her mouth in the mirror, she could not believe they were still hers. Maybe her eyes looked a little bloodshot. There was no other sign.

This had been the risk in coming to the conference: that being here would bring a headache on. Already Connie had seen a few flashing lights at the periphery of her vision. She dove a hand into her purse, searching for her vial of medications. Right at the end of the display of heads, beside a head cut open in slices, stood a thin, tall man with dark hair. He held a thermos in one hand. Her sense of smell had grown so acute that even from this far off she could tell, from the scent sharp on his breath and in the air around him, that he was drinking cup after cup of pitch-dark espresso, the way some people did when they felt the pain coming on because, if they got enough caffeine through their system fast, the rush might avert a headache. By now, through the dry air and endless fluorescence, she could pick out the lurid petrochemical whiff of a woman's perfume two aisles away. Down the long corridor of the migraine aisle, she stared at the man; the pupils of his eyes had narrowed, she was certain, in ever-increasing pain. He stared back at her. They stumbled towards each other. The pounding in her head grew stronger.

"Let's get out of here," he said.

"Why do you want to go to a conference?" asked Teddy, her husband, from across the restaurant table. They had gone out for dinner after a movie. Movies in a cinema were tricky: the barrage of sound, the visual onslaught. When they arrived at the restaurant, Connie had asked Teddy to sit with the restaurant interior behind him, because looking at him backlit by the bright window made her head pulse. "I mean, what good will it do you to go to a conference?"

"They're my headaches," Connie said. "You can't stop me." She had just taken a pill with a glass of water, trying to breathe deeply, willing her blood vessels not to start contracting. She ranged over the menu as if each item on it were weighted with talismanic value: There must be some food, the right food, that would calm her neurochemistry, at the very least would not make her sick, please not tonight. Already pain was becoming a slab behind her right cheekbone, inside her right eye socket. Sometimes the medications worked, sometimes they didn't. Taking a pill felt like playing a game of Russian roulette.

She had met Teddy during their final year at university, although they didn't get married until eight years later, after Teddy went to work as an editor for a new online politics and culture magazine, and Connie, having finished her PhD in history, had started teaching adjunct and doing some freelance copywriting. Marrying Teddy aroused in Connie a sense of achievement seamed with magnanimity, towards him and towards herself, which seemed to be something like what Teddy felt about her, which was how she'd felt when they first started sleeping together. And this was love, wasn't it? Teddy sat across the table in his black sharkskin jacket, his hair a straight blond fringe across his forehead, head resting on one fist, smart, articulate, moody, withdrawn, loyal, more like her father than Connie cared to admit. His gaze met hers then sidestepped. He ran a finger over his soft, full lips.

She'd had headaches when she met him, and long before she'd met him. She'd had them ever since she could remember, although the memory of pain tended to obliterate itself, because it had no form, it was impossible to hold on to, either it was there or not there. On days when she didn't have a headache, she could, like a child or an animal, forget about the pain completely, as if it didn't exist. Often she had some kind of headache four or five times a week. Teddy thought she had headaches once a week. Sometimes, she taught with what felt like an invisible axe driven through her forehead. She had never told Teddy this.

Mostly he left her alone when she had a headache. Usually all she wanted was to be left alone. She preferred not to talk about the pain. In the evening, Teddy liked to pour himself a whiskey and Connie a soda. No alcohol for her, said her head. Ensconced in the blue armchair, she would listen to Bach partitas through her headphones, while Teddy, in the other armchair, the one shredded to pieces by the cat, read a book that he had to review. Connie stared at him malevolently, but he didn't seem to notice. There were whole weeks at a time when she was working on her thesis that she had barely been able to read. When she tried, it was as if someone had stuck a pin in her eye and was poking it around. Teddy probably thought she was dreamier than she really was. He would rub her shoulders if she asked him to. Gently. On days like this she loved their cat, Ratso, with a matter-of-fact intensity she rarely felt for Teddy, because Ratso always seemed to know when she was in pain. He leaped into her lap, pressed himself against her, kneaded her, prick, prick, prick.

Once she asked Teddy to massage her neck, the back of her neck where the cords of muscle and tendon had turned to steel. Harder, she kept saying, harder, urging his fingers deeper and deeper, until she cried out and he stopped. "I can't, Connie," he said. "I can't do it anymore."

"Why can't you?" She turned until she could see him, feeling as if she'd been abandoned. He didn't say anything, but there was something in his expression that could have been fear. Did her pain frighten him? Did she frighten him?

One afternoon, about a month before the conference, they headed out together for a walk. Connie had no memory of what they'd been talking about as they ambled through the park, under the spiky, spring-green leaves, until the moment when Teddy said, "Well, yes, I think of you as fragile."

"You what?" She sucked in her breath as if she'd been hit. Teddy kept breaking a stick gently between his fingers, leather jacket slung open in the warmth, as Connie tried to convince herself that he didn't mean what he'd just said although she could tell by the quick, incautious tone of his voice that he did. "Why do you think of me as fragile?"

"Because of all your headaches." Now Teddy looked guilty. Cornered.

"But why fragile?" Connie demanded. She stopped in the middle of the path. "If you meet a man who's had a heart attack, you think, Okay, he's been through a lot of pain and maybe he didn't look after himself properly, but do you think of him as fragile?"

"Maybe not," Teddy said.

"I don't lie around with the lights off and drape damp cloths over my face and act like some kind of invalid, do I? So I won't get a full-time job, but why does that have to be a weakness? Why can't it look like a choice? Plenty of other people work freelance. You write reviews at home, don't you?"

"Connie, I just want you to do great things," Teddy said.

"Well, of course," she said, as tears welled in her eyes, "of course I want to do great things."

That night they went to a party hosted by Teddy's magazine at a club. Flashes of light sparking around her, Connie wove her way through the crowd, talking animatedly to people she knew, even taking to the dance floor, until she was on the edge of throwing up but was sure she'd kicked every image of nineteenth-century hysterics to death.

Between flashes, she caught Teddy observing her from across the room, a careful look from that distant archipelago of people who can take an aspirin and make a headache go away, if they ever got a headache. He couldn't see anything. He couldn't see her overcoming anything.

"Do you have a migraine?" he asked as they stood in line at the coat check at the end of the evening. He sounded as if he didn't really want to know, and Connie felt herself contracting, her whole body contracting away from him. He took her arm as they made their way towards the door and out into the street, through a line of parked cars.

"So," Connie said, as she concentrated on staying upright, staring down at the rounded surface of her pumps, the mottled, trembling concrete beneath her feet, "the fact of pain I am unable to get rid of makes me fragile."

SKIN

❖

At the headache conference, before she came to the aisle of heads, she'd encountered a glass display case fronted by a sign that read *Average number of painkillers consumed by a headache sufferer in one year.* Inside the glass, a pile rose in front of a long row of empty pill bottles: thick round pills, slim caplets, white, pale yellow, milky orange, all transformed into a carefully constructed object, a mountain of pills lit by a spotlight that cast a long shadow across the blue velvet beneath it. The display stopped Connie in her tracks. There was something awful and utterly satisfying about it. Out of a pair of overhead speakers, a hushed voice spoke: "Are you the kind of person who panics as soon as you realize you've gone out without your painkiller? How many kinds of painkiller do you carry on you at one time? Two, three, four? Are you addicted to the security of having your painkiller on you as much as to your painkiller itself? What would it mean to kill your pain? Can you kill the pain and not the person?"

She walked quickly towards the exit beside the man with the thermos. Then they were out in the street, hurrying together through the light drizzle. His name was Luke, he told her, and he got cluster headaches, which didn't necessarily come that often but seized him in massive, blinding flashes and could be so bad that he would bang his head repeatedly against a refrigerator or a wall. Once he'd had to stop himself from leaping out a window. Was he on the verge? Connie asked. He was, he said. And you? Connie nodded.

They stopped at a corner and he rested one hand against the side of her head until she leaned into the gesture. She touched his forehead with her palm.

"Let's take a room in a hotel," Connie said.

Streetlights flickered on. The air quivered. They stopped at a drugstore where Connie bought things she thought they might need, a box of crackers, bottle of ginger ale, lotion, muscle relaxants,

[102]

moving as fast as she could, pushing all her energy into a thin, clear strip on the outside of her forehead as her hands grew colder and her throat constricted. No painkiller could make a difference now.

They entered the room together, locked the door, drew the blinds. The room was dark, filled with the dark, hazy shapes of a bed and two chairs. The traffic seemed very far away. They turned off their phones. They barely spoke. Connie pulled off her coat. She took off her jacket and skirt. Clad in her slip, she lay down on one side of the bed. Jacket off, kneeling beside her, Luke turned her onto her stomach. Hands coated in lotion, he pressed his fingers into her shoulders, her neck, the exact point at the back of her skull from which pain radiated, but the pain was blooming behind her eye anyway, blooming into the room, until there was no longer any border between her and any object in the room. Closing her eyes was worse. A pit opened inside her, her self growing minuscule and huge. Luke took her lower jaw and shook it. He twisted the edges of her ears, hard enough to hurt, and she concentrated on that, to get away from the other pain.

"I'm all right for now," he said. The odour of other people's decades-gone cigarettes, the bitter scent of the aging polypropylene carpet filled her air passages, her lungs, then Connie was in the bathroom, blinded, slumped over the toilet, the man named Luke holding her hair out of her face. She thought, I cannot go on like this. Get me through this, and I will do anything to make it stop. She thought, I have my arms, my legs, my brain. I live in a safe country. All I have to do is make it across the room. She felt like Atlas. She was only trying to hold up her head. It was all in her head.

Time passed. They lay side by side on the bed. She could make out that Luke had finely lined skin and sharp features. "Sometimes I yell things when it gets really bad," he said. "Crazy things."

"Do you think of yourself as fragile?" Connie asked, turning to face him.

"Vulnerable. We're vulnerable. It's different."

"Yes," Connie said.

SKIN

They called room service and ordered toast and two cups of tea. She sat up carefully on the bed, ate a couple of crackers to settle her stomach, took a couple more pills. With enormous concentration, she went to the door and got the tea.

Beads of sweat stood out on his forehead. She massaged Luke's scalp, his damp hair, brushed away the line of sweat over his lip, worked her fingers over his forehead, his temples, the swollen blood vessels in his temples. Her hands squeezed the clenched rods of his shoulders, deeper, deeper, made their way down his arms to his wrists. He swore as she unclenched his fingers one by one and bit them. Somewhere in the darkness of her head she thought, I will have to call Teddy.

Luke moaned. "Oh God," he said. "Oh God, there is no pain like this. It can go on like this for days." Connie wrapped her arms around him. She poured all her strength into holding him.

Touch

Because the lockdown didn't come into effect until midnight, we decided to meet for a movie. This meant leaving the house outside the city where I had taken refuge after my divorce and riding the train into town. I felt desperate for company, however fleeting, still able to convince myself that I wore gloves only because it was the season for them, to protect my hands from the penetrating wind.

There she was, at dusk, riding towards me on her bicycle, wiry hair springing from beneath her helmet. Despite our happiness at seeing each other, we had misjudged. The café attached to the movie theatre had already closed. Only a single employee remained, a young woman in the ticket booth, waving us inside with one nitrile-gloved hand, pointing our way into the darkness where we would soon discover there was no one but the two of us.

About the movie itself, I can tell you only this: In one scene a young woman walks barefoot through a drafty manor house at night, in a sleeveless nightgown, not a single goose bump rising on her skin, and this unremarked-upon invincibility astonished, even disturbed me. It seemed as unreal as the moment when the same woman's bare hand drifts to caress another woman's cheek.

After the credits, the lights did not go up. From the exit, the sole employee beckoned to us once more with her black-gloved hand. When I picked up my bag in the dark, something clunked from it, forcing me to grope on the ground with panicky thrusts until I located my phone, by which point eager virions had surely sped from the floor up through my nasal passages to colonize every bronchiole of my lungs.

In the lobby, someone was banging on the outside door, as if to terrorize us or warn us of the future. But, no, it was only a red-haired young woman, another employee, who'd left an extra pair of gloves inside and wanted to retrieve them.

We found a café that was still open. We were instructed to sit with the span of an eagle's wing between us. The waiter measured, with gloved hands, the distance with a tape, each suite of customers separated, at his insistence, by an equivalent wingspan. There was still food on the menu and beer to drink, my phone now safely sealed within a zip-locked plastic bag.

Out in the street, I begged her to leave the city with me while she still could, suddenly obsessed with touching her in all the ways one might wish to touch another being. From the distance of a swan's wing, she looked at me as if I had gone mad.

Nevertheless, for a little while we had managed to distract each other, caught up in the old intimacies, and I carried that bittersweet pleasure with me as I set out for home. It wasn't until I was walking across the train station parking lot on my way back to my car, no other person in sight, that, scrambling in my bag, I discovered my keys were missing. Tugging off my gloves, I rifled through every crevasse of bag and pocket. I imagined calling her, imploring her to take me in, to accompany me back to the theatre, or to my place where I might yet touch her, balancing on her shoulders to break through my kitchen window.

But her phone might go on ringing, just as, when I tried the movie theatre, its phone line rang and rang, leaving me lost amid the world's broken circuitry, the night warping, traffic lights flaring over the empty streets, from green to yellow to red, again, again, from green to yellow to red.

Breath

As we rose to our feet, scores open, voices resounding through the hall, the bald man burst from the outer lobby. Like a tide, sopranos filled the orchestra, spilled into the balconies, altos squeezed to the left, tenors to the right, basses a small cloud floating in the rear. Every year, for years on end, we had surged into this hall in our thousands, massing to sing like angels, spurring ourselves upwards to this, the apogee of our Singalong *Messiah*.

Hallelujah! From our side balcony, my gaze snagged on the bald man's athletic suit, his waving arms.

Hallelujah! Grasping the edge of the stage, he hauled himself onto it, pale-skinned, long-jawed.

Hallelujah! The conductor who, an hour and a half before, had strutted into sight, wearing a topcoat and white wig, claiming to be George Frideric Handel himself, jerked at the interruption, baton mid-air. Powder gusted from him like vapour. The soloists startled. The soprano trembled in her blue gown. The alto, in red satin, went rigid. The bearded tenor puffed like an adder. Did the man intend attack? Assault? I saw no gun. Was he delusional? Psychotic? Only the bass, the youngest and tallest, kept singing, as if his voice had the profundity to move mountains. As soon as my mother, at my side, noticed the bald man, I felt her gaze shift, pass over me like a touch, even though she hadn't touched me.

SKIN

❖

Not more than a month before, my mother, aged eighty-five, had invited me, her only child, to accompany her to another concert, a performance of Schumann Lieder in a much smaller hall. As the singer and her piano accompanist approached the end of the final song, a rustle at my back caught my attention, movement forceful enough to make me turn. The woman seated behind me had collapsed. The man at my side, a stranger, bolted to his feet and clambered over the seat back to reach her. Those on either side huddled over her slumped form. Someone pulled out their phone. Had she fainted? Heart attack? Someone else muttered the word *stroke*.

Before I could make a move to help, my mother took hold of my shoulders. With a grip so strong it shocked me, she turned me to face the stage. Everyone, except those few behind us, had erupted in applause. "You need to clap," my mother said, her small face radiating happiness.

As the bald man struggled to his feet on stage, the phones of all those who had forgotten to turn theirs off or clandestinely refused to do so began to wail.

He shouted. The women in the rows around us murmured— What did he say? A what? What kind of airborne incident?

Our singing staggered into disarray. After a final blare of trumpets, the orchestra sawed to a discordant stop. Even the bass soloist broke off. The conductor swung to face the intruder, wig tilting into his eyes. Trained by our dopamine receptors, I, like thousands of others, scrambled for my phone, I, a middle-aged woman who loves to lift into the high notes but who had acquiesced to my mother's desire, her voice lowering with age, to transition to the alto section.

My mother does not have a phone. She does not concede to the needs of others who might wish to reach her in an emergency.

[108]

She stood there, a small woman, her posture only now slightly bent, holding her score.

I dumped my score onto my aisle seat, told her I'd be right back.

When I was a child, my father worked as a pharmacist in a drugstore some distance from our home. Sometimes, when my mother had errands or appointments that made her unavailable for some hours or when the kindergarten day ended, she left me in the care of a friend who lived not far off. One afternoon, this woman, Dorit, sent me home from her townhouse to ours, telling me that my mother would be there when I arrived. This was in the days when people still made a habit of sending small children off by themselves. When I rang our doorbell, no one answered. I did not have a key. I rang again. I have no idea how long I stood there. Hours? It could not have been hours. Surely someone would have noticed me. I wept. In my distress I peed myself, pee spreading over the concrete doorstep. At last my mother arrived to bustle me inside. Why hadn't I gone back to Dorit's house? she asked, seemingly flummoxed by my distress. This was what she would have done, so different from the sobbing child before her. I had no idea how to communicate to her the amplitude, the depth of my aloneness as I'd waited for her on the empty concrete, as if I were falling through some dark place, endlessly falling.

Out in the lobby, people raced for the main doors, shedding programs, hats, gloves, diving into their winter coats. It's amazing how fast people are re-seized by the ancient urges, fight or flight, even though an official-looking man had shouted at us from the back of the auditorium, exhorting us not to move. I ran my hands through my short, greying hair. Phone in hand, I wished for someone to call, but who?

SKIN

Ahead of me, a bottleneck grew by the front doors, cries rising from the crush of bodies. *Open the doors!* The outer doors were glass, guarded by ushers in blue greatcoats. The ushers' voices shouted in reply. *Locked! Management's orders!*

From my position a few steps above the crowd, I glimpsed, beyond the glass, shadowed forms and heard, from outside, a staccato banging, a crescendo of muffled voices. More shouts rose from inside the vestibule, a contrapuntal force of belligerence and horror. *Don't let them in!*

If the doors had been open, would I have run out into the street, along with that human tide, leaving my mother to her own devices? No.

I turned — in the direction of a nearby concession stand, already abandoned by the young uniformed man who had staffed it. I had to shove others out of the way, an aging man in a fur coat, a woman muffled by scarves, in order to grab what I had in mind, not mints or cough drops but boxes of chocolate-covered almonds, food or the closest thing to it. Moments before we had been singing, joy filling our mouths. I stuffed four boxes into my pockets, telling myself that, in the short-term at least, we wouldn't starve. To take more seemed like thievery. I ducked behind the counter to leave a ten-dollar bill under a dirty glass in the space where the cash box had been.

Decades ago, six months after my father's sudden death, the second heart attack having felled him, aged fifty-seven, in his hospital bed, my mother and I found ourselves stranded together in the vast grasslands of the Masai Mara in Kenya.

One afternoon, a month or so after the funeral, seated with my mother in her living room, not yet thirty, dazed by my own grief, I asked her if she had a longing to go anywhere. She was not a demonstrative griever but she'd lost weight and, in her bereavement, had the wan look of someone beset by sleeplessness. If she wished to travel, I said, wherever in the world she wished to go, I would go with her. Staring beyond me, through the white curtains of her living room, she told me at last that she had always longed to see a lion. Not in a zoo. In its own habitat. And so, perhaps, now was the time to do that.

From the moment she suggested the trip, I'd had to squelch my objections: Two white ladies, we were surely embarking on an ill-advised colonial misadventure. There must be some other animal she could set her sights on. But she remained firm. My mother's long-deceased sister, my aunt, had briefly lived in Kenya. And my mother's grief, layered and different than my own, humbled me.

And so, one morning at our safari lodge, we set our alarms before sunrise and rose to meet Simon, our driver, in the lobby.

In Simon's white Pajero, we drove out onto the plain. Left to my own devices I might have asked to linger among the tiny, delicate dik-diks, the browsing herds of antelope. Simon slowed and, whether his excitement was pragmatic, on our behalf, or came from a genuine wonder of his own, he pointed with a hushed cry—to a creature lounging along the branch of a solitary thorn tree. Not a lion. A cheetah.

My mother picked up her binoculars. Would this be enough, I wondered. The spotted cat's sprawled limbs, its louche, magnificent mystery?

I attempted to insist to myself, to her, that it was, wanting what from my mother—tears? Some sign of catharsis?

She lowered her binoculars and nodded.

Some minutes later, as we gained speed along the narrow road, an alarming guff, guff, guff came from the back of the car. After Simon had pulled over, folded his shirt sleeves to his elbows and performed an inspection, he announced that a large thorn had punctured the left rear tire. There were no other vehicles in sight. Purple clouds massed on the horizon. While he removed our bags from the trunk in order to unpack the jack from the emergency tire well, my mother, clad in cotton shirt and tan trousers, stepped out of the car.

SKIN

When I followed her, I fell—into a void, onto a vast plain that extended beyond the horizon, in which I recognized nothing, not even myself. The old, existential terror rose up, engulfing me. The clouds swelled. A bolt of lightning sluiced through them.

By this time, Simon had wedged the metal jack up against the vehicle and was turning the handle of the tire iron to ratchet up jack and car. A group of children appeared and stared at us in silence. My mother asked if she could help. Naturally Simon said no. She was likely old enough to be his grandmother. Small, as I have said. She didn't exactly wrestle the tire iron from him but something must have passed between them because, after a moment, he stopped what he was doing and relinquished the iron to her. All at once she, the oldest of us, was the one kneeling to crank the handle, raising car and flat tire into the air. I remember to this day how it felt to watch her: the sinewy strength of her turning arm. Simon, too, must have sensed something of her adamancy. Perhaps this action provided the catharsis she needed. It was impossible not to feel admiration for her will, her impressive tenacity, even as I wondered in what way she was aware of me, quaking on the road's shoulder. If lightning had struck and a blazing fire swept across the savannah, of course, in my panic, I would, like a child, have run open-armed to her.

At orchestra level, a group huddled near the foot of the stage. The choir stumbled down from their banked rows, Handel having vanished, leaving only an airborne trace of powder. Musicians wandered about, clutching their instruments, timpanist locked in urgent consult with a trumpeter. The tenor patted the heaving back of the soprano, collapsed in a pool of blue. My eyes kept returning to the alto: After gathering her red gown into a knot at her waist to reveal the tight leather pants worn beneath, she vaulted from the stage to join the crowd gathered around the bald man, the one who had first announced our predicament and who now gesticulated towards the rear doors.

They were planning a reconnaissance party, my mother said as I reclaimed my seat. They had shouted their plans to the auditorium moments before.

They were going to follow a route that led into the underground pathways linking the concert hall to the subway, through a warren of food courts and shopping malls that spread beneath nearby office towers, she said. Perhaps, that way, there would be an exit.

I did not share with my mother the images that, moments before, I had been scrolling through on my phone. A brief video came up on all the feeds. Glimpsed through the murky window of a streetcar, a woman beat against the outer doors, gasping for breath before sliding to the ground. The scene might have been shot blocks from where we were. A drone panned over traffic stretching as far as the eye could see, cars stalled along an avenue of plate glass and plastic signs as familiar to me as the lines of my palm. From street level, drivers and passengers waved frantically like the trapped occupants of small submersibles. Smudged forms sprawled on the sidewalk. An airborne threat, the feeds agreed. Particulates? Gas? Released in an accident? By drones, airplanes, aliens? Terrorism? Bioterrorism? There was as yet no consensus, only, whatever it was, it seemed to be spreading.

I pulled out the boxes of chocolate-covered almonds and handed one to my mother.

Sometimes I wondered what she saw when I appeared at her door, in my faded jeans and worn denim coat, bearing flowers or a loaf of bread. Did I disappoint her, living my quiet life, still working in the bookshop after all these years? Had she wished for other children, ghost children who still circled the air around me, as I had imagined sisters or a brother trailing behind me as I walked? She had never spoken of this. At times I thought I must appear to her as a kind of feral animal, stumbling out of the woods, given all the ways in which the texture of my being seemed inexplicable to her.

SKIN

    For several years I had been married, until the day when my ex-husband collapsed to the floor, crying, I can't love you anymore, I'm sorry, repeating the words as if asking for forgiveness, as if my inability to transform myself into the kind of person whom he could love demanded forgiveness, or his attempt and subsequent failure to love me left him wounded and unable to forgive himself so that I must find some way to forgive him.
    I had never found an adequate way to describe to my mother why he'd fled.
    I stayed in what had been our apartment. Each afternoon, in mid-winter, a beam of waning sunlight extends along the hallway. It is the cat, once mine and my husband's, now my companion, who, each day, follows the beam of light, making her way towards the kitchen as the light fades, a small, dark form who would be waiting for her dinner. How I longed to be hurrying up my block, turning the key in my door, gathering up her bowl and kneeling to ruffle her soft fur, her tail waving at me in the ordinary air.

I told myself: We still had functioning washrooms, water fountains, electricity. We could maintain ourselves like this for some time. In the line-up for toilets and at the washroom sinks, a cheerful camaraderie persisted among the women, altos mostly, a few sopranos, as we traded what little we'd gleaned. Our government had just declared a state of emergency, a tall woman said. My phone confirmed this. Many governments, said someone else. All flights were grounded, another woman claimed. All flights, globally, said another. Despite the camaraderie, we side-eyed each other's habits with the paper towels: Those who still, profligately, took multiple sheets to dry their hands while others made do with one; those who waved their hands at the dryers or gave up on the dryers to wipe their hands on their clothes. After refilling my water bottle at the fountain, I checked my phone once more, only to find a message saying systems were temporarily unavailable or overloaded. When I tried again, my phone flashed the same message.

Whatever the threat was, it would blow over, so I insisted to my mother when I returned to my seat. I didn't say to her: as rage or the feeling of being utterly inconsolable will, if we are lucky, blow over. She nodded, staring ahead of her. I swallowed my terror. Opening the box of chocolate-covered almonds, she shook a few into her palm and handed the box to me.

The doors at the rear of the hall burst open. Masked people surged in—the search party, wearing pieces of cloth or scarves tied over their noses and mouths, some of them grasping the bald man's inert limbs in the makeshift stretcher of their arms. A strip of red covered the alto's lower face, hers and that of the bald man—she must have ripped the skirt from her red dress, torn it again, tied the red satin behind their heads to hold it in place.

Amid the uproar, it was impossible from where we sat to hear what had happened. Once more I leaped to my feet. A cry for doctors went up. A woman in one of the rows behind us bolted through the door at our backs.

We waited, pacing and anxious, mumbling among ourselves, my mother still seated, staring straight in front of her. When, minutes later, the woman from our little group reappeared, she told us that the bald man had insisted on setting off ahead of the search party. He'd staggered back, only to collapse. Had poison rained down on him through a hidden air vent? Was the poison creeping closer? Neither she nor anyone else could say. I dug in my bag for my scarf and struggled fruitlessly to rip the wool in two.

From down below, and across the auditorium, a small movement caught my eye. Despite his slackened body and apparent stupor, the bald man turned his head. Across the distance between us, so it seemed, his gaze sought mine. Perhaps I imagined it—recalling how my father's weakened gaze had found mine from his hospital bed in the hours before his death.

SKIN

A line, a line and a half, from midway through the "Hallelujah Chorus" returned to me then. *The kingdom of this world is become.* All voices in the chorus join to sing these words. After a half-note of silence, the altos pick up the verse. Everyone else remains stilled for a whole note before they continue.

Whatever comes after the pause, what I hear in the pause itself is this: Breath. Breath determines meaning.

When the alto soloist leaped back onto the stage, all eyes followed her. It was she who declared we must sing once more. Where we sat no longer mattered, she said, arms outstretched, her red mask removed, attempting to rouse us from our stupor.

Should we begin at the beginning or where we'd left off? From the front of the stage, she called the question out to us. I handed my mother's score to her. Where we left off, I called from our balcony, the alto lifting her face in my direction as if she had, indeed, heard me. Weeping and shouts could be heard outside the hall.

Ever since she'd begun the slow, meticulous culling of her belongings, my mother's house had gained a haunted feel. Pale rectangles on the wall glowed where there once were paintings, which she had gathered into boxes, along with stacks of books, taking them to the Goodwill or leaving them at the edge of the sidewalk for others. We were to have returned to her house after the concert for a simple meal of lamb chops and broccoli, for dessert an apple snow — custard of apple and egg yolk topped with meringue, a dish she had made for me since my childhood. She would have set the table before heading out, two place mats, napkins, cutlery.

Only a few weeks earlier, arriving at her house one evening, I had come upon my mother outside, dragging a trunk across the sidewalk to the curb, her body bent to grasp the leather handle, the trunk's metal scraping over the cement. Singlehandedly, she must have hauled its weight up the basement stairs and into the street.

"Stop," I shouted, astonished, determined to wrestle the trunk from her—the same steamer trunk with which, at the age of six, she had been sent across the ocean during wartime, far from her own home. Repeatedly, when I asked, she told me she remembered nothing of this past. In any case, she said, it was best not to dwell on what lay behind you, only press onwards. This was what she'd been taught.

"Stop," I shouted again. "That's my inheritance." She stumbled, then flinched, as if she thought I might hit her.

A group of masked musicians straggled back to the stage. The alto took up an abandoned violin bow as her baton. I held my mother's elbow as she struggled to her feet.

Something else came back to me: When humans sing together, even if we start in disharmony, our voices find their way unconsciously into agreement. I kissed the papery skin of my mother's cheek. I took her hand and laced my fingers through hers, felt her fingers return the pressure of my touch. For a moment she rested her small head on my shoulder. I picked up my score.

We breathe in and then, as darkness falls, we sing, our voices soaring together and winging outwards the way a flock of bats will burst from a great cave.

Camouflage

One winter evening, at a Toronto bar called the Inter Steer, Danny sat listening to his friend Ethan and Ethan's girlfriend Anne recount how Ethan had won an all-inclusive week-long vacation at a Barbados resort, where they would be heading in two days.

"Three weeks ago, she drags me into this Portuguese jewellery shop in the Dufferin Mall," Ethan said.

"Not drags," Anne said.

"Convinces me to accompany her. When we step back into the mall, this very insistent group of middle-aged Portuguese men and women selling raffle tickets comes up to us."

"This woman really did grab me by the elbow—" Anne said.

"So I offered to buy a ticket. To free Anne. Actually, I bought ten."

"Then, a week later, Ethan gets a call from an unknown number telling him he's won an all-inclusive Caribbean vacation and hangs up—"

"I assumed it was a scam," Ethan said. "Wouldn't you? Wouldn't anyone? I'd forgotten about the raffle. Thankfully they called me back. They were very nice and persistent."

More snow was due to fall that evening. At Danny's back the window bled cold, the air's iciness crawling all over him, under his hoodie, into his jeans. "You're a lucky man," he said to Ethan. "You're both lucky," he added.

As soon as Ethan was out the door, off to buy cigarettes, his good spirits wafting around him, Anne leaned across the table. "Danny, can I ask you something?"

Danny nodded. He knew Anne only through Ethan, had known her only for the eight months he'd known Ethan, but people often confided in him, telling him secrets they'd kept for years. Was it something innate that drew people to him or the habit of sympathetic attention he'd cultivated since childhood?

Anne pressed her fingertips to the wooden table. "I don't know if I can go on this trip. I've been thinking about ending things, and if I go with Ethan and break up when we get back, I look like a hypocrite. If I break up with him now, I wreck the trip. What would you do in my shoes?"

"That's hard." Danny considered reaching out to touch Anne's arm in a show of sympathy. There was nothing he could say that wouldn't be tinged with self-interest. "No one wants to be a hypocrite."

He had to act surprised the next day when Ethan called him up. Distraught, Ethan said that after a year and without any warning Anne had dumped him. After sex. And right before their stupid fucking romantic vacation.

Danny offered up a profusion of condolences before adding, "In the end don't you think it's more honourable for her to do this before the trip than after?"

He felt for Ethan. Of course he did, though he had to ask, "Will you still go?"

"Are you free? It's a bit crazy. It means leaving tomorrow. We could make it a working vacation."

"I'm free," Danny said.

He'd met Ethan the previous spring at a house party. Searching for a bottle opener on a kitchen counter covered in empties, the air skunky with weed, Danny had become aware of someone entering the room and propelling himself towards him. A tall man, neatly dressed, good haircut, thirty-ish, held out his hand. "Danny Walsh? Reg tells me you're a screenwriter." Only then did the man introduce himself as Ethan Tepperman.

As an undergrad, Danny had won a school award for an autobiographical short film. Now, seven years later, he was in the midst of a treatment for a full-length feature about a girl gang in Scarborough; his collaboration with a friend on a zombie romance seemed to have stalled. In his day job, he translated TV scripts from English to French. His French was terrible: His charm and accent, or his charming accent, had been enough to get him hired was Danny's thought. Somewhere a source of public funding devoted to this project must flow like a magical tap, since no one had ever commented on Danny's whimsical or far-fetched or possibly execrable translations. He had a hunch no one even read his scripts. None seemed on its way to being produced. Nevertheless, he'd scammed his way into a regularly paying, if low-wage, job. "I work in screen and television."

It turned out that Ethan was a patent lawyer. He'd taken a screenwriting course and was working on a screenplay. "So far I have a treatment together and most of a first draft. People tell me the project has legs. I guess what I'm looking for is someone to be like a coach or consultant, give me a read-through, offer some advice."

"A script editor," Danny said. "Tell me a little more."

"Ex-Nazi war criminal's been living undercover in an Ontario town for years. Based on a true story. He's a local businessman, everybody likes him. One day the police show up at his door. Kind of like *Operation Finale* crossed with *The Stranger*."

"I see," Danny said, stifling his fear that the script would be awful. And did he even know a film called *The Stranger*?

"The early Welles one," Ethan said, "1946."

"Oh, right," Danny said. On the one hand, Ethan's presumption that all he needed to do was take a course in order to write a viable screenplay felt irksome. On the other, his admission of his limitations somehow redeemed the presumption. "I'd be happy to take a look."

Next thing Ethan was handing over a business card and typing Danny's contact information into his phone. An instant later, he pulled out a hip flask and poured Danny a shot of some complexly scented, amber-coloured liquid. Lagavulin, Ethan said. Twelve-year-old. Cask-strength.

"I don't offer this to just anyone," he added. The dark hair and not-quite-swagger of him. The earnestness. The way he threw himself into every gesture.

"Honoured," Danny said, taking the liberty of knocking his glass against Ethan's before inhaling a smoky, chokingly petroleum-infused sip, so very, very far from the three-dollar bottle of beer he'd been about to chug back.

"I'll give you a call," Ethan said, raising his own glass.

"Don't you want to know my rates?" Danny asked.

"It's okay, man," Ethan said. "I trust you."

They met at a café near Ethan's condo. Danny assumed the meeting would be a one-off: He'd pass along some breezily considered notes on Ethan's script, which was not as egregiously awful as Danny had feared; it had a half-decent three-act structure and some workable dialogue. But at the end of their first meeting, Ethan proposed another. It wasn't that he took all of Danny's suggestions. A definite no to Danny's pitch that they update the story by making the man a radicalized white supremacist. It'll make the project more hook-y, Danny persisted, for all that he was hardly an expert on the selling of screenplays. That's not the story, Ethan said. He was, however, willing to consider bumping up the love interest. What about turning the wife into a lover? In any case, Danny argued, more of her. She has to be our moral compass. (By this time Danny had gone out of his way to watch Welles's *The Stranger*.)

What was he, Danny wondered, as their meetings turned bi-weekly. Editor? Collaborator? Did it matter? Co-writer wasn't a term that Ethan seemed prepared to use while going so far as to insert some of Danny's lines into his dialogue.

And what was Ethan to him? Client. Friend? Sometimes the script sessions turned into drinking sessions. They'd ditch the coffee shop for a bar. Sometimes Anne came out to join them. Or else Ethan wanted to talk about Anne. Or Faith, the woman who had preceded her, with whom he'd lived acrimoniously for four years. Was Danny seeing anyone, Ethan asked over a round of Manhattans. He seemed curious about the rest of Danny's life. Danny offered up flashes of his boyhood in Scarborough and a wispy outline of his translation job. Not really, Danny replied to the dating question, preferring to keep his personal life, or the rest of his personal life, to himself.

There were the evenings when Ethan invited Danny back to his condo. Movie nights. Over a profusion of takeout food, often Chinese, sometimes Ethiopian, they settled on the couch to watch *The Boys from Brazil*. *The Night Porter*.

When Danny offered to chip in money towards the food, Ethan shrugged him off. Ethan was still paying Danny: for the coffee-shop sessions and whatever hours he clocked for reading and annotating Ethan's script. And Danny was careful not to overcharge Ethan, to seem to take advantage of Ethan's generosity, in the hope that, somehow, he'd prove himself indispensable.

There was the way that Ethan stretched out on his couch, long-legged. Or stood in a doorway, engrossed in thought, the hem of his T-shirt rucked up, stroking his abdomen as he spoke — consciously, unconsciously. Some old self-soothing habit? Whatever it was, Danny found it hard to look away.

Late in the summer Ethan invited Danny for a boys' weekend, just the two of them, up at his parents' cottage on Go Home Lake. They were thick into a revision of the first act, Ethan doing the writing, hunched over his laptop on the lumpy sofa, groaning sometimes, checking in hourly with Danny, who'd brought along his latest translation job—*Je reviens, mon petit brocoli*. Together they read aloud what Ethan had rewritten, Danny acting out parts, offering notes, lines. Sharper. Too on the money. Leave that out.

Then they went swimming.

The last night, under the spangle of a starry sky, Danny managed to coax Ethan down to the dock to go skinny-dipping. They were drunk. Danny had brought beer. A two-four. He wasn't a total mooch. Flinging aside his swimming trunks, he cannon-balled from the edge of the dock into the water. Surfacing, he called out to Ethan who, after a brief struggle with his own bathing suit, like some sleek, pale seal, dove in.

Ethan picked Danny up in an Uber en route to the airport for their obscenely early morning flight, Danny shivering with anticipation as he stumbled in the dark down the porch steps of the house that contained his grotty basement apartment. Ethan, Danny noted, was wearing layers that could be peeled off as they journeyed south: sports jacket, cotton sweater, hint of a T-shirt at his neck, the sight of which moved Danny inexplicably. When he asked Ethan how he was doing, Ethan shrugged. In his ordinary hoodie and jeans, knapsack dumped at his feet, Danny got up the nerve to admit that he'd never been south of Florida. Ethan, he knew, had been to the Caribbean at least a few times: St. Martin, St. Kitts, Dominica. "Your lucky day," Ethan said, before acknowledging that there'd been a bit of commotion switching Anne's name on the airline ticket to Danny's but he'd worked it out.

"Eternally grateful," Danny said.

Ethan said he'd tried calling Anne, but she'd texted back that she didn't want to speak to him. "She drops this and then doesn't even give us a chance to talk things through."

"So maybe this trip is for the best right now," Danny said. "Leave all that behind."

As soon as they were in the air and at cruising altitude, Ethan closed his eyes. This left Danny, in the middle seat, squashed between Ethan's slumped body and a large man who, hood pulled over his head, elbow bumping Danny's, leaned close and began speaking to Danny in a language he didn't recognize.

"It's Croatian," the man said. "My ex-wife's Croatian. Met her on the Baltic coast. Sometimes Croatian tourists come up to my counter at The Bay and you should see their faces when they hear me speaking it. My accent's that good. Then she dumped me. Six months ago. Feels like yesterday. I loved her, loved her language, loved it enough to learn it fluently. Now the language is all I have. I keep practising it, using one of those online platforms. Family thinks I'm crazy, but you never know, never know. Know what I'm sayin'?"

"That's harsh," Danny said. "About the dumping. I don't know Croatian, but it sounds like you have some real mastery. Maybe there's solace in the beauty of the language itself?"

"Going home to visit my grandmother," the stranger continued in his gravelly voice. "She's the one who raised me. Shipping out to Iraq next week. Operation IMPACT. Hoping for no big surprises over there, know what I'm sayin'?"

Danny nodded thoughtfully, although, again, he did not know. As the drinks cart drew close, Ethan opened his eyes.

"We didn't even argue," Ethan said, vodka and tonic in hand. "Ever. I thought that was a good thing. Then I thought she'd at least give us a chance to explore our options."

"Maybe not arguing was a good thing in some ways and not others," Danny said. "People are mysterious. And if she wasn't happy, would it really have helped if you tried to convince her to stay?"

Was there a way to break up with someone without being cruel? If there was, Danny didn't know it.

When he closed his own eyes, Eva B., met a couple of months ago on Match, hovered in the air before him. Photographer Eva with the shocking pink hair and cat's eye glasses that, not needing a prescription, she wore as a prop. On their first date, as soon as they'd stumbled in the door of her apartment, she'd pushed Danny onto the unmade mattress wedged so close to her kitchen table it would be possible to fall from a chair right onto it. She began immediately to rip off his clothes. He'd liked the bluntness of her lust, all he had to do was show up for it, which, at least for the first few weeks, had made everything feel uncomplicated.

Unlike his relationship with Jill D., met on Bumble a couple of months before Eva, whose initial enthusiasm had appealed to him, but whose rising anxiety when he failed to text her as often as she thought he should had made him retreat into a tunnel of silence.

Then there was Raj S., met on Tinder, who, every Sunday night for the past nine months, had taken Danny out for an expensive dinner before they headed back to Raj's apartment. Raj liked a routine and Danny appreciated this, no great depths but the comforts of attention, regular if unremarkable sex, plus fine food. Did it matter that Raj didn't know about Jill, or Eva?

Swipe-right Raj, who was as left-wing as you could be while working in finance, who favoured bespoke suits, and was devoted to Adele, the Persian cat who left her long hair on every surface of his house and clothes. As they'd idled in bed the night before, among the cat-hair-strewn bed clothes, Danny itching to be on his way because he had to pack for his next-day trip, Raj, patting the cat, had made a proposition: What about moving up to Tuesdays as well as Sundays?

"You mean like seeing each other twice a week," Danny asked.

"Exactly," said Raj. "Do Tuesdays work for you? If so, I'll put you in my book."

"Well." Danny slid himself from between the sheets. "This Tuesday, as it happens, I'll be out of town. For a week."

"Where?" Raj naturally asked.

"Barbados," Danny said. "A friend won a trip and he's taking me with him."

"I see," Raj said. "Do I know about said friend? And were you going to mention this trip to me? Because if you're away for a week, it seems to me you won't be around next Sunday either."

"Oh, right, right, sorry, hadn't got that far," Danny said, hiking himself into his jeans and searching about for his running shoes. "It's kind of a last-minute thing."

Raj ejected the cat from the bed.

"It's a working trip," Danny shouted. "I have mentioned him to you. We're collaborating on a screenplay."

"Right," Raj said. "And I was born yesterday. You're a little slut, Danny. You got a better deal, is that what you're telling me? Or not telling me?" The Oxford lace-up that Raj missiled at him just missed his shoulder as Danny bolted.

He was fifteen again: In sneakers blackened with a magic marker, a knapsack stuffed with gloves and cans of spray paint slung over his shoulders, he would slip out of his suburban apartment after dinner, telling his father, exhausted from a day spent building houses, that he was going to meet friends. Never once did his father, drowning in his own misery, attempt to stop him. By then it had been five years since Danny's Brazilian mother, after arranging for Danny to take Portuguese language lessons at the kitchen table with a young exchange student from Belo Horizonte, had run off with the exchange student, leaving Danny and his Newfoundland-born father stranded in their high-rise apartment in Scarborough at the corner of Victoria Park and Don Mills Road.

Alone, Danny would ride the bus to York Mills station, then the subway downtown, slipping along streets where he zigzagged his tags over the back walls of stores, garage doors in alleys, the Plexiglas sides of bus shelters. Sometimes he dreamed of encountering his beautiful mother — of his mother seeing his tags and, miraculously, recognizing them as his. Safe within some bubble of invisibility, he was never apprehended — until the afternoon when he cut school, headed downtown and took the streetcar east from King station, stepping out at Church Street, opposite St. James Cathedral. He had a plan and no plan. There was a car parked right in front of the cathedral. A police cruiser happened to be idling across the road. Pulling out a can, Danny began spraying *SIN* in large letters across the body of the car. When a uniformed officer burst from the cruiser, lunged across the road and grabbed him by the arm, Danny's whole body softened. It was a moment he'd never tried to explain to anyone but he felt something like it as he stumbled out of Raj's apartment: how the desire to be caught rubbed right up against the desire not to be caught.

A limousine and liveried driver bore them from the airport through the shimmering heat to the hotel, where, at reception, beneath whirring ceiling fans, a slim blond man and a light-skinned Black woman with relaxed hair greeted them effusively, offering up their congratulations. Yvonne, the Guest Experience Director, detailed all that awaited them: scuba diving, horseback riding, a tennis court, pool, a private Jacuzzi in their suite. Tony, the blond man, handed Ethan the plastic room keys with an expansive smile.

"You'll relax, the rest of your life will float away, and it will be the best medicine," Danny said as the cocoon of an elevator wafted them upwards. "Your script doctor says so."

Their room lay at the far end of a hallway. When Ethan unlocked the door, an ocean of pink filled Danny's vision: The sun shone through pink chiffon curtains; a pink satin bed cover enveloped the enormous bed; the quilted headboard had a huge heart appliquéd on it; pink balloons, tied to long ribbons, wobbled in the air. Ethan stepped inside and stopped. Danny kept going. On the gilded Louis XIV style desk, propped against an ice bucket, beside a vase of red roses and a profusion of food (fruit bowl, cheese tray, platter of desserts), a sign handwritten in curlicued letters read *Welcome to the Honeymoon Suite!*

Ethan sat down heavily on the bed, thumbs pressed to his closed eyelids. "I can't believe this."

On the one hand, it was hilarious, Danny thought, stifling the urge to laugh. It was, to be sure, a lot of pink. "Did the info they gave you say anything?"

"I don't know. I can't remember. I've had a lot on my mind." Ethan lurched for the room phone.

"Wait," Danny cried. "What are you doing?"

"Getting our room changed."

"Hold on, hold on. Let's think this through. For instance, the size of the room. Rooms, Ethan. The space, it's palatial. Jacuzzi in the bathroom." Danny checked. "Ocean view." He tugged open the pink chiffon curtains. "And look at this spread." In the bucket, a bottle of bubbly was chilling. Real champagne. Danny pulled the bottle out of its ice nest. "Ethan, you'd walk away from all this? Really? I'll sleep in the other room, there's a sofa." The bottle dripped as Danny padded across the floor. "Even more crass to vacate after we've opened the Veuve."

All Danny's days and nights as a waiter came in handy as he twisted the metal cap of the champagne bottle, pushed at the aerated cork until it burst against his palm, Ethan making no move to stop him as the liquid fizzed over his hand and into the waiting flutes.

"Come on, we're here to have a good time. Everything you need to have a good time is here. And if the pink gets to be too much, close your eyes or look at the ocean." Danny wiped his hand on his trousers. He opened the French doors that led out to the balcony, to the beauty of the view. The sound of the ocean sighed towards him. Before he could propose a toast, Ethan had downed his glass of champagne, leaving Danny little choice but to do the same.

Bottle in hand, Danny headed onto the balcony, hoping this would entice Ethan to follow.

"You know," Danny said, as an ocean breeze billowed in their faces, palm trees clattered, and the heat draped itself against Danny's skin, "it's a good set-up for a movie. They think we're newlyweds. We decide to play along so we don't get busted and get to enjoy all the pleasures of the Honeymoon Suite."

Whatever his mood, Ethan allowed Danny to refill his glass. Then Danny took a risk, clinking the edge of his glass to Ethan's. "To us, mon chéri." At which point Danny was convinced Ethan was going to pitch him and the champagne bottle over the balcony railing.

"I'm going to crash," Ethan said. Inside, tall and mournful, he dragged the pink satin bed cover onto the floor, yanked off his shoes and, throwing himself face first onto the bed, pulled a pink sheet over himself. "You go have fun, Danny boy."

Danny was sitting at the edge of the pool, in his swim trunks, waving his legs back and forth in the water, when a young woman in a bronze bikini slid to the edge of the pool deck beside him.

She had boyishly short hair and gently tanned skin — *gamine* was the word that sprang to Danny's mind. Her name was Agnes, she said, pronouncing the name with a soft *g*, in the French manner. She told Danny that she was on her honeymoon. She and Daniel — she pronounced this name, too, in the French way — had been married for two weeks. He was much older than she was, thirty-two years older — her eyes dared Danny to judge — but she'd found with him something she'd never discovered with anyone else. Protection and permissiveness. He gave her the freedom to do as she wished. Her husband was a jeweller, she said, renowned the world over for cutting and setting precious gems.

"Human beings are covered in approximately two square metres of skin," Agnes said. As she spoke, her fingers gestured with a prehensile dexterity, her tanned legs swinging close to Danny's in the turquoise water. On her wedding-ring finger she wore a large, diamond-encrusted band. "Our skin teems with nerve fibres, including C-tactile afferents, which exist primarily to register gentle, stroking touch. The CT afferents are spread in the highest density on parts of the body we can't reach, our grooming zones, in the back and shoulders, here, the places where we want others to touch us" — her fingers grazed Danny's shoulder. "I'm an experimental psychologist and this is what I study. Our need for touch in these places. Okay, now you tell me about you."

"Danny," Danny said. "Danny Walsh." He contemplated telling Agnes that he, too, was on his honeymoon. "I'm here with my friend Ethan." At least in this small way he claimed Ethan as his. Agnes's fingers brushed once more over his shoulder before she dove into the water and swam away.

Danny waited until Agnes had left the pool to slip into its amniotic waters. Later, when he returned to their suite, he found Ethan awake, showered, clad in his black swim briefs and white T-shirt, glass of bubbly in hand, his mood, to Danny's relief, altogether brighter. "Medicine's working," Ethan said.

"Huzzah," said Danny. Together, they finished off the champagne, made inroads into the mini-bar, devoured the cubes and triangles of the cheese tray, tackled both the fruit bowl and the cluster of tiny pink desserts. It was unclear to Danny how much Anne had truly meant to Ethan, if the loss of her was the unadulterated source of his distress or if the shock of being ditched had opened up some deeper vulnerability in him.

"When was the last time you were dumped?" Danny asked, picking up a slice of pineapple.

"University?" Ethan said. "You?"

"Well," Danny said, "I guess you could say I'm not so big into commitment so things usually just fade away."

After they had descended to the pool, and, in the wake of a few drunken dives, settled themselves on a pair of deck chairs, Danny caught sight once more of Agnes. Ethan, in the midst of lighting a cigarette, seemed not to notice when she appeared on the pool's far side, accompanied by a silver-haired man in a pale linen suit, a diaphanous robe over her bikini.

Daylight was dimming. The pulse of the ocean reached Danny from across the lawn. Little white lights flickered on amid the shrubbery surrounding them. His body eased happily, unequivocally into being where he was. Across the pool, Agnes removed her beach robe, folded it, and handed it to the man who must be her husband.

There was no one else in the pool when she slid from a ladder into the water, the pool lit now from within, illuminating Agnes's slender body from below. Diving beneath the surface, she turned in a somersault, the water parting with a gurgle around her shining head. As she rose, Danny had a sudden memory of turning somersaults as a boy in a community pool, the pleasure of being cut off from the rest of the world, becoming larval, rising dizzily to the surface through a cloud of air bubbles before somersaulting again. He had kept this up, back then, in the month after his mother had left, for what felt like hours.

He wondered how long Agnes would keep turning, if she was performing this action to please herself, seeking a specific sensation, or if she was aware of being watched: by her husband, by Danny, by Ethan now as well. If her desire was to prolong their gaze. The musky cloud of Ethan's smoke reached Danny. Part of him longed to get up and join Agnes in the water. He could. Who knew what might happen then. At his side, Ethan smoked and gazed. Impassively, the man in the linen suit took them all in.

Soft-footed Guest Ambassadors bore trays laden with glasses through the growing darkness. When one approached, Danny shook his head, only to find Ethan, T-shirt rucked up, beckoning to the man.

It was impossible not to be aware of Ethan's body—so close, the shape of his crotch visible even in the dim light through the tight fit of his bathing suit, Ethan's fingers gently caressing his own abdomen in that way he did. When Danny rolled onto his side, towards Ethan, an electric buzz from beneath his towel made him leap.

He pulled out his phone, a text from Eva B. lighting up his phone screen. *Where r u, Danny?*

He vaguely recalled an uncancelled date with Eva. He ought to be able to text back, *I'm at a resort on Barbados, can't make it tonight,* or even, *Sorry, something came up,* instead of sliding the glare of the screen back under his towel. Elusive Danny, slipping away while he still could. Really, he should turn data off altogether since each text, received or sent, was bound to cause more trouble as well as costing some huge amount.

One night, a few weeks before, as they'd sat in her kitchen, pink-haired Eva had taken off her prop glasses and asked him bluntly, catching him by surprise, "Danny, have you ever truly been in love?"

Now what kind of question was that, a trick, to which there was only one answer. "Yes," Danny said, convinced that he sounded unconvincing, certain that Eva was going to ask the follow-up question that opened like a sinkhole between them.

As he hung there, dangling, Eva asked something else. "Danny, have you ever truly been loved?"

Been loved? How was he supposed to answer that? How could he even know?

Now longing, longing was something he could speak to. Why desire what was within reach when instead you could fall for the reassurance of never getting what you wanted? Aspire for what you couldn't have or mangle what you did until it, too, became unattainable. In the end, how much safer it felt to let others desire you, curl to fit to what you thought they wanted, project an aura of sympathy, then vanish. All through his twenties, he'd become so good at that.

"Yo, Danny." How had Danny missed the moment when Ethan peeled off his T-shirt?

Once more Danny's phone buzzed. He was on his stomach, pressed against the webbing of the deck chair, and he didn't dare move because he had a hard-on.

"We'll start work in the morning and maybe institute a no-drinks policy then." Ethan's eyes travelled over Danny. He lowered his voice, so that it became, all at once, velvety and unaccountable. "But tonight's for relaxation. It's curative. Isn't that what you said, Dr. D? Only I've uncovered one small wrinkle. Alcohol isn't included in our free vacation. The man says it's printed somewhere, probably in like 8-point font, and you know I've not been great about reading the fine print. So here's my solution. You go score some drinks off the bartender. You're good at charming people. Tell him you want to do something special for me. It's our honeymoon. Make it a Manhattan, no, no, a Dark and Stormy. A double. Come on, Danny." Ethan's new, soft voice tendrilled between their deck chairs. "Do it for me."

Danny woke in darkness. The air conditioner thrummed waves of frigid air over them. He lay on one side of the bed, freezing and exposed, Ethan far away on the other, his back to Danny, fast asleep, all the pink covers pulled around him.

The sofa in the other room had not opened into a bed. Danny had said he would sleep on it anyway but there were no extra sheets, and Ethan kept repeating that the king-sized bed was big enough for both of them as he collapsed onto it, patting a spot beside him. Ethan was the one who'd insisted on air conditioning, rather than keeping the French doors open to the balcony and the susurrus of the sea. In minutes, he was on his side, softly snoring.

Mouth parched, Danny blinked at the stuccoed ceiling. His eyes throbbed. If he shifted his gaze slightly, the enormous appliquéd heart on the headboard hove into view. The balloons still jerked about in the air-conditioned wind. He tugged off his still-damp swimming trunks, dropped them over the edge of the bed, and lay there, naked.

He'd managed the first round of drinks as Ethan had suggested. Played the honeymoon card. Miraculously, his charm had worked. After that, he'd had to be more ingenious and circumspect: tried different bartenders, slipped on Ethan's shirt, borrowed his sunglasses as a disguise; at the end, he'd even resorted a couple of times to fake signatures, signing bills to other people's room numbers, bringing drink after drink back to Ethan, watching Ethan's body soften into increasingly drunken pleasure, his own pleasure suffusing him as Ethan's grew. Loose-limbed, they'd staggered back to the suite, Danny with one arm around Ethan's shoulder.

Stumbling to his feet, Danny pushed past the table full of fruit peels and drink detritus to switch off the air conditioning. He opened the balcony door.

The grounds below turned slowly grey. Pale deck chairs lay strewn about like lifeless bodies. Men who carried their own lives coiled within them moved among the pre-dawn palm trees, picking up the litter and abandoned glasses.

One path: He'd pull on his jeans, bolt downstairs and across the grounds, make for the slate-coloured beach and inky waves. Away. Already the roar of the sea grew louder, its insistence carrying other sounds towards him, the bleat of car horns, wind on corrugated iron roofs—a scream. Yet where could he go on a maxed-out credit card, having given his last American twenty-dollar bill to the chauffeur the previous afternoon, in the face of Ethan's insistence that everything was free?

As if registering Danny's absence, Ethan had rolled onto his back and lay sprawled in the middle of the bed, still in his swimsuit, pale limbs outstretched, pink comforter sliding to the floor beside him. In sleep, disturbance lifted from him. Danny picked up the pink comforter and pulled it around his body like a cape.

Something cracked in him, the crack spreading all the way through to his nerve-endings, a carapace, his own, splitting open. A new feeling stirred in him: not the desire to be caught but the desire to be revealed. No, the desire to reveal himself. Leaning over Ethan, Danny touched Ethan's bare shoulder. Tenderly. When Ethan groaned, Danny touched his shoulder again.

"Ethan," Danny said. "Ethan, wake up. I have something to tell you."

Roxanne
(after Edmond Rostand)

Dearest C,
    Last week I was sure you would say something. A certain anniversary is approaching. I do not need to remind you of what. And, recently, cousin, I've sensed a greater melancholy in you than before. Last week you arrived as you always do at the nunnery at the appointed hour, doffed your hat, bowed and, as ever, made no move to touch me, even to kiss my hand. Once more you walked with me into the garden, peered at my needlepoint and offered up your usual compliments, how beautiful my stitches are, what extraordinary verisimilitude I bring to the embroidered figures. Surely you must notice, week after week, through all these years, that I have failed ever to complete the scene. Each week it is the same one, half-finished, or unfinished, or not quite the same, the figures somewhat altered. Sometimes the woman on the balcony is opening her arms to the man climbing the vines to reach her. Sometimes she appears to be listening to a man in a broad-brimmed hat hovering in the shadows beneath her bower. Sometimes there is one man in plain sight and the trace of another man hidden beneath the branches of the orange tree. One thing I never change: the hooded figure approaching at the gate.

Each week, while you sit in the wooden chair the nuns have brought for you, out to the garden during the summer months, or set by the fire in winter, I take up my stitching. I thread my needle with silk thread and commence. I re-commence. And in the evenings, after you have left, I pull out my stitches. I unstitch.

Recently I have noticed, because I cannot fail to do so, that your clothes grow threadbare, there are mended squares on the cuffs of your faded shirt, patches on the elbows of your doublet. This pains me. Why, when, a few weeks ago, I offered to sew a new shirt for you, a thrifty solution, I thought, and I have time to spare, did you turn me down so adamantly, telling me you have a seamstress for such work. Would it have troubled you to accept a gift from me, stitched by my own hand?

Last week, I left the nightingale in the orange tree, unlike the week when I turned him into a parrot. (About which you said nothing.) For the first time, I gave him a mate, a second small dun bird nestled among the branches. I stitched the outline of a man about to clamber the vines, another man on the verge of bursting from beneath the orange tree, one wearing a black cloak, the other a blue one, which suggests, at least to me although perhaps not to you, that they are different men. Two men. Three men, if you count the hooded figure at the gate.

Last week, as every week, you peered at my screen.

Still, despite my provocations, you said nothing.

Why have I thought that stitching would be enough to induce you to speak, stitching and unstitching a shifting, never-finished scene?

You could, if you wanted, help me. You could elucidate, share with me something of what you know.

And so, on the days when you are not with me in the garden or by the fire, I have begun to write a letter. I write. I crumple the paper. I try again. Weeks have passed. Months. Years. It is hard to find the words. For all of this. Made all the harder, cousin, because, although you will not speak to me of certain things, you are so very, very good with words.

Roxanne (after Edmond Rostand)

Once, it is true, you asked me to describe what I am stitching. I hesitated, then said teasingly, Oh, do you not recognize the old story of the nightingale who must sing his heart out, seeking his mate, the bird whose song has such exquisite power it brings the dead back to life?

Ah, that old story, you said. Although I waited, you offered nothing more.

Sometimes, as I stitch in your company, I mutter under my breath.

You're mumbling, you say with a touch of amusement.

You know I have a habit of talking to myself when I sew, I reply.

Each week we speak of Christian. Of course, we must honour the dead. In ten years not a week has passed when we do not mention him.

As the scent of blooms from the rose branches tangled among the yews tumbles down upon us and a yellow cat darts between the vines, I might say, as I have said before, Do you remember how Christian loved to carve little animals out of wood, how, though his hands were not the white hands of a city nobleman, they were dexterous and gentle?

Were they? you might reply, pulling your worn gloves from your worn fingers and folding the leather pair over your knee.

I still have the little creature he whittled for me, a gryphon of all things, that mishmash of animals, part lion, part eagle, he gave it to me in my garden — so I might once more confide to you.

There's a scar that runs from your right thumb across your palm, one of several scars, but it's the one I note. Each week I notice it. Each week you flex and crack your stiffening knuckles.

Whenever I mention the figurine that Christian carved for me, I wait for you to ask to see it, but you have never done so. For some reason, I want you to ask before pulling out the little creature to show you. You say nothing. Or you change the subject.

Last week, resting my needle, I searched for a tassel of thread the colour of Christian's hair and said, Do you remember the first night Christian appeared at the theatre and the funny hat he was wearing?

After a pause, you answered, I remember that night, but not Christian's hat. As you know, I arrived late at the theatre, after Christian had departed.

Of course, I said. A silence descended between us. As I re-threaded my needle, I continued, Though his hat, and his clothes, made him look like some kind of bumpkin, and clearly, he wasn't one of us, that description hardly does him justice. I've spoken to you of this before. Of the quality of openness in him, the lack of guile, which gave him a singular kind of beauty, even a vulnerability. I find myself thinking about this. How he saw into you — at least that's what I felt.

In response, you looked away and murmured something inaudible beneath the stirring of the yew trees.

If you will not speak, then I will try, try what, not to goad you, no, I will try to write the things that I am not, as yet, able to speak. Because, as we both know, time is passing. I will not say, Time is running out. The things I want to say to you are complicated. I do not know if they will surprise you.

Here is one thing I have never admitted to you. In those weeks before I first set eyes on Christian, I fell to my knees every night offering up a particular prayer. Please, God, let me meet a man like no other.

I will approach all of this in a roundabout fashion.

As you know, my meeting Christian and the events that followed took place a little over two years after my father's death. Let us start with how my father brought me home from the nuns, where he'd sent me to be educated in the wake of my mother's passing. I didn't blame him for sending me away, even though I was distraught at being torn from his side so soon after losing my mother, and equally

Roxanne (after Edmond Rostand)

distraught when I returned to find him altered almost beyond recognition, bedridden with a hacking cough. Though you were my mother's not my father's kinsman, you stopped by the house in those days, as I sat hunched in the sick room, reading my father Montaigne's essays and feeding him bone broth. You passed across my vision like a ghost. I believe you asked me if I needed anything: More bones for the broth, more books? More books, I said, grateful for your solicitude. The next morning there was a stack of leather-covered volumes in the hall.

One night, my father showed me his will, in which he left me everything, enough money to live independently and run my own household, except that until I married or reached the age of majority I was to live under the guardianship of the Comte. Let us simply call him the Comte. It did cross my mind that my father might have appointed you my guardian. You were my kinsman. Although I understood why the Comte seemed outwardly more appropriate — richer, more powerful, more esteemed by society. Unlike you — flashy swordsman, acerbic poet, possessor of little social capital and no material fortune, skulking about with your soldier comrades, half the time smelly and unwashed. Perhaps, behind my back, the Comte had worked his sway upon my father, arguing for his own appointment, and I did not then know the Comte well enough to discredit him nor have the courage to dispute with my father on his deathbed. Am I telling you things you already know? What I want you to understand is that, while I might have brought up your name that night as I sat beside my father in the guttering candlelight, his breath no more than a wheeze, I did not.

Unlike you, the Comte was married. I didn't know whether the invisibility of the Comtesse was due to agonizing shyness, deformity or illness, or if, for his own reasons, he kept her out of sight. Whenever I pressed, the Comte brushed me off. Clearly, her invisibility suited him. But this was a fact: He was married. You were not.

And so, after a suitable period of mourning, my guardian came calling, bewigged, the heels of his brocade shoes clattering over our wooden floors. He told me it was time for me to remove my mourning dress, that his greatest desire was to continue my education. To do so I would need to accompany him to the opera, the theatre, a literary salon or two.

What choice did I have?

Did you not observe how painful this was for me when you caught sight of me with the Comte, his hand clutching mine? You had stopped coming by the house. Perhaps you considered your presence inappropriate after my father's death. But now and again we set eyes on each other as I travelled in my carriage or walked about in the Comte's company. You would be carousing, proclaiming your poetry amidst that pack of men, your comrades, or swinging your sword at some poor antagonist. Oddly, to my mind, whenever you saw me, you looked away as if you wished, for your own reasons, not to observe me too closely. I assumed you did not wish to witness my grief. Or my predicament. Your froideur or carelessness, whichever it was, provoked more pain in me even as I sensed, when I observed you, because I couldn't help doing so, some corresponding pain beneath your performance of élan.

One evening, as we descended from his carriage, the Comte rubbed his cold thumb over my knuckles, gripped my hand more tightly than ever, and told me he was introducing me to the man he intended to become my husband. I reeled in shock. In the theatre vestibule, the young Viscomte tottered forward on his gilded heels, circles of rouge flaming his cheeks. It took no time at all for me to understand the kind of man the Comte desired as my consort: a gallant, someone limp and simpering, willing to look the other way, whom he could likewise keep under his thumb. This was another shock and not a shock: Such was the nature of my education. As he bowed, I stepped on the Viscomte's taffeta-covered toes until I was certain pain swept through his body. I told him sincerely that I wished I'd never left the company of the nuns, that, at heart, I was a nun and, given any chance, I'd return to live among them. White-faced, the Viscomte teetered backwards on his heels as if I had the pox. In our theatre box, squeezed between the bewigged Comte and rouged Viscomte, I stared into all the other boxes, and everywhere I looked, this was the kind of man I saw.

I came home, undressed, fell to my knees, launched into my fervent prayer.

One night, a few weeks later, the Comte seated so close beside me at the theatre that the languorous feathers drooping from his hat brushed against my bare shoulders, back and forth, back and forth, I spotted a man entering the theatre stalls below. Wearing a wide felt hat with a turned-up brim. The hat and his plain clothes made him look countrified or as if he aspired to enter some religious order. Yet when our glances met, I saw no priest.

Something in my body stirred. The unknown man's gaze reached out with no hint of coyness. He seemed to have no idea why he was where he was other than to witness the strange manners of these parts. There travelled between us a sense of overwhelming sympathy as if, in that instant, without any need for explanation, he perceived the depths of my entrapment and I his estrangement—even though I could do nothing in that moment other than meet his gaze, breath gone shallow, and when I blinked, he was gone, swept away in the crowd.

Nothing the nuns had taught me had prepared me for such an onrush of feeling. The depths of it. Alive in my body. Perhaps you know something of what this is like. I believe you do, cousin. I announced to the Comte that I had to leave the theatre immediately. That night, alone in my chamber, stunned by the suddenness of what had occurred, what was occurring in me, I lay awake—but was this not what I wanted, the feelings I wanted, and for a man like no other? For, despite the brevity of our encounter, he seemed like no one I had yet met. I needed to meet him. I roused myself from my bed, flung open the window. In my desperation I called to my maid and asked her to reach out to you. Because—who else?

I wasn't sure if you would laugh in my face when I explained my circumstance to you the next morning, there in that hidden room at the bakery whitened by motes of pastry flour and dust. I was convinced you would think me such an innocent, your little cousin whom you had known since her girlhood. Once, long ago, we used to play make-believe games together in my father's garden, you, ten years my elder, graciously going along with whatever I made up. I thought to remind you of this even as I feared I would look ridiculous before you. Yet my conviction that this man, unknown as he was, offered me a route of escape was so strong that, however fanciful it seemed, I was determined to follow my impulse. And so I wasted no time in telling you I needed your help to meet a man I'd only fleetingly set eyes on.

All the while I spoke, you held onto your right hand, as if clutching a gift you'd decided not to give me.

I made you open your fingers, exposing the bloody wound. In those days you never wore gloves, disdaining them, and you flinched when I touched you. I prevailed upon you to let me clean the place where the knife had sliced your skin. I lowered your hand into a basin of water, washed away blood and dirt from the wound, scrubbed the ingrained dirt from beneath your fingernails. You will remember how, when I offered you the hem of my petticoat as a bandage, you refused to let me rip apart my clothing. You spoke teasingly but I sensed the iron beneath your words. Instead I wrapped your palm with a strip of rinsed linen torn from your dirty sleeve to hold the edges of the wound tight. Even though you wouldn't tell me in what fight or battle you'd been injured, your manner softened, as if you were allowing me to wash away some of your resistant armour in that basin of water.

I told you about the man I'd seen. As I described him, something shifted in you, which you struggled to hide.

Tell me, I insisted.

When you revealed that you knew who he was, through my body raced a new pulse. Fate. The good fortune of coincidence. You became the answer to my prayer. I was caught up in my own story, you understand. My face must have shone with heat and feeling.

Roxanne (after Edmond Rostand)

A new cadet in your regiment, you said. A young nobleman, a country boy from the southwest. You spoke his name with exhaustion, as if you hadn't slept, lank hair falling in your eyes. Your vulnerability, even though I had no idea of its source, met my vulnerability. I felt naked before you, exposed in my turmoil and desire, you who seemed so much more experienced in the ways of the world than I was.

Love, I said in a rush. I love him. When what I truly meant was All of This.

Help me, I said.

You stared at me through the haze between us, as if you saw into the roiling mess of me and in that instant could have articulated all that was happening in my body, my mind, my spirit, far better than I could myself. This was a new shock, which only ratcheted up my bewilderment.

You reached out as if to touch—*as if*, then retracted your hand. You said, I will help you.

In my agitated state, I said, You must let no one hurt him, cousin. No one. No man. No woman.

At first you said, I don't know if I can promise that.

Then, as you must surely remember, you nodded, your wounded hand folded against you like a wing.

I thought there might be a letter or two, then we'd arrange a meeting. Barely able to wait until the messenger had departed, each day I slit the sealing wax of a new letter, giddy with anticipation, grateful to you for arranging all this, for connecting me with Christian. The words. The flood of them. I still have the letters, every one. Signed with Christian's name. Sometimes I'll slip one inside my bodice, or inside the little leather pouch I wear around my neck, in which I keep the gryphon, its wood growing worn from contact with my hand, my skin.

I still read the letters.

SKIN

I listen to their cadences. What did I sense in those days? But I was not looking for recognition, I was looking for Christian, whose voice I did not know. I was being transported, I had never before been addressed by, beheld myself described by a lover, with such rivers of ardour, such beautiful rivers. Once more I was being schooled in something new. I wrote back, ardour for ardour, sending my love to Christian who had taken me in at first glance with such enlarging sympathy. The river entered my body. Words can move the body, this I learned. I touched my own body, breathlessly. Meanwhile, the Comte kept showing up at my door, grabbing my hand, demanding that I leave the house with him, forcing me to stuff everything I was feeling, the sensation of being opened up so rapturously, deep inside.

One day, when the Comte had driven me across town and pulled up his carriage to conduct a mysterious errand, leaving me momentarily alone, I spotted from the carriage window Christian seated on a bench outside a small hotel. I knew at once it was him, the homespun clothes, the floppy hat, his face. Beside him sat a small boy. In one hand Christian held a piece of wood, in the other a knife. He was whittling something, I couldn't see what, the boy's attention as rapt as my own. Despite his youth, there was something paternal in Christian's manner—a care that might or might not have been paternal, a kindness nevertheless. I wanted to call out to him, even as the Comte reappeared in a doorway, stranding me open-mouthed. Christian saw nothing. Absorbed in his task and the boy, he did not notice me at all.

The next afternoon, instead of waiting for me to receive him in the hall as was our custom, the Comte forced his way past my servants and strode into my chamber unannounced. I was at my writing desk and, as the door burst open, I had the startling thought that it would be Christian, my own words tugging him to me. But that voice—

When I turned, I found the Comte strutting towards me in a military uniform that on him looked like a costume, declaring over his shoulder to my maid that we were beyond such formalities as

Roxanne (after Edmond Rostand)

conversing in the salon. What was I doing, the Comte demanded. Writing a letter, I replied, ribcage contracting, hoping that he hadn't seen me shove the page of my writing into my bodice.

I had been describing to Christian how I had seen him outside the hotel with the boy, how the sight had moved me profoundly, because of the tenderness I sensed in him, but I told the Comte that I was writing a letter to the philosopher, the famous one, attempting to explain to him that it was not because I doubt or think that I know I am alive but because I feel, I breathe. I had discovered the philosopher's book among the volumes you'd left for me during my father's last illness and had begun to read it.

Examining the philosopher's words had become a curious way for me to converse with you, since I assumed, having left a copy of his book for me, you must think highly of his arguments. With hindsight, perhaps I should have paid even closer attention to his words. And yet I continue to insist, to argue, as we have argued over the years: Neither doubt nor reason can be the foundation for being or the world.

He was departing for the front in a few hours, the Comte announced. He'd been appointed commander of a new group of regiments. When he named them, I learned that yours and Christian's was among them. Perhaps he thought I would be awed by his appointment. Instead part of me fell out of the sky.

I endeavoured not to panic but to scheme, using the resources I had.

Why not leave your regiment behind, I suggested. I knew how much the Comte hated you, cousin.

It would be the greatest cruelty to you to be deprived of the chance for military combat, I argued.

To achieve my goal, I had to bargain, since the Comte was not a man who gave away anything for nothing. I told him I had lied. I had not been writing to the philosopher at all but to him at that very moment. To suggest a meeting. What else did I have to offer? I used the word he might have used when describing such an event. An assignation. I pulled the page from my dress and crumpled it in my fist. Now I didn't need to write the words, I said. I ripped the paper to shreds. His body shook, as if I'd flown willingly into the cage he'd fashioned for me. After he returned, we would make an arrangement, I said, blood draining from my fingertips. In the meantime, I would miss him terribly. Of course, I did not intend to fulfill my part of the bargain. Nor did I feel reason at this moment, I can assure you. When he drew close, I held out my hand, which he smudged with his lips and spittle in a manner that filled me with revulsion. Until you return, I said, praying with all my heart he would not.

So when Christian sent me a message that very afternoon, asking to meet me in person, I agreed with alacrity. I changed my dress. I washed my hands until the soap reddened my skin.

When I walked into the garden, there he was, the same dark-eyed young man, in his plain clothes, knees spread, hands clasped between them, seated on a bench as if I had willed him into manifesting. He looked up as I appeared, bashful, offering the ardent sympathy that I recognized. As I hadn't sensed the first time, he seemed mysteriously frightened of me. Why? Yet this was what I felt. His fear took me aback. Perhaps it was our new physical proximity, our attempt to navigate our bodies not just words. I wasn't afraid but nervous at the unknown in him, even as I knew clearly what I wanted, what I needed. Together, we had to resolve the impossibilities of my situation.

You look lovely, he said, which was not what I needed.

When I sat down beside him, his discomfort grew. He shifted his shoulders, his knees, as if there were things he wanted to say but could not find a way to do so. This unsettled me.

I'm not a scholar, he told me, squeezing his hat between his fists. I told him that he was being too modest, judging by his letters. I wanted to touch his skin, find him again through his body.

Roxanne (after Edmond Rostand)

I'm really not a reader, he said in a strangled voice.

But you read my letters? I was shocked by his admission, I admit.

Yes, he blurted. Although I had the bewildering sense that perhaps he had not.

I've lived all my life in the country, he continued, staring at the ground and wringing his hat as if he wanted some substance to fall from it. I would take you there. We would walk in the woods beside the little streams. We would look for the tracks of foxes and listen to the nightingale sing at dusk. There is such beauty in those places. The nightingale travels all the way from Africa. Did you know? Every year. I met a man who told me so. One year he followed a flock. I've loved you from the moment I set eyes on you.

He reached into his pocket and pulled out something. A small carved creature he said he'd made. When he handed it to me, I fingered it with even greater bewilderment because I couldn't figure out what it was. A bird, for it had wings, yet not a bird, for it also had feet and a tail.

It's a gryphon, Christian said. Part lion, part eagle, two creatures become one, do you understand?

I said I did.

It's for you.

At first I saw a toy, despite the delicacy of the carving, the art of it.

I made it for you, he blurted with even greater urgency. I want—

He took my hand in his warm palm, laced his fingers with mine. When he leaned close, I had a vision of our walking through bogs together, in the falling light of the countryside, then of the Comte's lips descending towards my flesh. A sudden horror filled me, that Christian wanted nothing more than what the Comte wanted, not marriage, but carnal passion and proximity, and I had made myself available in some way that suggested I, too, was amenable to this — I broke free of his touch and ran.

Inside my house, I dropped the wooden creature to the floor and burst into tears, convinced that I had ruined everything.

Were you watching, cousin, as all this occurred? Did you see me run?

I lay on the floor of my chamber, before pulling myself together. Dusk fell. I told my maid I had no appetite for dinner. And so she left. That was when I heard a voice calling to me from the garden. My name. Again. Again. Like a bird's call. The sky itself was calling. My hope returned. I blew my nose. I wiped my eyes.

It was late May, buds flushing, trees coming into leaf. I have no doubt, cousin, that you remember this.

All these years later, in the nunnery garden, beneath the yew trees, I will stitch once more the pink buds and the new leaves of my former garden, and the nightingale, such a small and unremarkable-looking bird, perched in his tree. You were the one who told me how the nightingale never repeats his call but offers up that intricate melody all through the spring night, note upon trilling note, as he tries to attract the attention of a mate.

Sometimes I ask you: Do you remember how the nightingale sang that night in my garden?

I do not need to specify which night.

You stare at my fingers as they stitch. You say, I do, yes.

That's as far as you will go.

Was the intensity of the nightingale's song that night a rare occurrence? I do know that I've never heard a nightingale sing like that before or since.

There's an impenetrability to the scene I am stitching, because darkness was falling, making it impossible to see much of anything at all, other than the darker blanket of trees, and, yes, the blue of moonlight—the bird, the human figures shadowy, at least from my perspective, so that all I stitch remains in the realm of the imagined, the possible, the improbable. Stitch. Unstitch. Re-stitch.

You could, if you chose, enlighten me, tell me what you experienced that night as I stepped onto my balcony. You could. But you

Roxanne (after Edmond Rostand)

haven't. Haven't yet. You do, at least obliquely, admit that you were there from the moment I appeared. When the bird sang. And so I will try, I am trying, with these words, to tell you how it was for me, on that night, and after that night.

Perhaps this way I can at last induce you to speak.

Out of the darkness below my balcony, a voice rose. Hesitated. Rose again. I moved towards the railing. I spoke.

Beloved, the voice called to me. The words were like and not like the words of the letters I'd received. At first they stuttered. Then they found a mellifluous directness. You are loved, the voice said with new fervour. I love you. I am here, telling you this with all my heart. As your words descend to my heart, mine ascend to your lips and ears. For this moment there is nothing between us. Tell me what happens then.

Your voice enters my heart, I said, through the rush of my blood. It enters through my ears and my lips and the air itself connects us. Can you feel it?

Through my hands, gripping the edge of the balcony, the vines trembled as if at another's touch. As if.

My recognition came slowly, then all at once. I knew this voice and it wasn't Christian's. I had never before heard it speak such words but I had known its cadences my whole life. With the letters I'd been able to deceive myself, allow myself to be deceived, but I was deceived no longer. Let me say this plainly. It was you down below, cousin, speaking to me as the nightingale sang from a branch of the orange tree. The knowledge shot through me. There are things one can know and not know. Then know anew. About one's self. Another.

I leaned towards you, in the trance of being transformed once more.

Even as I had to wonder if I were being played—was this all a game entered into by the two of you, and I your dupe? An image of Christian's toy, which I'd left in my chamber, appeared before me.

But why? Why would either of you do such a thing? I was convinced I heard no guile in your voice.

I wondered if I should call out your name, cousin, and put an end to the masquerade.

Where, I wondered, was Christian?

Except nothing in me wanted your voice, the song we were creating, our entwined voices, to pull apart.

I leaned over the balcony, made out your muffled form below and Christian pressed against the trunk of the orange tree.

Cleaved, I felt cleaved and doubled. Christian's extraordinary sympathy reached me, twisted now into an agonized rope. From you rose a sensation of wild horizons—I knew in the company of your voice I would never be bored.

Should I have called out, cousin? What would you have done?

When I demanded a kiss, I couldn't help myself. Was I surprised that it was Christian who leaped to seize hold of the vines, vaulted onto my balcony and, smelling of metal and crushed leaves, pressed his lips to mine? I was hungry for touch, hungry to be touched. I have wondered, I wonder still, what I would have done if I'd been you. Did Christian, down below, push you aside? What if you had been the one to clamber up the vines? Or climbed to push aside Christian, shouted an interruption, pulled me close, mouth to mine. On different days I imagine different possibilities. Just as I've wondered, without being able to obtain an answer, if Christian felt any remorse or anger or betrayal as he embraced me.

You did call out from below, shouting about an intruder. Did Christian, hands in my hair, register my lack of surprise at your presence? I almost laughed. An intruder? I assumed that you were simply announcing your own presence and trying to tear us apart.

Someone is at the gate, you cried. A monk.

Instantly I pictured the Comte in monk's clothing and broke from Christian's clasp. I tugged him inside and admonished him to stay in my chamber, not to come out no matter what happened. He swore

Roxanne (after Edmond Rostand)

he would not. After fixing my dress and attempting to reel in my flights of feeling, I descended.

To this day I can see you as I saw you then: at the bottom of the staircase, by the front doors. Since childhood I had been around your body and never before had I encountered you in this manner, as a sensual, radiant being. Despite your gaunt face and dusty clothing, I felt a radiance in both of us as we approached each other, yet I was simultaneously aware of your discomfort, embarrassment, mortification, as if you had been caught out and, even as we were both in the thick of a recognition of what had passed between us, you longed to deny our declarations. This shocked me. We knew what each knew. There was a seam of anger in you as well. And upstairs there was Christian.

The old man servant, Joseph, entered with a robed figure. A monk, indeed a monk, a wizened, tonsured man with no teeth and terrible breath, who held a letter out to me. You took the envelope and passed it over, my hands touching what yours had just touched. Splitting the seal, I spied the Comte's handwriting. The monk was his trusted messenger, he wrote. His words cut into me like scissors. He could not bear to wait any longer for our meeting. His anticipation would not stand for it. Instead our assignation would be his send-off. He would be at my house this very night, within the hour. I should prepare myself. If I refused to receive him, he would tell the world that, unmarried, I'd welcomed the Viscomte to my bed.

At my shoulder, close but not touching, you asked me who had written. I imagined turning to you and saying the blunt words that were in my mouth. The Comte wants my virginity. Here, tonight, he intends to rape me.

Help me.

Christian burst through the door of my chamber. As he stumbled down the stairs, hair a mess, hand on the hilt of his undrawn knife, I, too, felt a bolt of anger. Because I had asked him not to show himself and he had sworn to stay where he was. Now, in the presence of the monk and all my servants, by charging out of my room, where we had clearly been alone together, he had compromised my reputation irrevocably.

When I spoke, my mind became a flight of starlings landing in a tree. Monsieur le Comte has written to offer me his blessing in my upcoming nuptials, I said to all who had assembled, calmed by my own resourcefulness. He has sent this holy man to officiate this very night.

The monk turned from one of you to the other in surprise. My servants also turned between you, my ragged kinsman and the dishevelled young man who had galloped down the stairs. And I was drawn back to those old days in the garden, when you went along with whatever fanciful interaction I devised. I knew that you knew this was not what the Comte had written but you would agree with my words, whatever they were. We would make this into a game and play it together, one conducted now with utmost seriousness. I depended upon you utterly.

Which of you is to be the husband, the still-perplexed monk asked. The other, I presume, will give the lady away?

Here is the moment in which time alters and expands, unwinds like a spool of thread through the years between then and now. This is the singular moment that I would wish beyond all others to explain to you, the one, cousin, beyond all others, that it is impossible to stitch.

At the threshold of the hall, the Comte's letter in my hand, I understood with sudden foresight that if I pointed to Christian, he would never leave me, because he is in his deepest nature a loyal man. I would live within the circumference of his devotion and desire even as, year upon year, I grew frustrated by our incompatibilities, pulled back by his beauty and his sympathy then driven sometimes to the point of rage, my explosions entering him like a knife, because of all we cannot, do not share. Yet he would never complain. We would have children. There would always be loss in me. And in this ongoingness our lives, my life, would extend.

Roxanne (after Edmond Rostand)

There is a darkness in you, cousin. I am not alone in seeing it. You fight against it. You fight to escape it. You are, let us kindly say, for all your wit and generosity, a moody man. And for all your love, your passion, I saw in that instantaneous unravelling, the moment that became a span of moments, how, despite yourself, you would always doubt me — whatever words of love you bestow on me. Because I have also loved Christian, even declared to you my love for him. You would wonder about my honesty even as I declared my love for you. You would doubt me because you do not believe that you are worthy of love, a self-doubt that becomes self-annihilating and monstrous and scorches all around you. I have only felt singed by it. If you love from afar, you do not need to encounter the problem of reciprocity. If you were Orpheus you would sing and play your flute beautifully, descend to the underworld, return to the surface of the Earth and not turn around to see if your beloved Eurydice were following because you would be just as happy if she stayed underground. It would be safer that way. In that expanded moment, as I stood there in my hallway, I understood this, a new learning forced upon me with the greatest speed, although I could not have put it into these words then. I saw how I would never be able to heal the terrible wound in you, the wound of self-doubt.

I did not even know that you would agree to marry me. You might reject me out of a capricious act of self-protectiveness and self-flagellation. You would deny your own desire in order to hurt yourself while hurting me in the bargain. All this came to me, as you waited, along with the monk; Christian; Thérèse, my lady's maid; the old man servant Joseph; you with your self-cut hair, your jagged intensities, your fear, your terrible, incipient loss.

When I spoke Christian's name, perhaps this was my own gesture of self-protection. He turned to me instantly. I did not know if the Comte would be more furious at me for choosing Christian or choosing you. I took Christian's hand. I felt the contraction in your body and knew myself to be the cause of it. But I have wondered over and over, as surely you have also wondered, cousin, over these evenings, these years that we have sat beside each other in the nunnery where I live now—if, on that night, I had pointed at you instead of Christian, and said, This is the man I am to marry, would Christian still be alive?

I have long asked myself if Christian suffered any suspicions about the true, complicated nature of my feelings the night of our unconsummated marriage, when the Comte, upon arriving and discovering himself foiled, took his revenge by sending the two of you immediately to war.

I remember how my guardian stood there, in the great cloak he'd worn as his disguise, hurling fury at Christian, at you, and at me a kind of disgust, as if I were soiled. He sent the two of you out of my house—claiming that kind of authority. I didn't know how to challenge him, frightened that in standing up to him once more, I'd only heighten his ire and he'd find some new way to hurt you both. I gave one last, fumbled kiss to Christian, his words of love mumbled in my ear, a ring on my finger, and with you shared a hug that I have never forgotten, how its strength enveloped me and spoke without speaking. I hugged you back. Then, all three of you gone, I found myself alone with a violent suddenness that made my house feel not like my house but a shell.

I was married, therefore safe, at least temporarily, from the Comte's predations, he who, I was convinced, would never go near a battlefield, unlike the two of you, even if he had gone off to war. You two were not safe and now both out of reach, which frightened me. I touched the ring on my finger as I walked that night in my garden, listening to the lingering voice of the nightingale, going over and over in my head all that had happened, what I thought had happened—having no one to confirm it. A fantastical perplexity filled me.

The next day a letter arrived, signed by Christian. In its words I immediately recognized your voice. How, before, could I have failed

Roxanne (after Edmond Rostand)

to notice? I couldn't write back. For how was I to address a letter? To Christian de N—and Cyrano de B—c/o the Arras battlefield? If I wrote separately to each of you, you might share your letters and compare what I had written. What would I write? And why wouldn't you write to me as yourself, acknowledging all that had happened? I took long walks out of the city, across the countryside, listening to insects sizzle in the fields, shaking anxiety out of my limbs. In the afternoons, I read or, accompanied by Thérèse, went out to salons at the homes of other noblewomen, my head full of the two of you, praying for you both to remain invisible to the Spanish, or if not then for bullets and arrows to bounce off your bodies. At night, I struggled with the nature of my transformation. For the truth was, I thought of you both. In my head I spoke to one of you, then the other. I imagined walking with Christian through the countryside. A house. His kindness. A world. I imagined you appearing in the garden, smelling of horse sweat. I imagined us riding, riding, riding, my cheek pressed to your back, the two of us cutting a path through the theatre as others gawked. I imagined Christian coming to me in a bedchamber, his body. And I imagined your body as well, cousin, how you would insist, as you undressed me, undressed yourself, that our bodies meet each other only in the dark.

I discovered that it is possible to love like this, to feel an entwined love for both of you, because you had presented yourselves to me this way. And you seemed to want to go on doing so. Did Christian recognize the true nature of my love, foretell it? He isn't here to answer my question.

At night, sometimes all night, I wrestled with my sheets and argued with myself. Was it wrong to love thus? Was there something wrong with me? Had I not received precisely what I'd desired, what I had prayed for, a man like no other?

Who was I? What was I? I was still myself. I loved. I was beloved. Not just by one but two men. How, given all that had happened, could I chastise myself? But, in those days of your mutual absence and my penitential loneliness, I began to wonder, Did I know either

SKIN

of you at all? Perhaps you were no more than a fancy, a mirage I had created out of the double man you two had fabricated together. I was on my own. My restlessness grew. Wheat fields ripened and were cut down. To my mind the war seemed a pointless fighting over religion, that is to say, over scraps of land. Did Christian never once feel the impulse to write to me, I wondered. I mean, did he never desire to put his own words to paper no matter how crudely, to say, I miss you, I love you, I think of you every night as I attempt to fall asleep on the hard ground? Perhaps you stopped him from writing. Or he was content to put all his faith in your words, cousin, to live within the ruse of an assembled man. And you, cousin, did you not feel the urge to write directly to me of your love? Or was it better for him, for both of you, to believe me duped? Did you only love me, duped? Did Christian prefer a wife who was a dupe?

Your letters arrived, speaking of love, yet leaving so much out. I imagined you both to the north of me, towards Calais, outside Arras, which the Spanish held, intent on cutting off the besieging French army's access to supplies. It was only later that I learned starved French soldiers were reduced to eating rats. At first you signed your letters with Christian's name, then, it is true, came the ones signed only *C*, written in sloping, crowded letters as if with speed beside a sputtering candle or in fear that something would run out. In one letter, forgetting yourself, you went so far as to mention a moment the two of us had shared years before, when a butterfly landed in my hair and you convinced it to step onto your finger. I held this letter close. I wrote a letter to Christian and my words fell flat. I wrote to you asking if you felt love was a form of thought. It had to be more than that, I wrote. It needs a life in the body, a body flooded with life. Be honest with me, I demanded. At least offer me this, can you not? Tell me what is happening in your bodies, to your bodies.

I tossed both the letters I'd written into the fire. Ever more restless, my anxiety mounting, I could endure my circumstances no longer.

Roxanne (after Edmond Rostand)

❖

As dried leaves fell from branches, I called for my coachman, Barthelemi, told him to arrange my carriage for a trip. He seemed perturbed. Where did I intend to go? Alone? For how long? He would be the one to accompany me, I said. We were off on a mission to save people, only I didn't mention who or what kind of salvation I had in mind. To Thérèse, I said that I had been called away by a relative, an aged aunt. I packed sheets and tinctures as medical supplies and as much food as we could carry — breads and fruit and cured meats and wine. I donned a dark cloak and gloves, veiled myself beneath a large hat, reassured by my disguise. There was no one I could consult about my mission. I did not think about what would happen if we were stopped or caught or even what would happen once we arrived where I intended, only that I had to do what I was doing. Have you not wondered how I managed this? I suppose I believed that my conviction, some panache, would save me, and Barthelemi as well.

Charging through the northern countryside on half-frozen roads, when stopped by French patrols, I declared, from behind my veil, that I was off to see my lover, and although I know it will seem incredible to you, knowing men as you do, these soldiers, swayed by my act of devotion, at least sensing my urgency, let me pass.

We stopped at inns overnight. The less said about them the better. Trees grew more sparse, the ground trampled. On the one hand I felt bold, as if I were embarked on a noble exploit, on the other, guilty, alive to my duplicity, my recklessness. We began to pass wounded men, propped on crutches, limping by the side of the road. We got lost, repeatedly having to ask for directions. By some stroke of luck, we managed to avoid any Spanish patrols. I know the sight of me caused a stir and overheard the whispers that I must be a French spy. Perhaps in fact this helped us in our passage. Perhaps those who saw us, sturdy Barthelemi in his black hat and cloak, my veiled figure through the carriage window, didn't believe me to be a woman at all. In the depths of one night, thanks to Barthelemi's canniness, we slipped through a gap in the encircling Spanish lines. When, at last, we pulled up, exhausted, in the French camp, a little after dawn, some distance from your siege of the Spanish-controlled town, and were directed to the tents of your regiment, the lathered horses shook with relief. Relief flooded me as well.

Of course, nothing was as I'd imagined it, including the mud. There was no end to it. I'd brought clogs and had no choice, upon leaving the carriage, but to step into its depths.

You were the one I spotted first, gaunter than I had ever seen you, mud-spattered. You hurried towards me, holding out a lantern, the shock on your face like nothing I'd ever encountered from you. No embrace. Rather the opposite. You told me I had to leave at once. You will no doubt remember this. It's dangerous for you, you cried. I understood your anger as that of a man desperate to protect his beloved. It's dangerous for all of us, you repeated.

I declared that your comrades, busy unloading the food and drink and medical supplies I'd brought, might wish to complete their labour before sending me on my way.

Christian struggled out of a muddy tent, bearded and wan, almost stumbling to his knees at the sight of me.

I took a step towards him, calling his name.

I could not say: I want to touch your body, I want to ascertain that it is, you are real, that something real joins us. Instead I declared, I want to hear your voice!

My voice? His actual voice sounded croaky and tattered. Not joyful. Mud separated us.

Your real voice, I said. Written or spoken, I needed to hear something that was truly him. Perhaps having done something no wife he'd imagined would ever do, I had become unreal to him. Where was his sympathy? I couldn't feel it.

Say something to me, I urged him. Tell me what you feel. Give me your candour.

But I wrote to you —

Roxanne (after Edmond Rostand)

He went this far into the lie. At that very instant, you were darting a hand to me as I nearly lost my footing in the mud so that, yes, I did grab hold of you, aware, miraculously, of your pulse through your fingers, your unease, your ardour, and, despite the danger, a deep, surprising constancy that allowed me to steady myself.

What did Christian see when he looked at the two of us? His face rearranged itself. Perhaps, as I said, he could not live with the recognition that I had come for the combined man the two of you had created, and it is true, in that moment, I did not know where to fix my attention. Or he encountered something he had not yet allowed himself to acknowledge: the intensity of your love for me. When I looked at him, both these things were what I saw.

Christian, I said.

I was aware then, as I dropped your hand, how your hands have killed so many. This knowledge, so far from anything I know that hands can do, also lies beneath your skin. Killed both in self-defence and acid retribution—but the violence in you, there is no way around it. This awareness comes to me even now. Christian was a gifted swordsman and a crack shot, you yourself have said so. Snow fell on his bare head and ragged woollen clothes and he did not take a step towards me. I did not know if he had killed any men even as I understood that in a war he would need to do so. What did he see when he looked at you, and you when you looked at him?

Christian, I called again. He picked up his musket. I did not make a move to stop him, nor did you lunge in his direction—as he picked up his gun and strode in the direction of the Spanish line.

Some nights, as I stitch, re-stitch, I think, we remade him, you and I, into something other than what he was—we duped him, altered him, destroyed him.

What was he thinking as he stepped in front of the Spanish line?

If we speak of him, at least a little, each week here in the garden, we keep him alive. We bring him back to life. This is what I tell myself. We remake him once more. We owe him this. The three of us are bound together forever, cousin, are we not?

In the nunnery, I have discovered a freedom as a widow that I would not have anywhere else. To read, to walk, to be alone, to meditate. As I have said to you, I have no regrets about bestowing my inheritance on the nuns, after paying out the servants whom I released. I have a room of my own, far more commodious than anything the nuns live in. The Comte cannot reach me. I told him never to come. If he tried, the nuns would have refused him entry, although I am convinced I lost whatever remaining allure I held in his eyes when I chose a life among them.

I do not know how you imagine the contours of my life when I am not with you. We have spoken some of how I spend my days. How I rise with the nuns and pray with them: matins, lauds, prime. In the warmer months, I work alongside the sisters in the garden, they in their white habits, I in my black widow's gown. I roll up my sleeves, don a straw hat and clogs, grab a spade, trench row upon row of onions while the hot sun beams down on us. I am grateful for the labour. I find it meaningful. No, more than that, I find it pleasurable. I am physically stronger than I ever was. Christian, were he alive, might recognize something of what I have become. I speak to him sometimes as I work. I want you, too, to know what it is, my life in the body.

In the summer months, when done for the day, some of the sisters and I pluck and eat sweet strawberries. One afternoon, some years ago, I walked out along a grassy bank beside a field of wheat and stumbled upon one of the younger nuns lying outstretched in the grass. When she beckoned me close, I sank down beside her, our heads side by side. Our lips touched; our fingers began to journey beneath each other's clothes, at last finding their way to skin, across each other's bodies, until a saturation of feeling overwhelmed us both, small pleasures, which, she assured me, were a form of grace for women who lived among women or women like me who live with ghosts. Sometimes I walk out into the fields and we find each other again.

I am not Penelope, seated for ten years at her loom, weaving and unweaving her cloth in order to outfox her dreadful suitors while she waits for her husband to return. Nor am I Philomela, tongue torn out by the brother-in-law who raped her, who can only tell her story through the tapestry she sews. I have evaded rape and my husband is dead.

Nevertheless, ten years have passed.

All those years ago, in darkest December, my husband received a church burial. Even as the priest said the final prayers and I crossed myself, in my deepest heart, I was and am even now convinced that he walked in front of the Spanish line and didn't shoot but allowed himself to be killed—that is to say, he killed himself.

What do you believe, cousin?

Days have passed, weeks since I began this letter. The midsummer nights are growing shorter. Still the nightingale sings. It is the sisters who told me that only the male bird offers such an entrancing song, never the female.

There is also this—are we not a little happy, cousin, in our imperfect, damaged lives, despite the persistent presence of the past? I have chosen to live here. Each week you come to visit. Each week as I embroider my shifting scene, you tell me of your life in town, weaving stories out of your adventures, your words full of glitter, beautiful and at times a baffling wall. We argue about philosophy. We tease each other. Dualist, I accuse! Cousin, you call me, or, once, as if a slip, dearest one, only occasionally Roxanne. We speak of Christian. These are the confines we have set for ourselves. They are the ones that you, yourself, have taught me: to be this close to you yet no closer. That you have never asked for more from me remains a puzzle. Why haven't you? Why not confess to me your version of these events? Why not, knowing what I know, reach out and touch me?

And yet, for me, this is enough. To know you are there, as I am here. I do not reach out to touch you. Which is not to say that I am unaware of your body as you shift and settle into your chair, as you rub your forearm or your thigh. I have chosen this. All of This. The ghost of Christian threads himself through my needle and wanders among the yew trees like a cat. I carry one of your letters signed with the C of both your names tucked in the leather pouch hanging around my neck, Christian's wooden gryphon tucked beside it. When you ask me what is in the pouch, I tell you truthfully that it is a love letter. Some days I make the joke about our being a three-legged stool. Could we not say, seen through one window, that Christian is the one who brought us together?

Today I found a strand of silver in my hair.

Here is a truth, cousin: I have learned, like this, to be happy. Like this, I shall not lose you.

Here is another, inescapable truth: I would wish once more to behold you as I once did, declarative, open-armed, stripped to your heart's marrow.

This evening, as the light begins to fade, I will ask you to recite a poem for me, any poem as long as it is one written by you. Perhaps you will look befuddled, deeper lines creasing your brow. It's getting late, you will say. I must go.

Not yet, I will insist. First recite a poem.

I only have old ones, you will say, from a decade ago, I haven't written any since —

I will tell you it doesn't matter, only let it be a love poem.

Sitting back, needle momentarily idle, I will close my eyes.

We do not want the nightingale to find his mate, I will say to you as dusk begins to deepen, because then he will stop singing.

As darkness approaches, I will listen to the indelible rhythms of your voice.

Listen, I will whisper to my thread and needle.

Roxanne (after Edmond Rostand)

Soon I will seal this letter. Then I will hand it to you. For now, I will write these words.

I have loved you, cousin, the only way I know how. I will love you all my life.

R.

Mortals

White bag, body, flag fluttered in the middle of the road. In the half-dark she drove towards it. It raised a hand. Waved. Someone had been hit. Dear God. She hadn't hit them! Someone was dying in the middle of the road and she was hurtling towards them on a slick black course, the only person in sight. It had been a week, what a week. The white hand fluttered, wing, white wing. An angel. She was seeing angels at dusk in the middle of the road. Hallucinating. One angel. Could you stun an angel in a hit and run? She hadn't done it. Hadn't! If she drove over an angel she would go to hell. She veered the car onto gravel, braked, shut down the ignition as a cry escaped her. While not far off, a shrunken body twitched. Smaller than an angel — why had she thought angel? Yet who knew what size angels really were?

She wrestled with the thought of stepping out. Was she obliged to do so? Trees edged the tarmac. Someone might be lurking in the bushes and as soon as she left the car, they'd leap, grab her by the hair, drag her screaming into the underbrush. If, after the assault, she stumbled as far as the middle of the road, the next person speeding past in semi-darkness would plough right into her as she waved her arms, mash her bones, leave her twice-mangled body bleeding on the tarmac — atop the other body.

Impulsively, she unbuttoned her coat.

It had rained, and the air, when she stepped onto the gravel, smelled green and cool.

A bird lay in the middle of the road, a gull, a seagull, no, a lake gull, the sea a thousand miles away. Alive, hungering, one wing flattened, the other waving, stuttering. Blood pooled. And yet it waved, as if some alchemy of desire or terror or the spasmodic thrusts of a failing nervous system might lift it back into the sky.

She stopped. How best to approach it. Turn away. No. She stooped at the bird's side. One round, panicked eye met hers. The ragged, flapping wing—this was what she longed to touch.

In the grass beside the road, she scavenged until she found what she was looking for. The cool air feathered her arms.

Angel of mercy. She did not know how to do what she intended.

Folding her body over the other's, she swung, smashed rock to eye.

Derecho

He had always loved wild weather.

When Hugh was a boy, aged ten, his father, the marine ornithologist, had moved their family from a city in the middle of the continent to an island far off the east coast. For two years, they lived in a clapboard house in a village by the sea, only a ragged meadow separating their back door from the ocean. Now and again their father took Hugh and his brother Brian out in a metal motorboat to visit the small, craggy islands, home to the puffin and murre colonies that he studied. Above their heads, clouds of puffins whirled, red feet tucked, wings like propellers. Black-and-white murres dove out of holes in the guano-spattered cliffs. While his father peered through binoculars, Hugh rose to his feet in the boat, life jacket bumping his chin, arms spread wide, wind rippling through his clothes, waves surging and troughing beneath his feet, until his father, dropping the binoculars, pushed him back onto the metal bench with a shout.

Once, towards the end of their time on the island, in the midst of what could reasonably be called a gale, their mother, who talked back to the radio and read a new book every afternoon, chased Hugh and Brian outside to get some air. Rain and wind pelted them as they slogged up the hill beyond the house. Up there, rocks fell away to the wild ocean below. Spray splattered their faces. Brian, two years older, kept urging Hugh closer to the edge. Full of rivalrous, giddy energy, up above the smashing waves, they laughed and jostled, tugged at each other. Hugh grabbed Brian's arm, pulled, though what he remembered most vividly was the delirious fight to stay upright while being buffeted by the wind.

Some years later, as an undergraduate, plane after little plane bore Hugh north from Toronto to Frobisher Bay, where he stumbled through glutinous mud to stuff supplies into the canoes that would transport him and the rest of the research team across the summer sea. He'd been hired on to a geographical study that would repeat a series of magnetic measurements at sites in the Arctic one hundred years after the first set of measurements had been made. In this treeless world, more barren even than the island where he'd spent those two years of his boyhood, winds howled up the fjords unencumbered. That night, as they struggled to pitch their tents on a bare shore, gusts sent the nylon of the tent cloth flapping. In the morning, Hugh scrambled out of his tent on his hands and knees, two hats clamped on his head, riveted, the air bashing his face.

The following summer, having secured employment on a similar sort of expedition, as a fieldwork and data-reduction assistant in Iceland, he found himself out with a local guide named Árni, attached to a rope, knotted into a rope harness, walking backwards over the edge of a cliff.

Up on the cliff top, knobby-knuckled elders, women and men who'd arrived in pickup trucks, braced the umbilical ropes from which they descended. The smell of guano was overpowering. The cries of distressed birds seared the air. If Hugh looked down, he'd vomit. Árni was gathering murre eggs in the old way, eggs that would be distributed to the community. The murres only laid one speckled, pointed, turquoise egg a year. Árni wouldn't take them all. His ancestors had been doing this for centuries. He wanted Hugh, a small video camera attached to a cord around his neck, to film him.

Why had he agreed to this? Fighting his vertigo, Hugh gripped the lead rope with one hand and held the camera with the other, feet scrambling for purchase against the rocks. Gently, Árni's hand reached for an egg lying on an open patch of rock and slipped it into the plastic container strung at his side.

Hugh was getting the hang of the slow sideways walking when the wind rose, making the rope that held him judder. Letting go of the camera on its cord, he seized the rope with both hands and pushed out to stop from swinging into the cliff. Bile rose in his throat. If he let go of the rope, he wouldn't fall but, caught by the harness, would twist and hang upside down like a bat. The wind softened. After which came grace, the grace of feeling his body held aloft by the air, the careful presence of Árni beside him, the grace of being drawn upwards, at last, by the elders' hands.

Perhaps there was something epigenetic about his love of the wind, Hugh thought as he tacked a Sunfish across a lake at a cottage his parents had rented, the week before he entered graduate school. Air billowed the sail, Hugh's body counterbalancing the boat's tilt as he tried not to hit himself in the head with the boom when it swung. He'd grown up listening to his father's stories of a childhood spent in the cold and windy north of England. In his father's childhood home, there'd been no central heating, only a coal stove in the living room. On visits as a boy, Hugh headed down the flight of wooden stairs to the coal cellar, reached through a door in the side of the house, metal bucket in hand, to fetch the coal, which smelled of ancient, mashed-together life forms. His father had eaten beef tallow on toast, grilled over the coal stove, for lunch. Hot water bottles in bed at night. Walks through wind and rain to the water closet across the yard when you had to do your business. He'd wrestled and fought his way through the local grammar school before sailing across the Atlantic to a university where no one cared about his accent. Had there been pressure to follow his father into science? Lake water gurgled against the bow, the boat's movement thrumming into him. Not pressure, no. Yes, a need to live up to his father's insistent aspirations. But—Hugh turned to face the wind—he wouldn't be studying birds, he was pushing off in another direction.

In the helicopter, three of them sat strapped into their jump seats behind the cockpit. Wind poured through the open door to the outside, nothing between them and the white desert below, in which they would be crushed if they fell out. People died doing work like this, helicopters crashed. Opposite Leo, the animal-sedation biologist and the man with the stun gun, Hugh strained to see the ground. He loved flying low across the land, their pale shadow bouncing over the ice, over the bear's body as she cantered. He kept his eyes on her. They'd all received rifle training, but Hugh could never have done what Leo did, fix on a moving target from a moving gaze in such a constant blast of air, their propellers cycling shadows across the snow, the sound of the shot, when it came, no more than a pop. As the reverberation jolted through Hugh, a different ripple entered the bear. It didn't take long until she tumbled to the earth.

He laid a hand to the bear's rancid-smelling fur, feeling the amazing thwack of her heart, as if she were still running. Bearded, six-foot Derek, Hugh's supervisor, drew blood from her. Hugh, the doctoral student, transferred the vials of blood to the cooler. What he lived for was the physical contact with the bear, as they clambered over her massive body and rolled her into a sling to weigh her, estimating body-fat ratio with a pair of calipers. Derek, aided by Leo, opened her mouth to measure her teeth. Hat in hand, Hugh pressed his ear to her fur, even closer to the pulse of that astonishing heart. Meanwhile Derek fitted the $5,000 tracking collar, snug but not too snug around her neck, through which they would follow her movements, the signal travelling up to satellites, down to them. She would remember nothing of their encounter, Derek insisted. But she would smell them, smell and feel the plastic and metal collar, would in her way know something had happened, was happening, of this Hugh was convinced. Whether or not she bore traces of the encounter, surely their interventions were justifiable, useful in the bid to preserve her kind and the whole web of life that bound her.

Leo, he of the subtle fingers, injected her with the wake-up drug, because, out here, coming out of the anesthetic, she was vulnerable. Back up in the helicopter, Blaine, their pilot, spotted the black slink of a pack of wolves, and they hawed after them, chasing the wolves away across the tundra, before circling back to make sure the bear was shaking herself to her feet.

Months later, back in the city, spring coming around once again, as he stood in line at a university cafeteria, Hugh's gaze landed on the woman ahead of him. Around his age, she moved decisively, with a profusion of energy. Strong body, long hair, mobile face. A new exhilaration entered him. He could think of nothing to say, except, having caught her attention, to ask the most obvious question. "What do you work in?"

"I don't give out that information to just anyone."

"Fair enough," he said, almost tipping over his tray. "I'll go first. Arctic. Apex predator. Polar bears and their habitats. Shifting ranges. Sea-ice loss. Post-doc. Conservation biology."

"Nice to meet you, apex predator," the woman said. She took a neat-looking omelette from the server behind the counter.

"Hugh," he said, cheeks warming. "Hugh Robson." Unsaid: that he was already co-authoring papers with his supervisor, had a knack, when sifting through the slew of aerial images they examined, of finding bears out on the ice, white on white, his vision, particularly his distance vision, so acute that, when they were up in the western Arctic, the Inuit hunters they worked with jostled to have him join their hunting teams, to spot far-off seals or whales.

"Marine biology," said the woman. "Sea sponges. *Vazella pourtalesii*, I won't be offended if you've never heard of them, Hugh Robson. They're tiny and live in ocean-floor colonies all across the eastern continental margins of the Americas. Even if you've never heard of them, they're a crucial indicator species for the health of the oceans, as crucial a climate indicator as your charismatic megafauna. All hail, essential microfauna."

"Good to meet you, Vazella."

Meanwhile the server attempted to pass over his plate of poutine, gravy glistening over the sky-high pile of cheese curds so that the woman, whoever she was, would know him forever as the man who ate poutine for lunch.

"Paula Gasparovic." She set down her omelette and held out her hand. "Assistant prof. You can find me in the Aqualab."

"Lunch?" Hugh grabbed a salad for good measure from behind a little Plexiglas door. "Care to join me?"

Bony wrists. That eyebrow lift. The lanky stride. Hugh was immediately jealous of anyone who paid attention to Paula, any man, that is, even the university cleaner who, mop in hand, held open a door for her as she made her way along a cement-walled corridor towards him. Paula took him to a bar she liked on College Street, then back to her place, a small apartment up above a storefront farther west along College. Lying under the hand-stitched quilt bunched on Paula's bed, exhausted after all the drinking and fucking, Hugh had never felt so opened. And here was Paula turning to him once more, her fingers guiding him. Like this. Yes, oh yes. Her laughter in the dark. Her hands all over him. Her mouth. After more sex, Paula continued her stories: of the father who'd walked out when she was ten, the single mother who'd raised her in a one-bedroom apartment, her love of the ocean, her fears for the future of the ocean. Why him? Hugh couldn't help asking himself on his streetcar ride home the next morning. He carried her voice with him, her questions about the bears, her scent, her ambition, her ability to drink him under the table. How could such a person as Paula be so conveniently available?

In any case, she'd forget about him. In less than a month he'd be stuffed in a parka and teleported for the summer back up to the shores of Hudson Bay. He'd melt from her mind like a patch of snow.

When he told Paula of his fear, one night a few weeks later, at his place this time, bedclothes spilled across the floor, she laid a palm against his sweaty chest and said, "Really, Hugh? You think so?"

In the fall, she brought him along to a party full of aquatic biologists and introduced him as her partner. "Mr. Charismatic Megafauna."

"Accompanying the divine Ms. Microfauna," Hugh said, sliding an arm around Paula's waist.

They still indulged in joky, performative arguments, microfauna versus megafauna, alone or with others. Hugh found them arousing. In the midst of the joking, though, he turned serious, fixing on two of the marine biologists gathered over the punch bowl, a man with a ponytail, a woman in a button-up Icelandic sweater. "Of course, making people change their behaviour isn't the driver of our research but it's a wanted outcome. May charisma do some good, I say, since sea ice is definitely depleting, thanks to us, and our fate's inevitably entangled with that of the bears."

After a full day of teaching classes bulging with undergrads, Hugh made his way across campus to the Aqualab. He liked to approach Paula in her habitat quietly, letting himself in the door so that there might be a minute or two when she wasn't aware of him. By the tanks, back to him, she was giving instructions to a grad student, slinging her hands into the pockets of her jeans. In the bubbling water, the thimble-sized, glassine sea sponges, tiny ancient animals, swayed. Air, forced through a tube, blew sea-bottom sediment at them, turning the water dark and turbid, mimicking the effects of the increasingly industrialized ocean, the churning and re-suspension of particles due to bottom trawling, drilling explosions, deep-sea mining, all of this taking place in warmer and more acidified waters, which Paula and her team also replicated.

Sometimes he found Paula alone, sitting on a stool, staring intensely at the sponges. When she caught sight of him, she rose to her feet. He waited for exactly the right moment to touch her. Later they would walk home to their shared apartment, two floors of an old house in the west end, a study for each of them, he with a contract job, which might turn tenure-track. They'd grab hunks of cheese and bread, retire to the bedroom, strip off their clothes, but first, this particular afternoon, when they reached her office, Paula shut the door. Backing Hugh up against the wall, she slipped her hands inside his shirt. She smelled of the tanks, of salt water.

"Yes, the sea sponges are essential," he told her. How he loved the playful twist of her mouth. "They provide plentiful microhabitats for all sorts of other organisms. They filter sea water. Yes, our food and indeed our entire planetary life systems depend on them."

Her hands moved over his skin, found his nipples.

"Are you absolutely sure you want to marry me?" Hugh asked. A new wind blew through him: more excitement, nerves, desire.

"Yes," Paula said. "Oh, yes."

Sometimes, the bears they shot down had cubs with them. When they clambered out of the helicopter, onto the sea ice, the cubs would be with their downed mother, not anxious, exactly, still tumbling, curious, sticking close, the smaller ones the size of dogs but chunkier, and Hugh's own muscles flickered as they gambolled, a new longing entering him. The whole time he and the rest of the team worked on the mother, drawing blood, pulling a tooth, fixing on the tracking collar, he was aware of the little bears even as they shooed the cubs off, did not want them to come near. In his head, he spoke to Paula as he worked. Was it wrong to say he loved the bears? Surely love was as foundational as objectivity. Amid the granular snow, the cubs sniffing at the air, he'd be overcome by the beauty and vulnerability of everything around him. To his left, a small, watery hole had formed in the ice, not a hole, a declivity, a small stone at the bottom of it. Looking into its depths, he felt as if he were staring into the future.

Late August. One a.m. Arctic nights were beginning again. Twelve years into his life with Paula, Hugh tagged along with a team studying narwhals in the waters off the polar continental shelf, anxious to be out once again in this landscape. He'd proposed visually monitoring polar bear subpopulations, checking on body-fat indices through binoculars, though he also hoped to catch a glimpse of the narwhals, those single-tusked, ever-more-elusive unicorns of the sea. In any case, there was a job for him, someone always had to be on polar bear watch, up and about at all hours, tracking the flat, rocky coastline, keeping an eye on the water and the net that was anchored to the shore. Offshore, where the coast dropped off steeply and the cetaceans swam, the net stretched out across the water, marked by buoys and hanging like a curtain to a depth of twenty feet.

Through the dim light, his piercing distance vision, though bleary, spotted a white smear, perhaps thirty metres off, swimming in their direction. Rifle over one shoulder, Hugh pulled off his mittens and snatched at his binoculars. The calmed waters and lack of ice made it easier to see the bear and the two cubs paddling in her wake. A good heft to her. Healthy. What was she doing out in the water at this hour, with cubs, no less? Something must have spooked her. She was making steady progress towards the net and its row of orange buoys, oblivious to its dangers. If she didn't turn, she was going to swim right into the net. They were camped in the barrens, hundreds of kilometres from the nearest community. They had no tranquilizers with them. If she got tangled in the net, it would be too dangerous to attempt a rescue. They'd have to shoot her.

Hugh hollered to Elvira, narwhal researcher, on watch duty with him, and she set off at a run for the wooden hunter's cabin where their safety supplies were stored, while he grabbed the emergency kit out of the closest rubber Zodiac pulled up on shore.

Hugh shouted at the bear. *Don't come this way! Turn!* But, stroke by stroke, she kept up her approach.

He scribbled quick notes: estimate of body-fat ratio, the direction of her appearance. Back at his side, Elvira lit one of the emergency flares and passed it to him to hurl towards the water, a pink stream soaring before it sank. Ned, one of their local guides hired out of Pang, loaded shells into his shotgun, aimed the gun in the direction of the water, the crack of the shell so loud that Hugh's eardrums rang. Still the bear kept paddling, undeterred or determined to ignore their uproar, their existential threat. The racket pulled others out of their tents.

Far off, his own cub slept. Or Hugh hoped that she slept, Leonie, all of ten, string bean of a girl. Even as a baby she'd been a terrible sleeper, would often wake crying, cry for hours. Those nights, when nursing didn't help, Paula, sleep-deprived, undone, often burst into tears as well. If anyone had a knack for quieting Leonie, it was him, they both knew. He'd kiss Paula, take Leonie's small, heaving body from her. No love like his love for his child, the way it ran right through to his bones. If she grew warm with a fever, his skin heated. Those sleepless nights, he'd nestle her into the carrier, snug to his chest, hand pressed to her body still heaving with sobs, and walk with her, walk and walk, offering her all the calm he could muster, until at last, if he was lucky, she settled. What, he wondered as he walked, was he to do with the intensity of his own fear for her?

Later, when, as a toddler, then a child in her own bed, she still woke, crying and inconsolable, Hugh would lay himself along the covers beside her, stroke her soft hair, her quaking back. When she could, she'd tell him that she was frightened. Of what? he asked. This she didn't seem able to say. Then he grew frightened that the fear was something they'd passed on to her, he'd passed on, unconsciously, unwillingly, fear of the world they'd brought her into, despite their mutual, reckless desire to bring her into it. How could he undo Leonie's fear? Retrieve it?

Beside him, Elvira hurled another flare, yipping as she did so. Once more Hugh shouted, along with all the others. When the bear reached the net, she touched it with her great paws. Backpedalled. Hugh's stomach turned. Deftly, given her size and weight, she manoeuvred herself over the top. The wind fetched up, billowing the entire width of the net, blowing the cubs away from her. The bear beckoned to her young, directing them with her body until they paddled towards her. Easier for them, so much smaller, to scuffle their way over top of the net, between the buoys. Ned set down his rifle. Hugh's breath released, as the bears swam on, unharmed, at least for the moment, into the great sound.

Six years later, in Calgary for a conference, having delivered a paper for which he'd worn a suit and tie, such unusual attire that he felt like his own body double, Hugh was relieving himself in a hotel washroom when he became aware of a man standing behind him. Dark business suit. Combed hair. A white man. His first thought: The man was waiting to congratulate him on his documentation of how their satellite telemetry data revealed changing patterns of bear habitat range in the western Arctic; how the aerial infrared surveys the oil and gas industry relied on when locating drilling sites missed more than half the bear dens, buried in the snow but known

SKIN

to researchers. Then the intensity of the man's regard made him wonder—was his interest sexual? As soon as Hugh zipped up, the man seized his tie, twisted it, grip like a winch. When Hugh tried to break free, grabbing at the man's hands, trying to land a punch, grappling to loosen the cinch of the tie at his neck, the man used one hand to pry away Hugh's fingers with surprising force, tightening the tie against Hugh's windpipe with the other.

From the airless, panicked whirlwind in which he choked, spots forming in front of his eyes, Hugh heard the man say, "You and your fucking bears won't stop us. We want to drill somewhere, we will."

With one final tug, his attacker was gone.

Alone once more, clutching the edge of a porcelain sink, Hugh gagged. Gagged again. Should he run after the man? Couldn't. With shaky hands, he wrestled loose the noose of his tie and stuffed it in his jacket pocket. Touched his throat. Coughed. What had just happened? He couldn't stop coughing. How long had the throttling lasted? Seconds. Surely his attacker wouldn't have wanted to kill him. Hired gun? Renegade? Assassin? In mining? Oil and gas? The man would not have had to register for the conference or listen to Hugh's talk in order to confront him, yet had known enough about his work to target him. Presumably because the research he and others were doing was being used to argue for bear protection zones, particularly around denning habitats, thus hemming in resource-extraction expansion plans. He'd had the bad luck, the charisma, *ha, ha*, to have been singled out.

Another man entered the washroom, conference lanyard strung around his neck, stared at Hugh but made no move to speak to him. And Hugh, still coughing, had no desire to confide in this man, at a urinal, back to him now, mid-piss.

That evening, sitting in the hotel bar with Pawel Derksen, co-panellist and fellow polar bear researcher out of Edmonton, Hugh scanned the room for any sign of his attacker. A miasma of a man: This was all he could summon. Pawel passed him a shot of Norwegian vodka. After downing it, Hugh rubbed his neck beneath his sweater with the zip-up collar. Those instants when he'd fought for breath. The blank space inside him. "Someone attacked me in the men's room after our session." He coughed. His voice sounded odd.

"Attacked? Didn't like our maps or our numbers?"

"Definitely not. Grabbed me by the tie and tried to choke me. Said they'll drill where they want. Didn't leave a business card. I'll never wear a tie again."

"Jesus," Pawel said. "I've had the emailed death threats, a bunch, actually, some awfully explicit, but nothing physical, or at least not yet." He squeezed Hugh's shoulder. "You okay?"

"I don't think he's in here," Hugh said. "I'm supposed to keep a file of the emailed ones. Only a few so far. Maybe he sent one, didn't say. Stalker? Opportunist? My sense is oil and gas, but it's just a hunch."

With a sympathetic pat to Hugh's arm, Pawel waved at the bartender. "Not sure what happens next. Shit's getting nasty out there."

Arriving home from Calgary, Hugh dropped his bags inside the front door and stumbled into the kitchen to find Leonie, at sixteen spindling into the height and leanness of her mother, topped with a mop of mauve hair, pulling a dial of pizza out of the oven. She smiled at him. He couldn't tell her what had happened to him. When he attempted to ruffle her hair, kiss her forehead, she shook him off amiably, *Dad*, as if she were too old for such a greeting. Her voice focused his attention like no other. If Leonie called to him, he heard nothing else. His throat burned. His muscles ached. He hugged her. She hugged him back. He wanted to wrap her in his arms and never let go.

"Where's your mother?" he asked, wondering if Paula had heard his return.

Leonie passed a plate to him, pizza slice upon it, pointed with her own pizza slice. "Upstairs. She has a grant deadline."

SKIN

The next night, Friday, Paula ordered from the takeout Thai place up the street, the one she liked because it used tin foil and paper containers, not those unrecyclable black plastic ones most places used. She received the food from the delivery driver, set the containers on the counter, opened them, pulled out plates. Hugh lit candles on the table, the nice ones. He asked if the grant was in and Paula nodded. He noted, as he had that morning, the darkened skin under her eyes. He kissed her, still wearing his sweater with the zip-up collar. Everyone was so overextended, she said, and since she was one of the PIs, she'd had to do a lot of the corralling, of her own team and their colleagues down east in Dartmouth.

At the table, over a plate of green curry and mango salad, Hugh heard himself describe encounters with Indigenous hunters up north who resented the work that he and others were doing because their data collection revealed the drop in bear numbers, which in turn affected hunting quotas. Who saw their work as an imperialist intrusion which, you could argue, it was.

Why couldn't he speak of the attack to Paula, of all people? He'd worn his hoodie to bed the previous night rather than a sweatshirt, his more common attire if he wore anything at all. Paula had come to bed later than him, slid in silently at his side. Awake, he'd felt the fog of her preoccupation. That morning, after she left for the university, he'd stayed in bed for, what, a couple of hours, one hand laid gently over his neck. Shock still gripped him. He wanted to be released from the sensations that strobed back into his body: the man's grasp on his tie as, panicked, he lashed out. He fantasized about grabbing his assailant's tie and choking the man in turn. There was also the fact of the man: not only his violence but his implacability. There were so many like him, still so many, an army of them.

A week later, at the sound of Paula clattering in the kitchen, Hugh propelled himself downstairs and pulled a bottle of wine from the tall cupboard in the corner. "Something happened to me at that conference in Calgary. I've been meaning to tell you. A guy came at me in the men's room after our panel. Pissed off about our work and any way it interferes with whatever resource extraction he's involved in."

Paula, who had been chopping garlic at the counter, put down her knife. "Came at you?" She was, clearly, waiting for more.

"Grabbed me by the tie. Threatened me and anyone working with the bears. A white man in a suit."

"Did he hurt you?"

"A bit of bruising."

"Where? Can I see?"

He attempted to brush her off but when Paula persisted, Hugh pulled down the zip on his sweater, exposing his neck. She stared at the bruises, touched them gently with her fingertips.

"Hugh," she said. Then, "You went to the police?"

"I told the hotel and the conference. I didn't go to the police. I have so little memory of what happened. I couldn't have identified him. I don't even know the colour of his hair."

"Why are you only telling me this now?"

"I suppose I'm still trying to process it." He put the bottle of wine back in the fridge, realized it was a bottle of red, retrieved it. Their two filled glasses stood untouched. "And, in the larger scale of things, I didn't want to make a big deal of it."

"That's an assault," Paula said.

"A small one."

"Tell me exactly what happened."

So he did. The man going for his tie, tightening his grip, the choking, his words, his attempt to fight the man off.

"That's an assault, Hugh. People can't be allowed to get away with things like this. You need to go to the police."

"And what exactly will I say to them? I was attacked by an oil and gas thug, but I can't remember anything useful about the guy." He knew that Paula didn't intend to make him feel defensive. Her response to such an attack would have been far different than his. She was an agitator, her assertiveness one of the things he loved about her, her agitation, on his behalf, a form of care. "Pawel Derksen and I, and others, are already talking about removing maps from the end of our studies. At least that will make us and the bears harder to find out in the field. In case anyone really wants to take us out."

Two months later. May. The scent of lilacs spilled through an open window. From the sofa Paula eyed Hugh warily. He'd brought her downstairs, insisted that he needed to tell her something. "I've quit my job." He was on his feet in front of her. Outside, in their front yard, the ash tree, green but weakened by alien insects, was dying.

"Quit?" From the expression on her face, he could have made up the word.

"All you have to do is go up north and take a photograph of the Arctic Ocean with a credible GPS identification tag showing how little sea ice there is to confirm that polar bear populations are plummeting. No one needs us to be doing what we're doing."

"Data grounds observation." Bewildered, Paula was throwing him a life buoy, trying to pull back the version of him that she thought she knew. "We need numbers for anything to be credible. Long-term data. Your work's necessary, Hugh."

"Is data convincing anyone to change their behaviour? Are photographs of starving polar bears sent out by the conservation folk convincing anyone? Winsome pics of mama bears and their cute little polar bear cubs? They're not."

"You're still in the room with that man. It's your shock speaking—"

"Not shock. I can't bear the pointlessness of what I do. I can't get over the feeling of pointlessness. We've got bear protection zones. Still the ice melts. Bear numbers plummet. The drilling continues. We run risks to what end? We're all in the room with that man. I'm starting to believe disaster's the only thing that will change people.

And it has to be disaster that hits close to home. In the pocketbook. Not just once but repeatedly. Big disasters. Floods. Storms. Droughts. Atmospheric rivers. Maybe it's better not to resist but bring them on."

"It's not pointless to make threats to the world visible. Tell me what you're feeling."

"I am telling you. I sent in a letter of resignation this morning. I'm calling it that — not early retirement. I said I was resigning because I thought my work had become meaningless."

Paula gripped her knees, a compensatory gesture, when what she really wanted to do, Hugh was convinced, was shake him.

"Life isn't meaningless," he said to Paula. "I'm not saying that."

He took to walking for hours at a time, setting off south, through the neighbourhood and the dank concrete of the underpass, across six lanes of racing traffic until, on the far side, he reached the swelling, horizon-spanning body of the lake. Fixing his eyes on its expanse, he tramped from one side of the city to the other, east as far as the old water filtration plant, west as far as Humber Bay, following the trail that spanned the lakeshore, past industrially upheaved land and condominiums and the cranes and corporate towers of the downtown core, to the wide sand beaches and quaint residential neighbourhoods of the east, back again until he came to the west end's ribbon of grass and beach, squeezed against roaring roadway. Sometimes the man walked beside him. Sometimes he'd speed up, attempting to outpace the man. Sometimes the man became multiple. Staring at other men, Hugh wondered, Were they capable of doing what his assailant had done? Sometimes, amidst the humidity of summer, stopping along the eastern beach, he tugged off his boots, stripped to his skivvies and plunged into the water, as if this way he might shuck off the haunting. It wasn't precisely fear he felt. Was he being cowardly? Avoiding dangers that he should have stuck around to face? Sometimes, at night he dropped a line to former colleagues, Derek, Pawel, attempting to justify his decision. He'd go downstairs to the basement and shadow box.

On the beach, stumbling to shore, he shook droplets of water from his body, and this was something, compensation, consolation, the feel of the water, cold and ravishing against his skin. Rain didn't deter him, nor, when it came, the messy bluster of winter, the lakeshore path full of salt-laced sludge. He walked on and, when spring came round once again, flights of ducks drew close, settling on the water surface, buffleheads, mergansers, wood ducks. One morning, at dawn, on a tip, he hiked west into Etobicoke to watch the arrival of a flock of whimbrels, tracked now by app as they made their way up from Virginia, through New York State by night, across the lake, appearing in silhouette as the sun rose behind the old needle of the CN Tower, outnumbered by the birders in their bright Gore-Tex jackets who stood peering at the birds through binoculars and cameras. Yes, he was still processing something, he told Paula. Unsaid: An as yet indecipherable yearning pursued him. Yes, walking helped.

At home, he built Paula a wall of bookshelves, hammered a new fence into place in the backyard, hoping his labour might appease her, income-producing though it might not be. He had some savings, a modest pension. He shopped, cooked, dug out a vegetable garden, helped neighbours dig up their lawns and turn them into gardens, organized a community garden in a local park. Took heart when a group of youngsters—Niala, Rudi, Anwar, Kayal—decided to build another community garden and accepted his offer of help. Using his body in this way—digging, planting, mulching—brought solace and distraction. Satisfaction. He exhausted himself, which was good. And others depended on him. Nearing fifty, he was fitter than he'd ever been, which he hoped Paula noticed.

One July afternoon, coming in the back door with a colander full of sun-warmed cherry tomatoes, Hugh chanced upon Leonie, seventeen, sprawled on the living-room sofa, bare legs dangling, lost in her phone. He called her name. Miraculously, she looked up. His fingers smelled of the particular acridity of tomato plants, dirt, the day's labour. He tossed Leonie a cherry tomato, which, as miraculously, she caught. She popped it in her mouth, eyebrows lifting, just as her mother's did. With a groan of pleasure, she held out her hand for another. And another. Phone abandoned on the floor beside her. He'd managed this: to draw her back into the sensory world.

He found Paula on the front porch, frowning at her screen. She was, he knew, growing despondent about the results of her studies—the little sea sponges were having a hard time clearing suspended sediment from their systems after prolonged exposure, and out in the Atlantic, trawling gear, which whipped up sediments that might not disperse for days, was also ripping up their sponge grounds and so destroying them. He cupped her stern and beautiful face between his palms, noting the lines forming at the edge of her eyebrows. Close your eyes. The song of a cicada soared skyward. Listen. A breeze rustled through the ash leaves. Her face softened.

It was true that he missed the bears, the fieldwork, the peculiar intimacy of tracking them on his screen, the signals from their radio collars cast up into the atmosphere and tumbling down six times a day, the location markers making jagged lines as the bears wandered along the shore or out onto the sea ice of Hudson Bay, out and in, then farther out, chasing the ice. Yet these traces told him nothing of their specific circumstances, whether rain fell on them or snow, or what they hunted. Even if he'd kept on, the fates of individual bears would eventually have been lost to him. The signals faded away or ended; after a year or two the batteries in the tracking collars died. Knowing the precise location of Bear HB893 had never given him the means to intervene if she were starving, or shot, or do anything to slow the general drift of her species.

SKIN

❖

Three years later, coming in the door, grocery bags in hand, Hugh stumbled upon Paula on the bottom step of the staircase, hugging her knees, eyes red, Kleenex crumpled in her hand, phone at her side. Secretly he'd been wondering if this, the global sweep of a virus killing thousands, hundreds of thousands, millions, rushing over and through them, would be the shock they needed. To change them fundamentally. Which he longed for. Yes, there would be costs. Deaths. More deaths. He didn't wish for the deaths. He ripped off his face mask, dropped it onto the pile on the front hall dresser.

"What is it?"—thinking immediately of Paula's mother, two provinces away, querulous and out of reach for months; his parents, isolating on the other side of the province in their woodland house.

After blowing her nose, Paula said she'd just got off the phone with the university's animal ethics and security officer. Given the length of the lockdown and university closure, the officer was going around to all the labs and killing the creatures in them, by injection, in whatever way seemed most humane. "It's her job, Hugh. I know it's not the heart of what's going on, but we were discussing the Aqualab, how best to euthanize everything. The tanks full of fish, star fish, sea urchins, sponges, *Vazella pourtalesii*, it's a threatened species in its natural habitat, and I know some of the ones in the lab are already necrotizing, and, yes, we made that happen, but now they're all to be killed, which means all our ongoing experiments are killed with them—"

"Oh, Paulie." He pulled her to her feet and wrapped his arms around her, her distress not just about the lab or the sea sponges, he was certain. All of them were caught in this maelstrom.

One April afternoon, two years later, out on the lakeshore trail, Hugh was biking home when the air practically tore the bike from under him. The alert on the government weather app had warned of strong gusts as a cold front blew in but he'd gone out anyway, bike helmet clipped to his head, happy to be returned to a world that was sort of as they had known it, even if a mass of hot air, thickened with humidity, had for days refused to budge and shrivelled all the spring flowers.

Grit from the dust clouds rising off the lakeshore parking lots flew up his nostrils. He ran, which felt like stumbling, dragging the bike under a footbridge where a couple of runners had taken refuge. The four lanes of traffic beside them slowed to a crawl. The thin trees at roadside bent double, plastic bags howling in their branches. Coffee cups soared through the air. Banners on the street lamps ripped in two. Grip firm on his bike, Hugh turned into the wind. This was how weather fronts shifted now, hot to cold, cold to hot. Even as breath was socked out of him, a new feeling surged.

The gust passed swiftly, leaving in its wake cooler air. A moment later, his phone pinged. Paula, frantic to know where he was. *Power's out. Tree limb smashed onto a car in front of the house.*

In the neighbourhood, as he biked back through it, an oak branch lay sprawled across a lawn, pale, raw wood along its torn-off edge, a huge silver maple limb broken upon another. A downed power line sagged and sparked atop a car. A whoosh alerted him as, half a block ahead, another tree limb, chestnut this time, sank slowly to the ground, the damage so much worse among these streets because of all the trees. People stared from porches, clustered on the sidewalk. From his bike, Hugh waved at a woman he knew. Five minutes, this was all it had taken to cause such damage. The joy he'd felt moments before, braced under the footbridge, buffeted by the wind, returned. How could he be feeling joy? He tried to squelch it.

In June, as he returned from grocery shopping, on foot, sweating once again in the ostensibly unseasonable heat, the sky in the west, over the houses, surged mauve then swirled plum dark. Across the street, the remnant silver maple with its broken limbs shuddered while the dying ash in front of his own house shook. Hugh checked his phone app. That morning, an approaching cold front had spawned a band of thunderstorm cells in the Midwest. They were moving closer. A mass of cloud. No sooner had he picked up the grocery bags to make a dash for the front porch than the wind picked up with a frantic roar, and the rain began.

In the kitchen, Paula and Leonie, recently returned home after the final year of her microbiology degree, bent over Leonie's phone. The lights flickered and went out. The smoke detectors beeped. In the darkness, rain slammed the windows. The lights came back on. Half an hour later, at his computer upstairs, Hugh surfed through social media and the local news. There had been tornado warnings north of the city. Now there was chatter about actual funnel clouds. Posts surfaced. With prickling excitement, he followed the hashtags. There wouldn't be any official confirmation for at least twenty-four hours, but people had posted blurry phone videos of circular, spinning clouds. He scanned the radar map: red spots still active. Below the map, photos: a house stripped bare. Pink insulation exposed like flesh. Roofs sheared of shingles. Roofless. A crushed RV. Two.

He made his way downstairs, left the house, and, without thinking too much about what he was doing, got in the car and drove north. Though the rain had ended, the roads were slick. He passed the lumbering vehicle of a TV crew. The quickest way to where he wanted to be, he realized, rather than guessing from online posts, was to follow the media truck off the highway in Innisfil, along streets already jumbled with onlookers, wreckage, squad cars, stretches of yellow police tape.

Leaving the car parked by a residential curb, he stepped out, nodding at others, looking around, self-conscious and gratefully anonymous.

Police tape cordoned off more houses: the one canting off its foundation, the one next door with the entire second floor ripped off. Plywood, siding, drywall spilled into the road. A soccer ball and a motorcycle helmet lay on one debris-strewn lawn, garage door ripped away, windows blasted out. The hulking SUV in the drive next door lay overturned. Confronted by the force of the storm, had the people around him been fundamentally altered? He searched among them: Homeowners wandered about, holding projectiles of splintered wood and metal; someone sobbed. Above them all, the sky brightened. Cooled air cleansed them. Yet, as Hugh stumbled over more detritus, a plastic wading pool, an inflatable Christmas dinosaur, something else became clear. It wasn't aftermath he was after. Here was evidence of the wind's power, but this was wreckage without wind. Fingerprints not body, when what he truly longed for was contact with the amplified wind itself.

In July, as he was re-laying the flagstones of the back walkway, Hugh's phone let loose the wailing yodel of an amber alert. He was all set to ignore it, assuming the alert to be another broadcast about a missing child or missing children, a private disaster about which he could do nothing, when an impulse made him pull off his leather work gloves. No children were missing. They were being warned of a severe thunderstorm's approach.

In the kitchen, Leonie was breaking ice cubes from a tray into a glass. His twenty-two-year-old daughter. He rested a hand on her shoulder. Only a day ago, he'd run into her on the street with a friend, both with the same pale froth of hair, in jeans and oversized dress shirts, sharing a punnet of blueberries; he wasn't even certain of the gender of her companion; all he knew was that Leonie, happy to see him when they bumped into each other, willing to throw her arms around him, was nevertheless moving away from him, into her life. At the counter, when he showed her his phone and asked if she had any memory of receiving an amber alert about the weather, she said no. She'd heard the alert on her phone but hadn't bothered to look at it.

"You okay, sweetheart?" Hugh asked. Surely all that childhood fear must still be in her somewhere.

"I guess."

He kissed her wide, clear forehead, proffering what care he could. He did not want to frighten his daughter. "Stay inside for now."

Upstairs, online: A storm system, formed south of Chicago, fuelled by a heat dome over the eastern United States, was pressing eastward in the direction of Windsor and the rest of southwestern Ontario, already summoning heat-fuelled winds of almost one hundred fifty kilometres per hour. A widespread band of swift-moving thunderstorms would continue moving east across Ontario and into Quebec. Had the winds been this ferocious a year ago? He couldn't remember. Where they were nothing had happened yet. The air remained sultry and still.

After wiping himself down with a washcloth, a quick camper's shower, he knocked on Paula's study door. When he touched her bare shoulder, she turned from the screen and its rows of numbers, dazzled but smiling. He was going out to pick up some gravel to finish the backyard work, he told her, then planned to meet a friend, Mike, the guy he sometimes played tennis with, for coffee. "You got that alert, didn't you," Paula asked.

"It's just an alert," Hugh said, restlessness rippling through him. He assured her if the wind got up, he'd shelter, kissed her, as responsive as ever to the give of her lips, disturbed by how easy it was to lie to her.

Then he was driving north up the Parkway, east out of the city, recklessly burning gasoline. It wasn't that he hoped to outpace the storm, only that he didn't want to encounter it in the vast suburban hinterlands or while pelting along twelve lanes of mega-highway.

At the Newcastle exit, he pulled off the 401 and drove south towards Lakeshore Road, where, as he hoped, he came upon an unobstructed view of the lake across fields and there was almost no traffic. He sped some kilometres farther east, aware, in the rear-view mirror, of the sky darkening behind him, before he made a sharp U-turn. The clouds, mass, particles, whirl, velocity, tumultuous, gargantuan, slate-dark. Steroidal. This was what was coming towards them.

It was like and not like being in a helicopter chasing a polar bear. He was seized by the same adrenaline rush. He imagined tossing the man who'd attacked him out into the storm, watching him flail. As Hugh veered the rocking car onto the gravel shoulder, an oversized pickup truck pummelled past, speeding in the opposite direction, away from the storm, as if its occupants could outrun it. *Turn*, Hugh wanted to shout at them. *Look at what's coming! Turn!*

The air pressure inside the car dropped, making his ears pop. If he tried to open the car door, the wind would smash it shut in his face. Yet he wanted to be out there. He was downwind from a nuclear power plant. Two nuclear power plants. Over on the treeline, beyond the fields, raw wood burst into sight as trunks broke open and branches fell, a silent toppling within the scream of the wind. A moment later, although clouds still propelled themselves across the sky, and thunder distantly rumbled, the wind dropped as suddenly as it had arrived, leaving him spent, but still yearning.

As he flew east across the continent, first flight in two years, stuffed in amongst the masked and unmasked, *hypocrite voyageur*, since he had no particular reason to be flying other than his own confounding desire, Hugh tried to articulate to himself what held him in its grip. In the simplest terms: The wind drew him. More than ever. In the face of these swirling, human-magnified winds, his fascination had magnified.

As Hurricane Felicia, swollen by the ultra-warmed waters of the Caribbean, drowned Puerto Rico and seemed on course to take a swing at the Carolinas, before moving up towards Atlantic Canada, coastal Nova Scotia being the likeliest target, Hugh had written to his brother, suggesting a visit. It's been too long. We're both getting older.

Barely in touch for years, they'd managed dinner now and again. His entrepreneurial brother, the one who'd swerved farthest from their father's example, who'd made money in lasers, fibre-optics, something like that, sold stock options, put more money into some kind of medical R&D, before, once more, cashing out. There'd been a wife, Irene, who appeared, then disappeared, and was seemingly never replaced. No children. Did Brian judge him, judge them, in the same way that Paula could be so judgmental about his brother's overt pursuit of wealth? A decade earlier, when, over restaurant burgers, Hugh had told Brian about his conference attacker, Brian had shaken his head and muttered, Random sociopath. How can you be so sure about the *random*, Hugh had asked, but all Brian would do was repeat himself.

The last time they'd seen each other, the year before the pandemic, Brian had invited Hugh and Paula to his penthouse apartment for dinner. Apron over his dress shirt and wool trousers, he'd cooked for them, made something vegetarian at Paula's request, lasagna, opened a twenty-five-year-old Bordeaux, which, it had to be said, proved delicious. This was the night when Brian announced that he was selling his Toronto condo and retiring to a quaint Nova Scotia seaside village where he'd bought a renovated former bank.

Just as Brian had promised, a white pickup truck sped towards the curb of the Halifax International Airport where Hugh waited. A pickup truck! Jowled, a little more paunch beneath his windbreaker than when Hugh had last seen him, Brian burst out of the driver's door and came striding towards him, thrusting out a hand, a gesture that Hugh, stuffing his phone back into his pocket, intercepted with a hug.

On the flight, he'd been astonished at how packed the plane was — no one seemed scared off by the threat of a hurricane. When he'd told Paula of his plan to visit his brother, she'd voiced some surprise; why not wait at least another week, until after Felicia blew through. The timing worked for Brian, Hugh said. The converted bank was unlikely to blow down, and the thing about hurricanes was that you never knew exactly where they'd make landfall.

"How's Paula," Brian asked immediately, threading the truck towards the highway, Hugh's carry-on tossed in the cab behind them, as if he'd uncannily sensed something of the furtive energy that possessed Hugh.

"Great," Hugh said. In his late thirties, Brian had lost the hearing in his left ear in the aftermath of a virus. On his good side, in the passenger seat, Hugh didn't have to shout but raised his voice. "Back in the lab now. She comes down this way every now and again to check on a couple of offshore research sites. It's tough work. The news isn't always good from the ocean floor, alas." He cast a glance at his brother. Did Brian seem altered? The expensive if casual clothes; the truck was an electric one, there was that.

"Leonie?" Brian asked.

"Still sorting herself out, I'd say. How's the East Coast treating you?" He'd wondered if his brother, in moving to the Nova Scotia shore, was attempting to reclaim something of that briefly inhabited coastal landscape of their boyhood.

"Thank God the days of masking are over," Brian said. "That was brutal. No lip reading. Sure as hell felt deaf then."

"Granted," Hugh said. "Nevertheless, masks are epidemiologically useful." His phone pulsed in his pocket. Unable to bear the pressure any longer, he pulled it out: Felicia, still off in the Atlantic, a blotchy yellow-green sprawl on the planetary wind map, cycling, cycling, parallel with Cape Cod but moving closer with every hour.

"Worried about the hurricane?" his brother asked.

"Not really." Hugh turned over his phone, the wind map's pulse still felt through his palm. Outside, an earth mover, among the fir and birch trees, gouged out rock and soil at the side of the highway. "You?"

"Goes with the territory," Brian said. "I bought a place on a rise of land. Invested in a new generator. You batten down the hatches. Sometimes those weather warnings feel like freak-outs. Anyway, got a bunch more solar lanterns. Pantry's well-stocked. And, let me assure you, we're not going to run out of beer."

That afternoon, despite the oncoming storm and rising wind, Brian wanted to play a round of golf at the local club, where he was a member, up on a hill above the town harbour. At first Hugh protested. The wind, for a start. The waves, down below, were already surging. Not so bad, Brian said. What's wrong with you? And, indeed, given that he'd come all this way and was his brother's guest, it was surely churlish to insist that he hated golf, never played, had no interest in playing, and what was the point since Brian was likely to cream him.

Once, as boys, not long after they'd moved away from the island, back to Toronto, the two of them had come upon their father's bag of golf clubs leaning against the wall of their new rental house. Yelping at each other, they'd pulled out clubs, wrestling for the one each wanted, the one that, inexplicably, Hugh had managed to yank from his brother. All those years ago, as he'd stumbled into a swing, Brian had dashed behind him, and Hugh's club, in its clumsy backward arc, had caught his brother behind the temple. Despite Brian's wailing, there'd been no obvious damage: no concussion, no bleeding, only a bump. He wasn't the cause of Brian's deafness, although, later, when the deafness took hold, Hugh paused to wonder. Had the impact made any residual difference? Brian had never accused him of anything.

Up on the fourth hole, phone a burn in his pocket, Hugh took a swing without looking and once more almost hit his brother in the side of the head.

"For fuck's sake," Brian shouted.

What if, for the second time in his life, he'd hit his brother in the head with a golf club, and this time knocked him out or deafened him in the other ear? Had he wanted to hit his brother in the head? Brian seemed more incredulous than furious as he punched Hugh in the shoulder, his windbreaker billowing, making Hugh, the scrawny one, stagger about in dismay as he shouted apologies.

Later, in the room that had once been the bank's main chamber and was now Brian's living room, as rain from the hurricane sprayed across the windows and the voluminous clouds made an early darkness, Hugh, by the wood stove, under the tall ceiling, took the can of a local hoppy ale that Brian held out to him. Moments later, locked in the main floor powder room, he took another, less-surreptitious look at the wind map: Felicia swirling ever closer, her yellow centre still offshore but heading northward. *Come here*, Hugh wanted to shout. When he returned to the living room, Brian was nowhere to be seen.

His brother's voice drew him back towards the kitchen. A woman, their age, streaked hair, of solid build, in hooded rain jacket and rubber boots slick with moisture, stood inside the back door, holding a wet dog on a leash, she and Brian angled in such a way as to suggest familiarity, even intimacy.

"Hugh," Hugh said to the woman. And to his brother, "I'm heading out for a stroll."

"In that?" said Brian.

"Shirley," the woman said. "Not much more than a bad nor'easter. Landfall looks to be up on the western shore, more's the pity for them."

Before Brian could protest or wrangle him into staying back, Hugh set off through the bank. Grabbing his rain jacket from a hook, he tugged the front door shut behind him. The wind fought him as he tacked down the street. Where the street opened to the harbour, sailboats, including Brian's, lashed to their moorings, tilted and clashed against each other. Rain pelted his face. Yes, he was in the thick of a storm, but he'd been in far worse. Disappointment. He'd come all this way and been stood up.

Two days after his return from Nova Scotia, a new hurricane came pushing up from the Caribbean. A day after that, all of Florida was under a state of emergency and airports as far north as Orlando were on the verge of shutting down. After throwing some clean clothes into his carry-on, Hugh shouted to Leonie that he'd been called away by colleagues, texted Paula at the lab about a last-minute invitation, his old research team wanting him to join them, and he wanted to go, he would fly out that afternoon. On points, as it happened. He'd booked the Jeep on points as well. Bag in hand, he sat for a moment on the edge of his marital bed, the urge to go insistent, unignorable. A kind of madness?

In the baggage hall of the Orlando airport, he found himself for the first time among the storm chasers, sensing their presence again at the rental car kiosks, amid their piles of gear, the volley of their conversations about weather and tracking apps overheard as Hugh drew close. They were renting trucks or the heaviest, sturdiest SUVs they could find. He spotted a cluster of women. These were the ones whom he approached. The men intimidated him, with their particular brand of geeky machismo. One of the women reminded him of Paula.

He asked this woman—Jenny, he heard someone call her—who seemed to be leading the group, if he could follow them to the coast or if she'd care to share their routing. She had long, wild hair and a blunt attractiveness. He could imagine her navigating a truck through gale-force winds and slamming sheets of rain. He wasn't from these parts, he told her, he was a polar scientist who'd come south to observe the connections between what was happening up there and down here. He passed her a much-worn business card. He did not want her or any of the women to think he was coming on to her. They all looked tough and weather-ready, young and older, sizing him up, his windbreaker, his paltry knapsack.

"You're not with a partner?" Jenny asked.

Hugh noted the way she took him in when he said no. After consulting with one of the other women, also in knee-high rubber boots, hair a short Afro, Jenny said he could stick with their party. He texted Paula. Despite the weather, the conference seemed to be going ahead.

That night, after the hours on the road driving south as lines of evacuees nosed in the other direction, Hugh entered the bar of a hotel on the inland side of Fort Myers, where Jenny's group had a reservation and where he'd managed to snag a spartan room with two sagging twin mattresses. On his phone screen spread an enormous yellow-and-red spiral, radial wings circling across the waters of the Gulf towards them. One of the exterior doors to the bar had already been roped to an inner door to hold it shut.

From the tables their party occupied, Mae, with the Afro, beckoned to him. An aura of purpose emanated from the women, as if they were rescue workers or a choir. Their communal energy drew him, Jenny speaking to the others with the conviction that seemed to define her. Hugh heard her say the words, *Sense of shift*, as he pulled up a chair. "However you come to this work, as artists, scientists, citizen scientists, photographers, you're all super-sensitive to the shifts in air pressure before any storm, the electricity in the air before a thunder strike, the smallest alterations in wind direction. That's why you're here. You're also aware of much larger shifts of weather. You're paying attention to these shifts—and awareness like yours is needed."

"Unh-huh," someone intoned. Yes, said another.

"You will have to get used to the more-ness of it. More wind, more storms, more atmospheric rivers, more shift." Jenny tugged and manipulated the air with her hands as she spoke. "Your willingness, your desire to pay attention to all this, that's your gift."

Gift or curse, Hugh wondered.

"Gift," Jenny said, fixing on him, as if he'd spoken aloud. He nodded, wisdom received, the words lodging themselves in his chest, carried with him when he stepped outside, wind already rising.

The next morning, as rain lashed the hotel windows, Hugh approached Mae and Jenny at their breakfast table, a couple he now assumed, and asked if he could hitch a ride with them. "I can help with the driving. I've driven through blizzards, not hurricanes but other kinds of wild weather."

To his surprise, Jenny agreed, siphoning up the rest of her coffee before squeezing Mae's hand and launching herself to her feet as the power went out. She beckoned to Hugh to follow them through the darkened restaurant, into the driving rain, to their black rental truck where, already drenched, face dripping, he hoisted himself into the cab behind Jenny, in the driver's seat, Mae riding shotgun, for the drive north towards Punta Gorda and Port Charlotte.

Noon saw them entering the thick of the first eyewall, slaloming at slow speed towards a causeway Jenny said they needed to cross, around gushes of water, trees, sheets of twisted metal, the truck rocking with every blast, Mae, at Jenny's command, holding up her cellphone so that Jenny, white-knuckling, yelling instructions, could see through its camera, the windscreen impenetrable, the explosions of rain on the truck roof deafening, sensations so extreme that Hugh barely felt his racing heart. He could offer them nothing other than his attention, his willingness not to panic, as they offered their excited focus to him. He shouldn't be here. It was a death wish to throw himself into the path of a Category Four plus hurricane. A voice in his head spoke quietly to Leonie. And yet he gripped the handle above the window, mesmerized, his other hand pressed hard against the seatback.

Later that afternoon, back in Fort Myers, Hugh's whole body throbbed as, along with a cluster of others, including Jenny and Mae, he met the back eyewall, protected from the worst of its power by the concrete roof and pillars of an open-air parking lot. Rapids tore down the streets around them, marooning them. A street sign bent and crumpled before his eyes. It was impossible to see clearly, but the entire structure of a gas station seemed to be collapsing to the ground. The roar! Mae shouted, pointing to the roof of their hotel as it ripped free. Amid the grinding, the shrieking, pressed against a concrete pillar, water whipping against his thighs and rushing across his feet, Hugh tried to inch closer to the open air, holding tight to the metal of a car door in order not to be swept away, Mae and Jenny not far off. He caught Jenny's eye as she reached out a wet hand, taut grip, the two of them, three, Mae on her other side, leaning outwards, ardent, into the tumult. Was it knowledge he was after, knowledge that could only be reached through sensation? Yes! This was the world they lived in now, and he needed to meet it, not surrender to it but feel all its extremities.

At Paula's knock, Hugh leaped to heave a teetering pile of file folders from the second chair in his study. She hesitated before seating herself. For an instant, her features became unrecognizable. "There was no meeting of the Polar Council at the University of Florida, was there? It seemed far-fetched, but not impossible. Since they have a climate institute."

There wasn't, Hugh agreed.

"But you went to Florida—somewhere. Where?"

"To Florida," Hugh said, ghostly iterations of the wind and all its destructions still blowing through him. "To the Gulf Coast."

"The Gulf Coast? In that weather? Why, Hugh?" Paula rose. "Let's go downstairs."

"Now?"

"Leonie has something she wants to show us."

From the hallway, Paula called up to the third floor.

Hugh had been distantly aware of Leonie using the spare room across the landing from his study, though when he'd asked what she was up to behind that closed door, she'd been noncommittal, self-contained as he could be, holding her secret close. At the sound of Paula's voice, she opened the door, as if the two of them had planned all this in advance.

In the living room, side by side on the sofa, Paula clasped his hand with a firmness different than Jenny's in the midst of the back eyewall. Hugh returned Paula's grip. Minutes later, Leonie entered the room.

She ran a hand through her short blue hair. A bathrobe. No, a lab coat. He saw it now. She turned in a circle, pointed to the waistband, adjustable to fit both small and full-figured bodies, particularly female bodies with waists and hips. "The elasticated wristbands keep foreign or toxic material from slipping up your arms. The multiple pockets include interior pockets for tucking away things like tampons and Kleenex. The collar can be folded down or raised if you need protection from potentially volatile or harmful substances." She was earnest, lovely, her slim hands in motion, her small voice explaining all this with a bashful smile.

"I thought about going to grad school," she said, as if she had prepared these words just for him, "but then I started talking to people, to Mum and friends and peers, women and female-identifying people in the scientific community, and I realized there was this need. I like to make things, and here was something I could make that would be useful for anyone whose dimensions aren't the same as a typical male scientist. A better protection garment."

Protection garment. All through her childhood, Leonie had collected things: leathery oak leaves, acorns, cicada casings, milkweed seed pods, marbles, gentle in her attentions. Hugh had watched her store these beloved objects in wooden boxes. She'd crafted little houses out of popsicle sticks, carefully sculpted tiny bowls of clay. He'd been aware that she'd installed a sewing machine in the room across the landing, the sound of the machine's treadle coming to him distantly as, after hours spent weeding in their garden or the community garden, he stared at his wind maps, wondering what kind of future lay in store for her and all the other young ones.

"It's innovative and fills a gap," Paula said.

"This is the prototype," Leonie said. "A few people have been trying it out. So far they really like it."

Hugh leaped to his feet, enfolding her in a hug. Nothing in him was inclined to mock her practical, generous hope.

"Leonie wants to put the coat into small-scale production," Paula said. "Create a beta run. Offer it to a group of scientists to try out. I thought we could provide some financial help to get her started."

He saw what Paula wanted from him, solidarity, commitment, for them to rally around Leonie and press onward together. "Yes," he said.

Paula waited until they were in bed that night before asking him outright, "Are you having an affair?" The bed shook as if from the reverberations of her body.

"No." How was he to put it into words? "But I'm having a kind of a thing with the wind."

"A thing, Hugh? With the wind? What the hell does that mean?"

"I want to be close to its extremes. Know what wind is these days. Somehow it feels necessary."

There, it was out in the open. What would she make of this, of him as he lay beside her, newly exposed? Could she share this knowing? An image returned to him of Jenny, storm chaser, biophysicist, soaked to the skin, fervent eyes on the sky, phone camera raised, up to her knees in water on the edge of that parking garage in Fort Myers, Florida. "I love you," Hugh said. "Believe me. I love you and Leonie more than my life. I'm trying to explain something I'm finding hard to explain even to myself."

Paula said nothing.

"The winds are getting wilder. Don't tell me you haven't noticed."

Paula gave a grunt of assent.

"Sense of shift," Hugh said aloud. "In Florida I spent time with a group of storm chasers. Women. Scientists, some of them. Following Juan in Fort Myers. It's what they say we need to hone. In these days. To be as aware as possible of what's coming, given what we can't change. They're tuning themselves to the shift. That's how they put it. And I suppose, that's what I'm trying to do as well."

Did what he was saying truly make no sense?

Paula turned away from him to face the wall, the bed still shaking. Hugh thought she might be crying but couldn't bear to find out if she was.

He stopped up his ears. He stuffed Kleenex into them, foam earplugs. He bought noise cancelling headphones, a good pair, and clamped them on, autumn, in the onrush of another intense weather front marauding out of the Midwest. He made it through this one. Didn't go out. Branches rushed wildly outside the windows but the penetrating voice of the wind barely reached him. He barricaded the door to his study with a box full of books. He would lash himself to the mast of his home. Headphones pressed to his ears, groaning, he stumbled to the day bed in the corner of the room and collapsed, pillow over his head.

One night in December, Paula shook him awake and Hugh pulled out his earplugs to hear what she was saying. Deep in his body, he'd felt the thump of the gate between walkway and backyard unmoored from its latch, crashing against its wooden frame.

"The latch must be broken," Paula said in the dark. "I went down already. I tried to get it to catch. The latch bent. The wind bent it. It won't stay and I can't sleep."

"It's not the latch, it's the wind." Wind coming strongly at a precise angle and with a force that had heretofore been unusual, or had never before occurred, the hapless latch caught in its crosshairs, the funnelled, augmented air speaking directly to them. To him. Bang. They needed to change. Bang. They all did. Bang. And had they changed? Bang. Were they changing enough? He'd go down there and play with the latch, reset it, and the noise would keep happening. This night, another night. "It's not fixable. I could get a new latch and still the wind will bash it hard enough to loosen it, I promise you."

He placed a hand on Paula's shoulder, the faint curve that had come with age, work and care tracing themselves into her strong body. He gathered her to him, kissed her mouth, her throat, the coolness of the wind a layer over her skin, over the startling warmth beneath. Hand on her hip, on the small of her back, helplessly acknowledging all the ways in which his body was aging alongside hers, he beheld an image of himself standing at one end of a great mansion, Paula at the other, rooms multiplying between them, all the chambers of time that bound them. "Paulie, what do you want me to do?"

In the dark she pressed herself against him, touched him in an old way that aroused him. "Not abandon me. Let's not abandon each other."

He would learn to live with the rising winds. They all would. They had to. For two days before Christmas, the wind blew, as it had blown all the way across the continent, bringing with it lake-effect snow and tornadoes in December while, to the east of them, huge drifts closed highways, downed power lines, left people trapped in their cars. All they had to contend with was air, frantic and moaning, creaking the tree branches, banging the gate, flattening the remains of the garden, like an Arctic blizzard, only in the cities of the south the wind didn't blow at such speeds for two days straight, or it hadn't before, it did now, and in the midst of it, people were still trying to fly to Cuba, despite the after-effects of the fall's hurricane damage there, or to Mexico, and the air was full of stories of stranding and delay. Elsewhere there were earthquakes. Or fires. And fires. It was hard to keep track. Hugh roamed about the house with a tube of draft-proofing silicone. In the kitchen, Paula and Leonie were baking. The aroma of whatever they were baking reached him. As he traced a bead of silicone around the edges of the hallway window, he heard them adjusting social plans now that it was once more virtually impossible to go outside. They didn't have a tree, only the delicate,

SKIN

coloured lights that Leonie had strung across the mantelpiece. She was still at home with them. Hugh did not know whether she would ever move out or if he wanted her to. Some nights he still shadow boxed in the basement. Lifted weights, his mind travelling out into the inescapable world and towards all the creatures in it. Upstairs, Leonie was working on a trial run of the lab coat. She'd insisted on drawing up a contract for their investment, adamant that as soon as she could she'd pay them back. On the upstairs landing, she'd modelled the newest coat for Hugh. Pale green. It fit her perfectly. He told her so. Surely life could be made meaningful through such moments, such endeavours. He longed for this so deeply.

Springtime again. He'd just turned fifty-five. Like most storms, this one was pressing east across the continent, out of the west, into the Midwest. *Derecho*, the severe weather meteorologists were calling it. A huge band of cloud was proceeding towards them, intensifying winds blowing straight at them, not in the usual tornadic swirls. Projected gusts of over two hundred kilometres per hour, risk of downed trees and power outages. On Hugh's weather app, out of the mouths of the warning-preparedness meteorologists: Extreme storm warning. Wind gust warning. Already the usual pictures of destruction were coming in.

He went around the house checking doors, windows, and, outside, the latch on the gate. He stood, eyeing the garden, all the tender little shoots pushing up, wished them luck amidst whatever was coming. He thought wistfully of the bears. In the kitchen, Paula used the sink hose to fill a big blue container made specifically for storing potable water, plus a few extra jugs, then hurried upstairs to fill the bathtub. She'd called her mother, Hugh had called his parents, safe where they were for now. On the counter, Paula had left a list and was crossing off items. They had a good stash of batteries, different sizes. Flashlights. Candles. Canned food. Peanut butter. Preserves. No generator yet but a solar-powered battery backup to charge phones and electronics, the solid green light of its full charge shining. They had all plugged their phones into wall sockets, charging them proactively. Leonie capped three thermoses full of milky tea. They would have no way to boil water if the power went out other than on a small propane camping stove, only for outdoor use, but at least they had the stove. Hugh hauled it out of the basement.

"I suppose you could say," he'd said to Paula that morning when word of the approaching storm first reached them, "that what I feel for the wind is love."

"Love?"

The house creaked, now, as he climbed the stairs, phone in hand, wind rising. As far as he knew, there was no better word. Was it not better to feel love than the opposite? The opposite being: Fury? Terror? Inattention? There was no comfort in this love. No complacency. It did not offer solace. Already gusts whipped through the one-hundred-fifty-year-old oak in their backyard, the neighbour's white pine. Outside the window, leaves were beginning to push out of the dendrites of oak branches, a frail and citrine green. And the birds, all the little birds on their long journey north, what would happen to them as the wind sucked at them, crashed their fragile, continental formations.

At his desk, he rubbed his hands over his thighs. Another of those emergency alerts wailed from his phone, telling them: Stay home, do not go out, do not go anywhere. Hugh checked the wind map and there it was, a yellow-red line driving towards them. He paced. From across the hall came the sound of Leonie at her sewing machine, binding the future into a cord, a thread.

The wind abated, grew louder. Dark clouds ranged across the sky. What was there to do other than love—the world and those who loved you—love harder? Hugh opened his study door and called to Paula. The sound of the wind became a clanging, hollow reverberation shaped by wind tunnels funnelling between the new apartment towers to the west, making the sky itself sound metallic and tubular, air on the march, socking them in with its force.

He took to the stairs. The wind was in him, of him, they were all part of its hugeness, in their significance and insignificance, and it wouldn't stop. Yet he couldn't deny the exhilaration, the extraordinary alertness the wind called out of him, spurring him to where life felt most vivid and keen. How best to be alive amidst whatever was happening—this was the crucial question, the singular urgency that drove him onward.

When he opened the back door, air burst around him. Dust filled the yard where the garden had been. One of their plastic garbage bins shot upwards and smashed into the windscreen of the neighbour's car. The oak tree cracked, a branch loosening. Somewhere behind him Paula screamed. Once more, the world as he had known it broke open.

Glacial

As they sail into the fjord, the woman's eyes catch on the wooden hut, alone on its white slope, melted snow leaving black patches like spores on the rocky heights behind it. From its small, single window some trick of the light winks at her as she stands on the boat deck in parka and mittens, she and the others who have come on this expedition to an archipelago in the high latitudes, only a few hundred miles from the North Pole. This is as far north as she has ever been in her life, or ever expects to be. All of them are eager to experience the glacial landscape during the white nights of endless summer light in the high Arctic. Some of them sketch as they travel; one drops a recording device deep into the water; another sings. They take photographs. The woman writes in a small, waterproof notebook.

The sight of the hut amplifies a desire that arose in her early in the trip, as they travelled over turquoise water, past glacier after melting glacier. The longing surprised the woman when she awoke in her tiny cabin, shared with a young cartoonist from San Francisco. When she stepped onto the boat's deck by the pale bright light of noon or midnight, the longing made itself felt. Even as the virus ran through her blood and body, as it ran through so many of them that they joked they should raise a black flag announcing they were a plague ship bringing their stew of viruses to the Far North, the desire to be alone in this landscape rose in her, plaintive and fervid. Alone and so to find, perhaps, an echo of its fragile vastness in herself.

She has been alone in other landscapes: In a city far-off across the sea, she lives on her own in an apartment, two floors of an old house surrounded by oak trees. Though not entirely alone. She has a dog, athletic and inquisitive. Her lover, a man of quick attentiveness, lives not far off. Squirrels rustle in the branches of the oaks outside her windows. The sirens of ambulances wail past day and night on their way to the nearby hospital. She has lain in a tent in the middle of a desert; spent nights alone, unafraid, in a house in the country, where, every now and again, a pickup truck will streak past along the dirt road, a white arrow searing through the dark.

On their voyage up the coast they passed other huts, even walked as a group to one perched on a flat plain surrounded by pale water and distant mountains. Their guides staked themselves on nearby rises, rifles slung over their shoulders as they scanned the land for polar bears. They were to go nowhere without their rifle-toting guides.

Why this hut? The woman doesn't know. All she knows is that when she glimpses it, something speaks to her. Approaching the man in the red down jacket, one of their guides, she finds herself asking: Would it be possible for me to spend some time on my own, out on the land—alone, that is, in the old hunters' hut we passed on our way into the fjord?

The man, younger than she is, a blond fringe of bangs protruding beneath his wool cap, takes her in, her face, her body, as if assessing her request, its seriousness or its folly, and the woman feels briefly seen. He is considering her query, not brushing her off as indulging in caprice or selfishness. He nods, then sets off across the boat's wooden deck to consult with two of the other guides. When he returns, he tells her, Yes, it's possible.

He will take her ashore and lock her inside the hut for her own safety, he says. For an hour or so. After that, he will return to fetch her. They can spare no guide to guard her. This will be the only way.

For a moment, the woman wavers. Then she says, That's fine. That's great, actually. Lock me inside.

When the man in the red jacket reappears, on the water, in a rubber Zodiac, the woman clambers down a ladder from the boat's deck to meet him, waving goodbye to her companions, who wave back. The roar of the motor is so loud as she and the man speed off, bouncing over the bay, that it is impossible to speak. Upon arrival, as they climb the slope towards the hut, across rock and moss and over dirty, melting snow, the man remains quiet, so self-contained that she has no idea what he is thinking.

There are two doors enclosing the hut. The first, made of nailed-together slats, is secured by two wooden planks. These are slotted horizontally into carved holes at the top and bottom of the wooden posts that frame the doorway. The man pushes the planks out of the slots, then lifts the door itself aside, leaning it against the tarpaper wall of the hut. The inner door is simple, covered in tar paper on the outside, the wood of its exterior oblong handle so worn it appears to be bone. They enter a tiny vestibule.

On the inside, wooden slats reinforce the door, which is solidly made, and from which protrudes a smoothed wooden knob. The hut's contents are minimal: a table, a chair, a bed, a wood stove. The woman drops her knapsack onto the chair, her hat and mittens onto the table. Beside them the man places a walkie-talkie, which he will leave with her, he says, in case of emergency. He shows her how to switch it on, how to connect to the ship.

When he leaves, he gives a little wave, before closing the first door behind him.

The woman hears him, outside, wedge the second, safety door in place over the first. Ordinarily, this door would only be used when visitors, hunters or hikers, left the hut behind. He slides the upper plank into the groove of the upper slots, then shoves the lower plank into position. It is impossible now for her to get out on her own. Behind both doors, she will be safe from predators. Three small slivers of light beam through a crack at the top of the door frame.

SKIN

Through the wooden walls of the hut, she follows the crunch of the man's footsteps as he makes his way back down the slope towards the water, where the Zodiac lies pulled up on a pebbly beach.

She watches as, head bowed, he passes in front of the hut's small, Plexiglas window, nailed into place in the wall's wood. Although he waved at her on departing the hut, he does not now turn to glance at her through the window, as if, already, he has moved on and she has vanished from his mind. However much she wants to be alone, this disconcerts her. Her hand twitches with the urge to wave, but she doesn't.

It is June, close to the solstice. Somewhere in that huge white sky the sun circles day and night, but the sky has been hazed for days, the air windless and becalmed, so that the woman has not seen the midnight sun, only gradations of endless, clouded brightness that expand above the motionless waters of the bay and the low, black-and-white mountains on the bay's far side, colour vibrating from a single, sapphire-blue iceberg.

After pushing the Zodiac off from shore, the man leaps aboard and flings an orange life jacket around his shoulders. Crouched over the outboard motor, he tugs until it catches. Without looking back, he sets his course for the far end of the bay, the grey Zodiac slicing into the water's stillness, the muted purr of its motor reaching the woman through the little window. The water, fine as glass, shatters as the boat speeds across it, shard upon shard, until man and boat disappear around the curve of the shoreline, the shore swallowing every smash of wave, every bulge and ripple of disturbance. Calm reasserts itself.

She is alone. The woman considers the initial timbre of this aloneness. It's a kind of intimacy she longs for. Not awe, not grief in this melting world. Yet her mind leaps like a rabbit. She picks up the walkie-talkie. When she flicks the switch, as the man showed her how to do, voices from aboard the ship tumble out, calling to each other. Sarah! Tomas! Marius! The woman pushes the tab that will allow her to speak but doesn't say anything. A light glows. It works.

That's all the reassurance she needs. Switching off the walkie-talkie, she returns it to the table.

The hut is small and dim in the face of the bedazzling expanse outside which, from where the woman stands, looks empty, the black and umber rock of the low mountains stippled by ribbons of snow, the mountains doubled by their reflections in the still water. This hut, like the others that infrequently dot the land, would have been cobbled together by hunters from salvaged wood, here in a land without trees, hunters of seal and fox and polar bear, some of whom built traps to hunt the bears, affixing a rifle to a wooden frame baited with meat, so the woman has learned. When a bear, often a mother bear, approached, drawn by the scent, the frame collapsed on her, triggering the rifle, which shot her in the head, leaving her to bleed to death or the hunters to finish her off, hunters who might also capture her orphaned young. There is blood here, on the land, under the melting snow. The whale and walrus killers gathered elsewhere, on wider shores where they stripped the huge carcasses, rendered blubber to oil, discarded cascades of bones to be cleansed and whitened by time. She has no history in this landscape, other than that her skin binds her to the white-skinned hunters, Russians, Norwegians, English, Dutch, no ties to root her here, but she knows enough to know she isn't entirely alone. She stands in a land full of ghosts.

It takes four steps to cross the hut from the small bed built into the wall, its mattress little more than a husk covered in worn fabric, to the entryway, where there is a simple wooden bench and where, if one were a hunter, one might leave one's heavy boots and jacket and rifle, store whatever driftwood one has hauled in or dragged up from shore. Up here, logs float in from the Russian coast like exiles. Or refugees. Elsewhere, war is raging. It is summer, warm enough for the woman to unzip her parka. She doesn't need to light a fire in the tiny wood stove behind her, or attempt to light one and possibly fail. With every step she sways; after days at sea, her body carries the movement of water within it, deep in her inner ear, making the cabin around her sway along with her body. She reaches out an arm to steady herself.

Beside the wood stove, a cast-iron pan and an antique kettle sit on a shelf. On a shelf above the pan and kettle stands a row of bottles: whiskeys, tequila, even a bottle of Texas hot sauce. She eyes them: Jameson. Johnnie Walker. José Cuervo. Texas Pete! Interlopers all. There are, it seems, many ways to stay warm here. Swaying, she picks up one bottle after another, shakes them—empty, every one, save for the hot sauce, which she opens, taps a tiny amount of sauce onto her palm, licks it. The heat searing through her guts like a meteor makes her shout and toss the bottle back onto the shelf.

On the window ledge a stubby candle keeps company with the jawbone of some creature, teeth embedded in it, a relic that someone has gathered, abandoned, left for another to encounter. The woman touches the bone and moves the candle to the table, plucks a match from the matchbox also left on the ledge and lights the candle wick. Who has been here before her? What will she do with her time here? She will sit, she will listen, she will grieve, she will think.

Somewhere over the ocean, her lover has been following her journey by satellite link, charting the boat's coordinates up the island of Spitsbergen, but he doesn't know that she is in this cabin. No one knows exactly where she is other than the man in the red jacket. This pleases her, the beautiful disorientation of it. She has a phone in her knapsack but there is no reception given the remoteness of her location. The phone, a shell, is usable only to take a picture, which she does, aiming its camera into the bright glare of the outside world. Across the bay a glacier spills from the base of the low mountains into a wide, white mouth. Click. This time, when she glances away from the window, her vision, polarized, sears green, the contrast between the radiant outside and dim interior so great that, for a few seconds, everything inside, table, chair, her hand held out in front of her, are burned away.

Take off your coat, a voice says.

The woman recoils in shock.

Across the bay, the glacier moves. Because this is what glaciers do. It's what glacial means, the ice is always moving.

There is so much that is invisible in this landscape: mountains that descend underground as far as they table above; polar bears that roam out of sight; kittiwakes that wheel, tossing their high-pitched cries before diving into their cliff burrows along the walls of rock farther into the fjord; the ice that runs deep beneath the glacier's surface, channels of water tunnelling through it, the movement of ice and water carrying the upper ice with it towards the bay, towards the sea, where the ice will disappear into the dark blue Arctic waters. All this the woman knows as her gaze turns outwards, unsettled, eyes straining.

Again, a voice says, Take off your coat.

But she is alone, as alone as she has ever been. Unnerved, she looks about. Perhaps she has no business being here, despite her wonder and desire, yet this is where she is, breathing this air, asking the air, How am I to be in this landscape? What am I to be?

When the voice asks a third time, she struggles to shuck off her parka, to work her arms out of the sleeves and hook the coat's shoulders over the back of her chair, not cold but shivering a little, because who knows what will happen if she doesn't do as the voice commands, or what will happen if she does. She makes a choice.

There is no presence in her vision as powerful as the glacier, which seems to loom the longer she stares at it through the little window. The harder she stares at the mobile whiteness the more clearly she takes in its mouth, wide and white and scarred with crevasses. You? Is it you? Once more, she checks over her shoulder into the green, polarized air of the hut but sees no one, no glimpse of movement, not even of ghosts. She leans to peer out the window at the ground below, the space to either side of its frame. No one. Only the trickling sound of melting snow. Is she hallucinating? No sound of any person or creature stirring on the gritty roof.

How does one address a glacier, so ancient, such a miracle of compressed time, time turned to ice. Should she? Yet isn't this why she came? To open herself to some kind of encounter. Which may be hubris. And yet.

What she knows: On the surface of the glacier lies snow, beneath that, ice crystals, beneath that finer firn, which thaws and refreezes and slowly turns into the deep, compacted, deformed ice, that, stressed under its own weight, begins to move. Moves and turns to water. Time turns to water, the great mouth across from her cracking and breaking open into the bay. As the air warms, the water warms. Faster. Days ago, she sped with others of the expedition in one of the Zodiacs through open water where their GPS said there should have been nothing but glacial ice.

Thou. The word comes to her. How art thou?

She speaks. In response, there is only silence. How dare she ask a glacier how it is and, ridiculous, expect a response? Yet the lack of response is, despite everything, a disappointment.

She sits, she waits, she listens, she breathes. Her skin crackles. Not silence: Water trickles over the ground outside. Everything feels still but isn't. She casts her mind outwards.

Take off your skin, the voice says, the voice that may or may not belong to the glacier.

The woman jumps, startled all over again. She stands stock still, listening, her ears abuzz.

You heard me, the voice says. Take off your skin.

I don't know how to do that, the woman says, still coursing with shock. Somehow, with something or someone, she is having a conversation.

Well, the voice says. Figure it out.

◆

The woman's skin has always felt thin and porous to the world around her: to the cries of others, the way leaves grow flaccid in a drought or browned after spraying, the pores, the spores, the vines brought across the world from one continent to another that scramble and spread through their millions of seeds, metastasizing in the woodland park near her apartment. At night sometimes, as if in response, her body will twitch and vibrate.

The woman presses her face and chest to the window of the hut and as she stares down the slope to the water, the convexity of the slope seems to enter her, pulling her out through the window. Somehow, she's not exactly sure how, she is stumbling down the slope to the shore. Perhaps there was, indeed, some hallucinogen in the hot sauce. At the shore, the water laps against her bare feet, annihilatingly cold. Somehow, she does not know how, only that she feels compelled to do so and can do this, she finds herself wading into the water, an explosion against her, so cold on her skin it is like being irradiated, her blood vessels contracting until they are as thin as hair, her head throbbing so relentlessly it pushes out all thought. Somehow, she doesn't know how, she is in the water, swimming, hard and fast, trying to warm herself, limbs thrashing as they carry her across the bay.

She hears a sound, like a wire being unspooled, which, the first time she heard it, she was convinced was some peculiarity of the engine of the ship that brought her here, something mechanical coming terribly undone, but now knows to be the song of the bearded seal, thin, piercing, alive, coil after coil unwinding deeper and deeper into the water. She has seen the seals on shore, on ice floes, their dark heads surfacing in the water, staring at her. They are here, somewhere.

She finds herself close to the glacier, the wide spread of its mouth, a quiet one, this one, cracked ice trickling, not like some of the thunderous ones she has recently encountered, which crash and calve repeatedly, hurl ice into the water, blue floes that spin and disperse, still melting. There is the one blue iceberg slowly circling and dissolving in the water, becoming water, its colours a spectrum from near white to azure, light piercing the thickness of time as it disintegrates, the jostling of waves smoothing the ice into curves near the water's surface, granular, melting snow still coating the top of the iceberg. She finds herself touching the ice with her fingers, her lips, with as much tenderness as she can muster. Thou, she thinks again, oh, thou. This is the amount of sadness she can hold within her human body.

Elsewhere, not far off, a young polar bear ambles down from the hills and stops to sniff the air in the direction of the hut before setting off into the water, swimming across the bay to a small island where, shaking droplets from her yellowed pelt, she meanders among the seagull nests, beneath the screeching gulls, marauding and gulping down eggs full of unhatched young, swallowing the shells and warm yolks, until, sated, she sinks to the ground, among the flowering saxifrage, and, limbs outstretched, pillows herself against the land's undulations as if they were her own.

In the still white light it is impossible to say how many hours have elapsed. Inside the hut, the woman finds herself seated on the floor, the small window above her. Her head throbs. She rubs her eyes. On the table the flame of the squat candle flickers. She pats her hand about until she finds her phone.

 On its screen, only minutes have passed, it seems. Clambering to her feet, the woman returns to the chair at the table, facing the window. The same still light illuminates the land outside. And yet it might have been a day. Two days? It strikes her that some time has passed and no one has returned to fetch her.

In a sudden panic, she fumbles for the walkie-talkie, switches it on, and out spills a nearly incomprehensible barrage of human voices. What are they saying? She struggles to decipher them. She clears her throat. She presses the *on* button. She attempts to speak. Hello, she says. Hello? The voices call to each other as if they haven't heard her.

She tries again. Hello? She turns the walkie-talkie off and once more flicks the *on* switch. Hello? She shakes the plastic. Hello? Hello? The voices give no sign that they can hear her.

Coatless, she stumbles to her feet, and there, in front of her eyes, through the window, a boat floats past, across the bay, a sailing ship with three tall masts, the boat that she travelled in on. There are tiny people on deck, including a man in a red jacket with his back to her. Another figure perches high in the rigging. No one looks in her direction. She waves her arms within the small cabin, but the gesture is useless. How can they see her, so far off and trapped within the hut? She shouts. Of course no one can hear her.

The woman doesn't feel fear exactly. Once more the light pries open her eyelids, the green world entering her, emptying her, until, slowly, she begins to see again.

Take off your skin, the glacier says. All of it. You haven't gone far enough.

What does that even mean? The woman takes off her boots. Her socks. Wriggles her bare feet.

The world is still cold, at least for now. Somehow, she doesn't know how, she is once more outside the cabin, her skin thin as a breeze. Out on the water, the boat of her little life floats past, unreachable, dwindling, small as a leaf.

The woman slides her legs under the snow, into the rocks, into the earth, her arms into the cool melt-water. This time, the shock of the water is much less.

SKIN

There is no other way to move. She is moving, finding the depths of the rocks, the texture of water, the shifting border where water meets ice, salt water meets fresh, grief meets tenderness. She is taking off her skin, and it may be that, soon, there will be nothing left of her, but she is doing it, becoming skinless, expansive, she has no choice but to continue, no other way onward other than to abandon all that was for all that is.

In the Park, the Great Horned Owl Summons His Mate

Below, as darkness grows, rabbits leap over melting snow.

I call.

A spray of pellets skitters. Voles crackle dead leaves as they pass.

The ones blued by little fires held close to their chests stumble out of the woods, into their land of lights.

Later, in darkness, Coyote, scruffy Emperor of the forest, and his limping Queen bolt out of the trees, through the park gates, pad along the hard tracks. A wrestle of bodies reaches my ears, scream of a creature, cat guts ripping.

You. I call. And again: You.

Soon you will come — perch high on a pine branch. As you exhale, the feathers at your throat will flutter. Mottle, flicker, swerve of neck, twitch of feathered horn, burn of yellow eye will fix me as, from branch to branch, we speak to each other: You, yes you, yes you.

SKIN

For so long we have done this.

The sun turns, fades, returns.

How can one who was here be not here?

I call again.

I listen. The screech owls stir in their hollow branches. Chipmunks, tucked in their burrows, quiver. Fox sniffs and lifts a paw. Beavers, in their stick house, chew the green wood. Sap runs—a soft gush.

All day, the bright-eyed hunters soar, talons flexing. Higher than birds, a flash of flint circles with a great groan. At night, in this aged forest, ghosts cross paths with the living. Beyond the spell of the gnarled oaks, blinding lights roar along black ribbons.

Free of ice, the creek trickles. The Queen and her Emperor are digging a den for their young.

Where are you?

Dogs ransack the woods. Again, the trees turn into silhouettes. The vast lake, out beyond the blaze of racing lights, gurgles and lisps.

How can I be here without my other? Alone, I wait in this high pine, amid the rustle of needle and creak of wood.

If I call into the space where you were, into the silence that expands into absence, will you hear?

With my call, I draw you close. Conjure you to return, across time, out of the ether, out of the earth.

Acknowledgements

I'd like to acknowledge the land on which these stories were written and my debt to the lands where I've lived while writing them: Toronto/Tkaronto, where I was born, the Treaty Lands and Territory of the Mississaugas of the Credit and the traditional territory of the Anishinaabeg, Wendat, Métis, and Haudenosaunee; the countryside of Hastings County, where I live part-time, traditional territory of many nations including the Huron-Wendat, Anishinaabeg, and the Haudenosaunee peoples; and Bavaria, Germany.

While working on the collection, I received support from the Rachel Carson Center for Environment and Society of Ludwig-Maximilians Universität, Munich, Germany, in the form of the 2024 Writer-in-Residence Landhaus Fellowship, and from the Ontario Arts Council and the Government of Ontario, a Literary Creation grant. Much gratitude to both. The Dark Mountain "How We Walk Through Fire" workshop series, particularly the "Kinship with Beasts" workshop, proved inspirational, as did my 2022 Arctic Circle Residency off the coast of Svalbard. Thanks to the Canada Council for funding this residency.

To those who read the manuscript-in-progress, especially Martha Baillie, Mike Hoolboom, and Shyam Selvadurai, thank you for your brilliance and for pushing me further when I needed it. Your faith was instrumental. Thanks to my fellow 2024 Landhaus Fellows for cheering me on during the final stages of revision.

To my editor extraordinaire André Alexis, this collection would not exist without your desire to shepherd it into the world. Thank you for your keenest eye, passionate attention, and visionary rigour, and for the opportunity for us to work together in this way.

To Bethany Gibson, my editor at Goose Lane Editions, gratitude for your bountiful and ongoing editorial acumen. To Paula Sarson for astute copy editing. And to everyone at GLE.

Thanks to Pete Ewins for invaluable polar bear lore; Dona Ann McAdams, my East Village go-to; Stephen Hubbell for Brooklyn tips; the Shaw Festival for their 2022 production of *Cyrano de Bergerac*. To the University of Guelph for its support of my research.

Heartfelt thanks to all those who provided love and support as I saw this project to completion.

Thanks to Jack Wang and Jenny Ferguson, judges of the 2024 *Malahat Review* Novella Prize, for selecting an earlier version of "Derecho" as a finalist.

Earlier versions of some stories have been published as follows:

"Voices Over Water," *Canadian Fiction Magazine*;

"The International Headache Conference," *The Idler*;

"Skin," *Brick*;

"Touch," *The Quarantine Review*; and

"In the Park, the Great Horned Owl Calls to His Mate," *Dark Mountain, Eight Fires*.

Catherine Bush is the author of five novels. Her work has been critically acclaimed, published internationally, and shortlisted for numerous awards. Her most recent novel, *Blaze Island*, was a *Globe and Mail* and Writers' Trust of Canada Best Book of the Year, and the Hamilton Reads 2021 Selection. Her other novels include the Canada Reads longlisted *Accusation*; the Trillium Award shortlisted *Claire's Head*; the national bestselling *The Rules of Engagement*, which was also named a *New York Times* Notable Book and an *LA Times* Best Book of the Year; and *Minus Time*, shortlisted for the City of Toronto Book Award. The recipient of numerous fellowships, Bush was the 2024 Writer-in-Residence/Landhaus Fellow at the Rachel Carson Centre for Environment and Society in Munich and previously a Fiction Meets Science Fellow at the HWK in Delmenhorst, Germany. An Associate Professor of Creative Writing at the University of Guelph, she divides her time between Toronto and an old schoolhouse in Eastern Ontario. *Skin* is her first story collection.
www.catherinebush.com

Photo by Arden Wray